ADVANCE PRAISE FOR THE BAD BREAK

"A ray of sunshine cloaked in a mystery. Orr is one to watch— the best humorous mystery writer around, with a voice all her own."

— **Laura McHugh**, internationally bestselling author of *The Weight of Blood* and *Arrowood*

"Here comes Riley Ellison, the journalist-slash-hero we need right now. She solves murders! She writes obits! She gets life coaching from an app and somehow makes it work! I loved this fresh page-turner—it's fun, funny, and moves like lightning. Jill Orr has created a complex plot and complex contemporary characters that make murder quite delightful. Can't wait for the next in the series."

— **Lian Dolan**, Satellite Sister and author of the bestselling novels *Helen of Pasadena* and *Elizabeth the First Wife*

"Deft at imbuing her pop-off-the-page characters with both humor and heart, Jill Orr also spins a gem of a twisty mystery that will leave readers breathless as they chase a huge (and dangerous) headline with Tuttle Corner's sassy, scrappy new star reporter, Riley Ellison. Utterly delightful—don't miss this one, y'all!"

— **LynDee Walker**, Agatha Award–nominated author of *Lethal Lifestyles* and *Front Page Fatality*

Praise for *The Good Byline*

"Jill Orr has put pure joy on the page."

— *BOLO Books*

"Fresh and funny, romantic and sunny, Jill Orr's book checked three genre boxes for me: a smart cozy series, a Southern small town setting, and, my favorite, a newspaper mystery... I loved the hilarious emails the author interjects into the narrative from Riley's Personal Romance Concierge."

— **Carole Barrowman,** *Milwaukee Journal-Sentinel*

"Riley 'Bless Her Heart' Ellison is a breath of fresh air—a funny, empathic, millennial heroine. She kept me turning the pages well into the night."

— **Susan M. Boyer,** *USA TODAY*–bestselling author of the Liz Talbot mystery series

"A fun romp... Recommended to admirers of Janet Evanovich's Stephanie Plum capers." — *Library Journal*

"Who knew obituaries could be this much fun?"

— **Gretchen Archer,** *USA TODAY*–bestselling author of the Davis Way Crime Caper series

"In this irresistible page-turner, Jill Orr delivers a funny, smartly written mystery featuring a charming heroine."

— **Ellen Byron,** author of *Body on the Bayou* and *Plantation Shudders*

"The methodical local reporter, Will Holman, is a standout—here's hoping he will appear in more of Riley's adventures."

— **Naomi Hirahara,** *Edgar Award*–winning author of the Mas Arai and Ellie Rush mystery series

For my Ellie, my Fletcher, and my Jimmy.
You guys are all the reasons and all the rewards.

THE BAD BREAK

Jill Orr

Prospect Park Books

Published by Prospect Park Books
2359 Lincoln Avenue
Altadena, California 91001
www.prospectparkbooks.com

Distributed by Consortium Book Sales & Distribution
www.cbsd.com

Library of Congress Cataloging-in-Publication Information

Names: Orr, Jill, author.
Title: The bad break : a Riley Ellison mystery / Jill Orr.
Description: Altadena, California : Prospect Park Books, [2018]
Identifiers: LCCN 2017040323 (print) | LCCN 2017042433 (ebook) | ISBN
    9781945551215 (Ebook) | ISBN 9781945551208 (pbk.) | ISBN 9781945551321
    (hardcover)
Subjects: | GSAFD: Mystery fiction.
Classification: LCC PS3615.R58846 (ebook) | LCC PS3615.R58846 B33 2018
    (print) | DDC 813/.6--dc23
LC record available at https://lccn.loc.gov/2017040323

Cover design by Susan Olinsky
Cover illustration by Nancy Nimoy
Book layout and design by Amy Inouye
Printed in the United States of America

Special Limited Time Offer!

Dear Miss Ellison,

Although we were sorry to see you deactivate your account on Click.com, we are thrilled that you found love through our advanced technological algorithms and are enjoying the satisfaction that comes from being in a committed, fulfilling relationship! #feelthefeels #reallove #wearehereifthingsgosouth

But we at the Click Thru Life corporation understand that there is more to life than just romance. That's why we want to make you aware of a special opportunity for former Click.com customers who are looking to bring their lives and their careers into MEANINGFUL ALIGNMENT.

Bestmillenniallife.com is the preeminent online clarity coaching service offered specifically by Millennials, for Millennials. Bestmillenniallife.com takes a client-centered, results-oriented, SYNERGYSTIC approach to helping you connect with your AUTHENTIC SELF so you can live your life to the fullest extent possible.

As a special parting gift from Click.com, we would like to offer you a 30-day FREE trial membership to Bestmillenniallife.com. To redeem this offer, simply fill out the attached intake form, use activation code: GETALIFE,* and we will connect you with your highly trained Personal Success Concierge™, Jenna B.

It is our deepest wish that you will continue on your journey toward SELF-ACTUALIZATION and allow Bestmillenniallife.com to be your guide.

➤

Warmest regards,
Gordon A. Fancher
CEO (Chief EXCELLENCE Officer), Click Thru Life, LLC

CHAPTER 1

S o how long will you be gone?" I asked Holman, trying to keep the panic from my voice.

"Depends. Could be a few days or a few weeks."

"Uh-huh. Yeah. Okay. I gotcha." For reasons I didn't understand, I kept spitting out affirmatives. I could feel my head nodding up and down like a bobblehead on the dashboard of a monster truck. "I see. All right. Mm-hmm."

Holman arched an eyebrow. "Riley, are you okay?"

He had clearly not anticipated the effect the news that he'd be taking leave to go undercover would have on me. I was a little surprised myself, but the idea of working at the *Tuttle Times* without Holman had me feeling panicky, like all the air had been sucked out of the room. Or like I couldn't find my cell phone. I guess I'd come to depend on him more than I realized during the past month.

"A few weeks? Really?"

He shrugged. "The first trip is scheduled for seven days. But if I don't see anything, I may have to do another."

For the past few months, Holman had been working an investigative piece on the TransVirginia Shipping Company. A former employee had tipped him off that the company had been ordering its workers to illegally dump barrels of toxic waste in the ocean to avoid the high cost of proper disposal. Holman had found several former employees who corroborated the story, but all refused to go on the record. As the son of a maritime engineer in the Royal Canadian Navy, Holman knew his way around a ship. So he'd been trying to get a job as a handler on one of the ships, which had proven more difficult than he anticipated. But after several weeks, he'd finally been hired. It was a great break for him. For me, not so much.

"You'll be fine," he said. "You're ready."

"But what if I'm not?" I let my insecurities bubble up to the surface. "I have yet to write a single story without going over it with you first."

"You bring your work to me because it makes you feel better. Not because you need to."

"But who will edit me now?"

"Kay, of course," he said. Kay Jackson was the editor-in-chief of the *Times,* and although she was technically my boss, I think I'd spoken a total of seven words to her since I started working there. She was nice but scary. And therefore my tenure at the *Times* so far had been spent comfortably in Holman's shadow. I liked it there. He had become my personal safety net, my insurance against failure.

"Fine," I huffed. "Leave me all alone with the jackals."

"Spencer and Henderson aren't jackals—"

"Well, they don't exactly like having me around."

"—if anything, a more apt comparison would be vultures, as they're waiting for you to die, metaphorically speaking, of course, so they can pick off your stories," he completed his thought.

"Is that supposed to make me feel better?"

Holman blinked, surprised. "I wouldn't think so."

The guys in the newsroom had not been thrilled when Holman convinced Kay to hire me. The *Times* was a small weekly newspaper, and everyone who worked there had worked there forever and had their own turf. Holman was the paper's crown jewel, having received the Worth Bingham Prize for Investigative Journalism some years ago, and I was hired mostly to assist him. But at a small paper, everyone pitches in, and over the past few weeks I'd been assigned stories from multiple departments. This wasn't always appreciated.

"They think I'm an *intern*," I said, sulkily. "Spencer called me Lewinsky yesterday."

"Who cares what they think. You're not an intern. You're a paid employee, same as me."

"Are you sure you won't be available at all, even by phone? Text? Email?" My desperation ticked up as he packed up his files and loaded them into his briefcase.

"Listen," Holman said. "You are going to be fine. And who knows, maybe Flick will even let you help with obits while I'm gone."

I knew he was just trying to make me feel better. Hal Flick hadn't let me do anything for the obituary department except research on the "pre-dead." Even though Kay told him to train me, Flick had stubbornly refused to let me write a single obituary since I'd been at the *Times*. This was partially because he was an old curmudgeon who didn't like change, and partially because he and I shared a long and complicated history. Either way, it sucked.

People in small towns read the newspaper for two main reasons: high school football and obituaries. Flick had been lobbying Kay for years to let him expand the obit section to include more than just death notices sent in by families or funeral homes. He wanted to run editorial obits, like the kind in *The New York Times*, true news stories about people whose lives have influenced our community. Kay finally agreed to give him the space for one news obit per issue, and the response had been amazing. People in Tuttle were loving the longer obits. Personally, I felt vindicated that I was no longer the only person in town who realized the simple beauty of the form. Plus, I was thrilled that I was going to get to learn the craft of obituary writing like my granddaddy had done. But so far Flick had kept the juicy assignments all to himself, leaving me the scraps, spell-checking death notices or doing research for our advances, which basically involves calling healthy people and asking them to verify information to be used . . . "later." Needless to say, people don't always appreciate these calls.

"What am I supposed to do if I need you?" I whined.

"You won't. This will be good for you—a natural way to bring your training to an end. I have provided you with the knowledge, insight, and experience gained during the course of my career to help launch yours. As the sculptor molds the clay, I have been able to shape you—"

"*Holman!*"

"What?" He looked surprised. "I didn't mean that in a sexual way, if that's what you were thinking—"

I held up a hand to stop him. I simply could not have this conversation again. "That was not what I was think-ing. That is *never* what I am thinking. It's just . . . what if I'm not ready?"

"You're going to be fine," he said again with a confi-dence I envied. "But there is something I'm going to need you to do for me while I'm gone."

"Name it." I got out my notepad to write down the assignment. Was it research for another investigation? Following up with a source? Looking for the proverbial smoking gun?

"I'm going to need you to feed Aunt Beast."

"What? You need me to feed your aunt? Is she ill?"

"No, she's not ill," Holman said, looking at me like I was crazy. "She doesn't have any arms."

This was the first I was hearing about a relative of Holman's with no arms. But before I asked any more questions I paused, waiting for the rest. With Holman I'd learned that sometimes when you thought you were talking about one thing, you were actually talking about something else entirely.

"She gets one pinch in the morning and one in the evening. And if I'm gone for more than two weeks, you'll need to change her."

Before I could object to feeding, pinching, and changing anyone, he pulled out a large cylinder of Bettamin Tropical Fish Food and set it on the desk in front of me.

And there it was: a fish.

Holman pointed to the electric-blue betta fish swimming in a clear glass bowl atop his credenza. I realized that although I'd seen the fish nearly every day, I'd never asked if it had a name.

"You named your fish Aunt Beast?"

"Yes."

"Any particular reason?"

"Aunt Beast. You know, from *A Wrinkle in Time*?"

It sounded familiar, but I was going to need a little more to go on.

"Aunt Beast is the beloved monster who helps Meg heal and teaches her not to judge people by their appearances."

I looked at Holman and didn't know whether to laugh or cry. It was one of the sweetest and saddest things I'd ever heard. Before I could stop myself, I threw my arms around his neck and squeezed him as tight as I could. "Do you really have to go?"

Holman, for his part, stood quite still except for his long, spindly arms that he stiffly wrapped around me and crossed at the wrists, being very careful not to touch any part of my torso. He'd tried to hug me once before and I remember thinking the experience was akin to being embraced by a stick bug. This second attempt was not much better, but I appreciated the effort.

"Who will protect the coastal waters of mid-Eastern Virginia if not me, Riley?"

I released him and tried not to be offended by how relieved he looked. "Fine. Go save the environment. Leave me here all alone."

Holman picked up his briefcase and turned off the light. "You won't be alone. You'll have Aunt Beast."

———•———

After Holman left for places unknown, or at least unknown to me, I skulked back to my cubicle and was about to text my boyfriend Jay to tell him I was thinking about his cute face when my phone rang.

"Riley, thank *God*! It's me."

"Me" was Tabitha, my former library co-worker and current bridezilla. I'd been covering some shifts for her at the library as she prepared to marry her blue-chip doctor fiancé, Thad. She'd complained bitterly when I handed in my resignation. *"How am I supposed to plan my wedding and do all of your work for you?"* I agreed to help out here and there mostly because I loved our boss, Dr. Harbinger—and he loved Tabitha and me. We were both like daughters to him, which I suppose made us like siblings, rivalry and all.

"Can you come meet me? Like *now*?" she snipped.

Tabitha was an unrelenting taskmaster and no matter how hard I tried, I never seemed to be able to do anything to her satisfaction. I wondered what cardinal sin of information management I had committed this time.

"I'm at work. Can I do it later?"

"That depends," she said. "How long after finding a dead body can you wait before calling the police?"

CHAPTER 2

"Are you okay?" I asked Tabitha as I stepped into the massive foyer of her fiancé's family home.

"I'm fine," she said. But she didn't look fine; she looked pale. True, Tabitha's skin was always pale, however it was usually an aristocratic pale—farm-fresh cream with a hint of peach—that paired perfectly with her raven hair and haughty attitude. But when she opened the door her cheeks had more of bad-shrimp pallor. In five years of working with Tabitha St. Simon, I'd never seen her look so fragile.

"It's in there," she nodded toward a long walnut-paneled hallway, at the end of which was a door that stood halfway open. The "it" she referred to was the lifeless body of Dr. Arthur Davenport, a prominent local cardiologist and her fiancé Thad's father. I walked down the hallway and peered into the room. Seeing him lying on the rug made me feel a little like I'd eaten a bad shrimp myself, so we walked back to the foyer to wait for the sheriff, whom I'd convinced her to call as soon as we had hung up.

Tabitha told me on the phone that she'd come over to get some measurements that the wedding planner needed—some crisis about the antler arch possibly being too wide for the terrace doors. And since Thad was out of town at a conference and Arthur was supposed to be at work, Thad told her to just run over and get what she needed. She heard the family dog howling from Arthur's office when she got there, which was weird, so she went to go see what was the matter. And the matter was Dr. Davenport lying dead on the floor.

"Do you know what happened?" I asked.

"I have no idea. Maybe a stroke? Heart attack?"

"Is there a reason you didn't call 911 right away?"

Tabitha paused before speaking, as if it was difficult for her to remember what she'd been thinking. "When I saw him lying there like that . . . completely still, eyes open . . . it was very unnatural-looking, you know? I felt his neck for a pulse and his skin was cold and stiff like leather." She shuddered. "It was obvious he was already gone. I didn't know what to do, so I called you." She looked up at me, her eyes shining with emotion.

She looked so vulnerable in that moment, I was actually rather touched. Maybe I was more important to Tabitha than I realized. Maybe after all these years of working together we were forming a friendship, despite her outward hostility toward me? I moved to give her a hug, but she took a step back.

"Besides, a dead body doesn't need an ambulance. It needs an obituary. You *do* write obituaries, don't you?"

Okay. So maybe she didn't call me for support.

"Why don't we go sit down?" I said. I was a bit stung, but more than that I was eager to change the subject. I may have slightly exaggerated the level of my responsibility in the obits department to Tabitha. But when she kept pressing me to cover more and more of her shifts at the library, I felt it sounded better to refuse because *I'm swamped at the paper*, rather than *I just want more time to hang out with my hot new boyfriend Jay*. And besides, it wasn't my fault that I wasn't writing obits yet. That was on Flick.

"Don't worry about the obit," I added. "I'm sure we can get it in for this Sunday, or worst case, next week's edition."

"Next week?" Tabitha rounded on me like a cage fighter. "Do you know what is happening here exactly twelve days from tomorrow?"

Of course I knew, but I wasn't about to answer her when she asked me like that.

"The wedding event of the *season* is going to be held in this very house. Have you ever planned a wedding for 450 guests, Riley? I doubt it very much. So let me tell you, it doesn't just happen. It takes time, precision, and decisive action." She spoke of it more like a military operation than a wedding. "And it's not like I'm getting a lot of help or anything. So I'm sorry that Arthur is dead, I really am, but you will excuse me if I'm being proactive in getting the ball rolling on his obituary. If it doesn't get in this Sunday's paper, there is no way we can have the funeral by next Thursday, which needs to happen because the antler artists will need to get in here by the following Monday, *latest.*" Her face was flushed, eyes wild. "The arch takes four days to be constructed, which only leaves us a one-day cushion for contingencies. Not to mention the flagstone path that needs to be finished up, final alterations on my dress, confirming the musicians, the caterers, and the florists"—she was really working herself into a lather—"so as sad as it is, you'll understand the importance of getting the show on the road so-to-speak. Life doesn't just stop because someone dies!"

"Okay, just calm down, Tabith—"

"Why am I even explaining this to you?" She turned away, cutting me off like a boil. A second later we heard the sound of sirens screaming up the long, winding stone driveway. It was acting-Sheriff Carl Haight and his deputy

Chip Churner, who everyone called Butter.

"Miss St. Simon. Miss Ellison," Carl said as he stepped out of his cruiser. Even though I had known Carl Haight since I was four years old and we used to play Teenage Mutant Ninja Turtles together at preschool, he preferred that we keep things professional while on the job.

"Acting-Sheriff Haight," I said. "Hey, Butter." Butter didn't stand on ceremony.

Carl tipped the corner of his hat toward Tabitha. "I'm sorry for your loss, ma'am. Coroner's on the way."

Tabitha's arms were crossed tightly across her chest. "I'll show you to the, um, body." She led the two officers toward the back, leaving me alone in the foyer. "Riley, don't go anywhere," she called over her shoulder.

As I watched them walk away, I couldn't help but wonder why Tabitha had called me before she called the sheriff. I wasn't buying her obituary story, and it wasn't like we were exactly friends. We were more like frenemies, if anything. And it's not like a girl with nine bridesmaids would call a former co-worker-slash-frenemy for support. There was something weird going on with Tabitha.

I heard the click-clack of shoes coming back down the long hallway as she walked back toward me holding a neat manila file. "This should get you started. If you need any interviews, I've listed family names and numbers on top. The theme we're going for is understated heroism, okay? And we want maximum number of inches allowed—at least a half page; a full one, if possible. This will need to run in Sunday's paper. Got it?"

I looked at her, stunned by the businesslike way in which she was handling all of this. I knew Tabitha wasn't the dissolve-into-tears sort, but she had just found her future father-in-law dead. You would have thought at least a short period of mourning or shock would have been in order.

"Does Thad know yet?"

She looked away; emotion rolled across her face briefly. "Yes. I called him before you got here. He's on his way home from a meeting in Richmond."

The front door was still standing open and the sound of another car pulling into the circle drive drifted in. We turned to see the red pickup truck of the county coroner roll into the Davenport driveway.

The Tuttle County government was like many other rural communities in the United States: economically disadvantaged. So they had to make some concessions. For example, we didn't have a medical examiner; we had a coroner. The difference is that while a medical examiner has to be a physician trained in forensic pathology, a coroner simply has to be elected, like a member of the school board or the president of the PTA.

Tuttle County's coroner was Tiffany Peters, a former beauty queen (five-time Miss Junior Johnnycake) and the current owner of the county's only dance studio, Jitterbugs. She ran for coroner in a surprise move after Tuttle's longtime coroner (also our longtime veterinarian), Willem Graham Suppes, died last August. No one ran against her. I guess people figured someone was better than no one. And after all, the only thing she really had to do was show up at the scene when someone died and say, "Yup, he's dead." So far, she'd been right almost one hundred percent of the time.

"Hey, y'all!" Tiffany called to us as she stepped inside the house, a huge grin on her heavily made-up face. She never tried to hide her excitement at being called out on a job. "Thanks for calling me! Sorry I'm late, but the junior bugs had their dress rehearsal for the Halloween Spooktac-ular and I had to make sure all the little ghosts and goblins were scary enough." She laughed and the tinkling sound echoed through the entry. As Tiffany followed Tabitha back to examine the body, I heard her say with barely contained glee, "I'm so glad you called, I was beginning to think no body was going to die this week!"

But before they got to the office, Carl and Butter walked out of it. "I'm sorry, ma'am," Carl said to Tabitha, who by the look on her face did not appreciate being called *ma'am*. "I'm going to have to seal off this space. Ms. Peters, you can go on in, as you are official county personnel, but everyone else is going to have to stay clear of the area."

Tiffany preened at her VIP status and scooted past Carl into the room.

"Carl, what the hell—" But Tabitha's rant dried up as she turned toward a sound in the entryway. Her eyes went wide with shock.

"What's going on here?" It was Thad Davenport wear-ing a brown leather messenger bag and a confused expres-sion. "Tab?"

Tabitha's face instantly drained of color. "Thad, honey . . ." she started to say, but then stopped, as though she suddenly forgot how to speak.

"Mr. Davenport," Carl said. "I'm very sorry for your loss. I'd like to—"

"What loss?" Thad asked.

"You said you told him," I whispered to Tabitha.

"Babe," she said, rushing to his side, "I was . . . I just came over here and . . ."

Just then, Tiffany walked out of Dr. Davenport's office, pulling off her blue latex gloves. "Yup, he's dead all right. Poor Artie."

"*What?*" Thad's face was now as white as Tabitha's. He charged through our group, but before he could get into his father's office, Carl grabbed his arm and stopped him.

"I'm sorry, but you can't go in there."

"The hell I can't—" Thad struggled to free himself from Carl's grasp as Butter grabbed his other arm. "Let go of me. . . *Dad! Dad!*" Thad's anguished cries reverberated throughout the cavernous house.

"Let him go!" Tabitha ordered.

"If you'll both just calm down a moment," Carl said. "I can explain."

Thad stopped fighting and yanked his arm back from Carl's grasp. "What happened? Why can't I see my father?" His voice cracked, anguish radiating off of him in waves.

"I'm afraid it looks as though your father has been the victim of a homicide."

"A homicide?" I couldn't stop myself from voicing the question out loud.

Carl's mouth hardened into a thin line. He nodded once.

Tiffany broke the silence. "Stabbed. Right in the ticker." She pantomimed sticking a knife through her own heart. "I didn't realize it at first, but then—"

"Thank you, Ms. Peters," Carl cut her off.

"Oh, sorry," she said. "I forget with murder cases you have to follow certain protocols, like not telling all the details. You see, I took this online course called Death Scene Investigation? And I learned that—"

"*Thank you,* Ms. Peters," Carl said again.

Thad looked like he might be sick. "Murder?" His voice was almost a whisper. "No—I just saw him last night and . . . I . . . he was fine."

"Thad, Tabitha, I'm going to need you both to come down to the sheriff's office and answer some questions, fill out paperwork, that kind of thing." He turned to Tiffany. "Can you call Dr. Mendez? I think we're going to need to loop in Forensics on this one." Dr. Mendez was the medical examiner from Richmond. Then Carl turned to me. "Riley, we do not have a statement for the press at this time."

I'll admit I had almost forgotten I worked for the newspaper until he said that.

"Sheriff, do you mind if I call my brother first?" Thad asked. "He needs to know."

I snuck a glance at Tabitha, who stood completely still except for her eyes, which floated between Thad, Carl, and the office where Dr. Davenport lay dead. Something was going on with her; she looked upset, but not surprised. And she should have been, especially since she told me earlier that she thought Arthur had died of a heart attack or stroke. She never mentioned the whole "stabbed in the heart" thing.

"Can we meet you down there, Carl?" Tabitha said. "My fiancé needs time to call his family and gather his thoughts."

Carl was already shaking his head before she finished. "I'm sorry, but procedure is, we have to take statements right away."

"I just . . . don't understand . . ." Thad was saying, more to himself than anyone else.

"Please, Carl," Tabitha said, more firmly this time. "He's had quite a shock. Can't you just let him absorb this for one hot minute?"

Carl wouldn't budge. "We need you both to come along now."

Tabitha St. Simon did not like being told what to do. Which is why it was even stranger when her voice softened and she instantly replaced her look of outrage with one of contrition. "Okay, then. We'll just take my car and see you down there."

"No ma'am."

Tabitha's nostrils flared at the second *ma'am* in as many minutes.

"Mr. Davenport will have to ride with me," Butter said.

Struggling to maintain her composure, Tabitha said through clenched teeth, "Why on earth would he have to ride with you, Butter?"

"Oh, I know!" Tiffany said, her hand shooting up into the air like she was answering a question in class. "Murder suspects must be transported in official vehicles, alone, so as not to allow them the opportunity to collude with another suspect or suspects."

"Suspects?" Tabitha lost any control she had had over her anger, and her sharp tone reverberated against all the stone in the large foyer. "Are you freaking kidding me with this, Carl?"

Carl tried without success to interrupt Tabitha's rant. Tiffany stepped outside to call the Richmond medical examiner. Thad stared at the floor, looking shell-shocked from the events of the past few minutes. And Butter reached into his back pocket, pulled out an Oats 'n Honey granola bar, and ate it while the whole scene unfolded.

As for me, three thoughts flashed into my mind simultaneously: *Tabitha is hiding something. Thad doesn't look like someone who just killed his father. And, ready or not, I have some work to do . . .*

CHAPTER 3

I raced back to the *Times*, hoping to catch Kay Jackson before she left for the day. On my way back I practiced my pitch, listing all the reasons why she should assign me this story. But as it turned out, I didn't even have to plead my case. She agreed as soon as I asked.

"This would normally go to Holman," she said. "But before he left he said you were ready to fly solo, so that's good enough for me."

All it took was that tiny measure of success, that small vote of confidence to convince me to push my luck. "Can I have the obit too?"

Kay arched her eyebrows. "You'll still have to keep up with your other responsibilities, like covering the community and education pages. Think you can handle it all?"

"I do. And actually, I think the obit and crime story go hand-in-hand."

She looked skeptical.

Now was my chance to use what I'd rehearsed. "No, really. Think about it: since I'll be covering the developing story about how Arthur died, I'll be in a good position to learn about his life, too. Most of the time the way someone dies has very little to do with the way they lived—but a murder turns that whole concept on its ear, right? Because unless Arthur was killed by a random act, which seems highly unlikely, something in his life led to his death—and our readers are going to want to know what that something was. I think I'll be in the best position to write about it, given the reporting I'll already be doing about the investigation."

She thought about it for at least five seconds, which was a long time for her. Kay Jackson was not an indecisive woman. "All right," she said. "File your stories electronically to the central database. We'll run updates online as quickly as they occur, and do two separate print stories in Sunday's edition." She paused and then added, "If you get in over your head, I'm here."

I felt like doing a victory dance. I'd done it! I'd asked for what I wanted and gotten it! This was a big moment. The old me would have been too scared to ask for this sort of opportunity, but I was no longer that girl. Overcome with gratitude and emotion, I started to gush, "Kay, thank you so much for believing—"

"This isn't charity," she cut me off. "I'm giving it to you because I see talent and, quite honestly, I like the idea of having another female reporter around here. We've got something of a testosterone imbalance in case you haven't noticed. But the guys aren't going to be happy about it. So my advice to you is: don't screw this up."

<hr />

Kay's "pep talk" didn't dampen my enthusiasm (even though I knew she was right about the guys not liking it) and I still felt excited as I gathered my things and headed over to the sheriff's office to see if I could get any updates before heading home for the day.

Tuttle Corner was built on a square like so many of the colonial towns settled in the late 1700s. This meant that nearly all of our municipal buildings and most of our local businesses occupied a four-square-block area around the green space in the center, Memorial Park. Years earlier, my mother had been on the committee to spruce up the park, which included resurfacing the walkways that snaked corner to corner, installing black wrought-iron lamps along the paths, and offering residents the opportunity to sponsor a bench. I remember Janet Gradin and Charlotte Van Stone going nine rounds over whether the plaques on the benches would be black plastic or engraved metal. In the end, Mrs. Van Stone won out (as if there'd been any doubt), and as I wound my way from the *Tuttle Times* office on the northeast side of the park over toward the sheriff's office on the southwest, I passed the bench my family had dedicated to my granddad. The golden plaque read, "In Loving Memory of Albert Christopher Ellison, beloved father, grandfather, and obituarist." I probably passed this bench ten times a week, and never without feeling his loss deep down inside my soul. But as I walked past it that day, I couldn't help but think Granddaddy would have been proud of me. He always encouraged me to consider a career in reporting, but I'd lost all interest in journalism, among other things, after he died under what I still considered suspicious circumstances.

The official cause of death had been suicide, according to the former Tuttle County sheriff, Joe Tackett—a man who thanks to Holman and me now stood on trial for fraud, corruption, and attempted murder. Despite Granddaddy's supposed-best-friend Hal Flick's refusal to consider alternative theories, I felt it in my bones that Granddaddy hadn't left this world by his own hand. And I'd be a liar if I didn't admit a part of me hoped that becoming a reporter would help me prove that someday.

I walked inside the sheriff's office and Gail, the receptionist and my ex-boyfriend's second cousin, greeted me.

"Hey Riley. What can I do for you?"

"Hi Gail!" I said brightly. I'd always liked her and even though I wasn't dating Ryan anymore, we were still friendly. "I'm actually going to be covering the Davenport story for the *Times* so I wondered if I could talk to Carl about the investigation . . ."

"Good for you, sugar! Look at you go!"

It had been no secret in Tuttle Corner that I'd had a bit of rough patch for a while, but ever since Holman and I broke the story about the corruption and murder of my friend Jordan James, people around town no longer looked at me as an object of pity.

I tried to play it cool. "Thanks, I'm excited. I mean, I'm not excited about Arthur Davenport's death—oh gosh, that sounds terrible. I'm just excited, you know, for the opportunity to . . . cover it . . . for the newspaper." So much for playing it cool.

Gail laughed. "I get it, honey. No worries. But it's gonna be a couple of hours till anyone's free. If I were you, I'd come back by after a little bit."

"Okay. Hey, would you mind giving me a shout if there are any developments? I'm going to run to dinner." I jotted down my cell and handed it to her.

"You going with that new dreamy man of yours? Mmm-mm, I'd like to sop him up with a biscuit!"

My face turned bright red. Gail knew Jay because he'd done some consulting with the sheriff's department over the past few months and she loved to flirt with him on his frequent visits to the station. But since she was Ryan's mom's first cousin, it also felt a little weird to be talking about another guy with her. Even though for the first six weeks after he broke up with me, Gail had referred to Ryan as "my stupid cousin."

"I'll tell Jay you said 'hi' . . ." I said, as I headed home, now excited about the evening ahead for a couple of different reasons.

CHAPTER 4

I barely had enough time to take Coltrane for a quick walk, change clothes, and swipe on a little lip gloss before I heard Jay's car door close in my driveway. I bounded to the front door to meet him and planted a big old kiss on him before even saying hello.

"It's nice to see you, too," he said, coming up for air. "Looks like someone had a good day . . ."

"I can't wait to tell you all about it," I said, grabbing my sweater. "We can talk on the way."

We walked hand in hand over to the Shack, which was about four blocks past Memorial Park along the river. It was mid-October and still warm, but not hot—and perfect for dining al fresco. Louis seated us at a table for two out on the deck overlooking the water.

The Shack, or James Madison's Fish Shack, was Tuttle's nicest restaurant by far. Originally a family home, the Shack was a two-story house with gray shingles punctuated by crisp white trim around the many windows. Inside, two dining rooms sat on either side of the narrow staircase that led upstairs to the bar area, which was always crowded on weekend nights. Instead of having tables up there, Louis and Dahlia had put in a bunch of couches and overstuffed chairs, and some low coffee tables filled with board games and trivia decks. But by far the Shack's best attribute was its large deck that overlooked the James River. It was a wide-plank cedar deck dotted with small tables for two or four, each one covered by a black-and-white striped umbrella. It was the perfect place to unwind after a long day at work. And I was with the perfect companion to do just that.

"You got the story," Jay said after I'd finished telling him about my day. "That's great!"

"Yeah," I said, grabbing a strand of hair just below my shoulders and twisting it. "It is. It's just . . ." I stopped. Ever since I'd left the sheriff's office, a kernel of doubt and insecurity had started to take root. This sort of thing had been happening a lot since I left my comfortable job as an hourly worker at the library; I'd go from wildly excited about my new career to desperately insecure in three seconds flat.

"What's wrong?"

"Nothing, it's just—what if I mess up? What if I miss an important element of the story? Kay told me I'd better not screw up."

"So you won't screw up," he said, making it sound so simple. He leaned across the table and took my left hand in his right and knitted our fingers together. "Just promise me you'll be careful."

"Of course," I said. "Okay, enough about my day. How was yours?"

Jay was a DEA agent who had moved down to Virginia from New Jersey less than a year earlier. He was brought here to go undercover to investigate Juan Pablo Romero, a restaurateur suspected of selling drugs out of his taco trucks. That's actually kind of how we met. Holman and I were also looking at Romero's involvement in the death of our friend Jordan—we sort of stumbled into Jay's investigation. The spark had been instantaneous, and though it had only been a couple of months, I felt like Jay and I were on our way to something pretty special.

"It was work, you know, fine."

Jay didn't talk about his job much. I wasn't sure if that was because he was working on something super secret or some other reason, but his reluctance to talk about work had started to pique my curiosity. "Oh yeah, what'd you do today? Did you catch some bad guys?"

He leaned forward with a sly smile on his face. "Yeah, four or five big ones. Got 'em with my bare hands, too."

"Seriously," I laughed. "You've never really told me what you do all day."

"That's 'cause I haven't been doing a whole lot lately," he said, leaning back in his chair. "It's been pretty slow. The Virginia office is nothing like Jersey—which I guess is a good thing."

"I like to think so."

"Plus, Virginia has one particular thing that Jersey doesn't."

"Oh yeah?"

"Definitely." He gave me a look that could only be described as smoldering. "See, there's this girl . . ."

I felt color rush to my cheeks as the server came over to take our drink order. The Shack was famous for its themed cocktails and Jay ordered a Yankee Doodle Dandy brandy punch, but since I knew I'd have to head back to work, I got a Boston Tea-Totaler.

When the server walked away, Jay pivoted. "Have your parents made it back yet?"

My parents were in a band and spent a lot of time on the road. Wait—that makes it sound too cool. Let me rephrase: my parents made up the two-member singing group The Rainbow Connection and toured the region performing at libraries, private birthday parties, and preschool graduations, delighting the under-six set with their pun-filled songs about such topics as woodland creatures, making friends, and learning to go pee in the potty.

"They get home Sunday," I said. "Maybe you could come for dinner next week?"

Jay and my parents had really hit it off. My mother was fascinated by Jay's Indian heritage and had used it as an excuse to try out to several new vegan dishes of Indian inspiration, often asking him if this or that tasted authentic. Jay was an omnivore born in Massachusetts who had never visited his parents' country of origin—but he always told her she had a real flair for Indian cooking, which made her love him. And my father liked everyone. Literally. In almost twenty-five years on this planet, I had never heard him say anything remotely negative about anyone—except once when he said Kim Jong-un seemed "a little unstable."

"I'd love that," Jay said. "I actually promised your mom I'd bring her some of the *amchoor* I had my mom send from home. She wants it for her mango curry."

"Mom really likes you, you know."

"I like her too, but not half as much as I like you." Jay reached across the table and grabbed my hand again. I linked fingers with him and squeezed back. It was probably a combination of the fresh air, the low light, and the fact that we were smack dab in that dreamy new-relationship phase—but I felt like I could stare into his eyes forever.

"You're going to make everybody sick if you don't stop that." A voice as familiar as my own intruded into the moment. It was Ryan, my ex, and he was walking up to our table.

Ryan had been my first love, the guy I was sure I'd spend the rest of my life with. He was also the guy who'd broken my heart into a million tiny pieces when he'd de-

cided after seven years that I wasn't enough for him. He'd
run off to Colorado (literally in the middle of the night) and
called me from the road to break things off. But he never
really let me go, giving me just enough hope that we'd
get back together to keep me on the line for nearly a year.
And then a couple of months ago, he'd come back home,
told me he loved me, and that he wanted us to be together
forever. I found out approximately twenty-four hours later
that while living in Colorado he'd gotten a woman named
Ridley pregnant and that he planned to move her to Tuttle
Corner to raise the baby around family. He begged me to
stay with him, saying he loved me and that Ridley was just
a fling. But there are flings and then there are babies that
result from flings. The whole thing was a little too complicated for me. While I believed Ryan loved me, I'd come to
realize that the way he loved me wasn't good enough—not
anymore. I deserved more. Making the decision to move on
was one of the hardest things I'd ever done but it set me on
a new, brighter path forward. I hoped Ryan would accept it
eventually and find his own brighter path.

"Hi Ryan," I said, pulling my hand back from Jay's.

"Hey," Jay said, and I could hear a faint weariness in his
voice. Ryan was as much a part of Tuttle Corner as I was,
and it seemed we were forever running into him.

"Hello, lovebirds!" Ridley, who was a step behind Ryan,
floated up to our table and bestowed upon us a blinding,
thousand-watt smile. How somebody that pregnant could
be that graceful I would never understand. Every head in
the place turned to watch this vision of maternal loveliness
glide by. When Ryan first told me about Ridley, I thought of
her as the bizarro me—my complete opposite in every way.
This image was confirmed when I actually met her. Ridley
stood six feet tall and had long, toned limbs and a thick

swath of white-blond hair that fell effortlessly to the middle of her back. She had startling blue eyes and approximately twelve perfect freckles distributed evenly across the bridge of her button nose. Her lips were full, bow-shaped, and naturally pink; her teeth straight and white; and, as if that weren't enough, she had one of those raspy voices like a DJ. Oh—and at eight months pregnant she looked like most of us do after a big meal. There was no evidence of any sort of pregnancy weight gain other than the tiny bump just under her tanned, pierced, and always-exposed belly button.

Ridley and I were learning to coexist, but I'll admit it hadn't been easy for me. I was over Ryan, but seeing his perfect Amazonian baby mama and the way everyone fawned over her made me feel things I wasn't proud of—things I didn't want to examine too closely.

"You remember Ridley," I said to Jay.

Jay smiled politely, but when he didn't blush or stammer like every other man in town did in her presence, I fell just a little deeper for him.

"So, what are you two kids up to tonight?" Ryan asked, as if the appetizers and drinks offered no clues.

"Just having a little dinner," I said, unable to keep the sarcasm from my voice.

"Us too," he said and clapped Ridley on the back of her shoulder. "Ridley can really tie on the old feedbag now that she's in her third trimester."

Ridley, instead of being offended, threw out a throaty laugh. "Yeah, I can't seem to get enough these days." She swirled her hands around her perfectly shaped bump and I felt a pang of something deep within. "I sometimes wonder if I am incubating a baby lion with all the cravings for red meat."

"Oh, that's just a Sanford for you." I said it before I even thought about it, and then immediately regretted it. It was an intimate comment, exposing my deep and thorough knowledge of the Sanford family. Ryan's eyes found mine. I felt the unidentified emotion again and wondered if my ovaries hadn't heard the news that Ryan and I were over.

"Well, I think you look super healthy," Jay said. "Enjoy your dinner." Translation: *move along, people.*

Ryan held my gaze for a moment too long. "Yeah, you guys, too." But before he turned to walk away, he said, "Hey, did you hear about Thad Davenport getting arrested?"

"Wait—*what?*" I said. I dug out my phone from my purse and sure enough, Gail had texted me fifteen minutes ago: Thad arrested. Tab throwing one hell of a fit.

This was big. I looked up at Jay, an apology cocked and loaded.

"I know that look—I've given that look. Go."

"You're the best." I kissed him goodbye. "I'll make it up to you."

Without so much as a glance at Ridley or Ryan, he held the side of my cheek close to his and whispered, "I'll hold you to that."

Chapter 5

I heard the yelling before I even walked inside the sheriff's office.

"Are you out of your mind?" Tabitha, red-faced and wild-eyed, was screaming at Carl Haight. "You let him go right this minute or I will sue every last person in this room!"

"Tabitha—I mean, Miss St. Simon," Carl struggled to retain his professional demeanor. "You need to calm down or I'm going to have to ask you to leave."

When I walked in, no one even looked at me. Every employee of the Tuttle County sheriff's office was watching the dramatic showdown between Carl and Tabitha.

"How could you even think Thad could do something like kill his own father? It's ridiculous!"

"Miss St. Si—"

"He's a well-respected cardiac management specialist!"

"Miss St.—"

"He can't even kill a spider! He puts them onto little slips of paper and takes them outside, for Pete's sake! In all my life I have never seen such a gross miscarriage of justice, not to mention complete idiocy!" She spat the words like bullets from a machine gun. No one dared interrupt her or attempt to step in between the two.

As the former target of several Tabitha rants, I wasn't

intimidated. I walked over to her and put a hand on her shoulder. "Tab? Can we talk for a second?"

She had the wild look of a jaguar that had been interrupted mid-kill, but after a second, sanity returned to her eyes. "Fine," she huffed, then jabbed a finger in Carl's direction. "But this is not over, Haight. You got that? I'm going to get the best freaking lawyers money can buy and sic them on you and this two-bit operation you're running!"

"C'mon now." I led her toward the front steps of the building.

"Can you believe this?" She leaned against the railing just outside the building. "Thad—a *murderer*? It's insane."

"Just slow down a minute," I said in what I hoped was a soothing voice. "Tell me what happened."

Tabitha smoothed her long dark hair and tucked both sides behind her ears. She took a deep breath before explaining. "*Acting*-Sheriff Haight said he wanted to take our statements, but I knew something was off when they separated us. I was with Butter, who basically just asked me a bunch of inane questions that I'm pretty sure he was reading off of a Google search of 'What to ask people after they find a dead body,' all the while eating an entire pound of pistachios, mind you." She rolled her eyes.

"But Thad was in another room with Carl *forever*. Once they finished up, everything seemed fine, and Thad and I were about to leave when Carl got a phone call from Dr. Mendez in Richmond. He said that in addition to the knife wound in Arthur's chest—which we already knew about—there was something else. Results from the quick tox screen showed high levels of digitalis in Arthur's blood."

"What's digitalis?"

"They use it to treat heart-rhythm problems. But Arthur didn't have any heart problems."

"Okay..." I waited for her to put this all together for me.

"Duh. Thad sells Digoxigon, a form of digitalis."

"Wait—what? I thought Thad was a cardiologist?"

Tabitha gave me a look that might as well have turned me to stone. "No."

"But you just said that he is a cardiac management specialist, isn't that the same thing?"

Two peach blooms appeared on her cheeks. "He *is* a cardiac management specialist—for Helder Pharmaceuticals."

"So he sells drugs?"

Tabitha's blush deepened, the peach blossoms morphing into the redder blotches of anger. "Yes, technically he is a pharmaceutical sales representative. But he is in the upper echelon of sales for Helder, and reps their cardiac-care medications."

I was dumbfounded. Tabitha loved to throw around that her fiancé was a cardiac specialist, and even inserted herself into conversations with library patrons about heart health issues, citing her expertise as a result of her fiancé's line of work. She knew people assumed he was a doctor and never once corrected that perception.

"I never said he was a doctor," Tabitha said. "Anyway, do you want to know what happened or not?"

I nodded. I put a pin in this whole Thad's-not-really-a-doctor thing and made a mental note to come back to it later.

"Okay. So since one of the drugs Thad reps is Digoxigon, which, like I said, is a form of digitalis. Naturally, he carries samples of it in his car and stores samples at home..."

"And when Sheriff Haight heard Dr. Davenport had toxic levels of the drug in his system, and then found those same drugs on Thad, he arrested him." I finished Tabitha's thought for her.

"Exactly."

"But wait," I said. "I'm confused, did Arthur die from digitalis poisoning or from being stabbed?"

"The medical examiner hasn't determined the official cause of death yet. But Carl—in his infinite stupidity—decided to arrest Thad anyway."

Tabitha was so distressed I felt sorry for her. She seemed genuinely concerned for Thad. I could imagine that spending any time at all in jail would be pretty hard on a guy who had grown up on the Davenport estate, and it was touching how scared she was for him.

"I'm sorry, Tab," I said. "This must be so hard on you."

"Yeah. His final tuxedo fitting is in three days! Can you imagine if I have to ask the tailor to come to the jail to do it?"

Just then the door to the sheriff's office opened. Butter leaned halfway out and looked at Tabitha. "You can see him now if you want."

Tabitha said nothing but gave Butter the evil eye before twitching past him into the station.

"I was there when that girl was born, did you know that?" Butter said, shaking his head. "Marge was the on-call nurse at Tuttle General the night Patricia's water broke. I was up there bringing Marge some dinner. Anyway, little Tabby was born just after 8 p.m., I remember, because there was a Nationals game on and Dr. Benton was itching to get home to watch it. She came out all pink and wrinkly, like we all do I expect, but I remember she had a set of lungs on her like I'd never heard. Marge and the other nurses joked she was gonna be an opera singer." He laughed at the memory. "I guess she found another use for those lungs of hers."

I smiled. Tabitha was well known around town for her robust rants. "Hey, how's Carl holding up?" I asked him before he turned to go back inside.

"He's doing all right, trying to conduct the investigation to the absolute letter of the law—with so many eyes watching and all. And the mayor's had that little minion of hers calling over here every hour to get an update."

"Ugh, *Toby*."

Mayor Shaylene Lancett's nephew, the only son of her only brother, was her unofficial second-in-command. Even though Toby Lancett held no official post within our government, he was continually dispatched by the mayor for anything she couldn't, or didn't, want to do herself. This gave Toby, an otherwise excellent candidate for Most Likely to Be Shot by His Own Troops, an inflated sense of power.

"I can see why the mayor's upset though. Two murders in about as many months does not exactly reflect well upon Tuttle Corner now does it?"

"No, it does not. Carl would sure like to solve this one quickly and move on."

"How about Lindsey Davis? Has she been by yet?" Lindsey Davis was the new prosecuting attorney in Tuttle County.

He nodded. "She was here about a half an hour ago—" Butter stopped midsentence. He'd said too much and he knew it. "Nuh-uh." He wagged a finger at me. "No comment. That's what I'm supposed to say to all-y'all right now. Carl'll make a statement soon. Until then"—he mimed locking his lips with an invisible key and then, in true Butter form, he ate it.

I hung around the sheriff's office a while longer trying to get anyone to talk to me, but they were all on message with "No comment." Once I'd hit a dead end I decided to go by the office quickly to log the story. It was a short piece, reporting only the news that there'd been an arrest in the case. I had just uploaded the article and was getting ready to head home when I got a text. I assumed it was from Jay checking on me, but I was wrong. It was from Tabitha:

I NEED TO TALK TO YOU ASAP. MEET ME AT LIBRARY NOW. COME ALONE. PLEASE.

CHAPTER 6

Tabitha, red-eyed and blotchy-cheeked, sat across from me in the children's section of the library. Even though it was way past closing time, we both had keys and knew the code to the alarm system. Plus, we knew Dr. H wouldn't mind us meeting here. And back in the children's section, we could sit with the lights on and no one would be able to see from the outside. Tabitha said we needed absolute privacy for this conversation. And after hearing the story she just told me, I understood why.

"Tab," I said after she'd finished unburdening herself. "I'm not a lawyer and I'm not a priest. I work for the newspaper, you know."

She shrugged. "It's fine. I'm planning to tell Carl all of this tomorrow anyway, but I wanted you to know what really happened because once I tell Carl what I did—" She broke off for a moment. "—I'll probably be in jail right beside Thad."

I nodded. I wasn't certain about the particulars of the law, but I knew enough to know that what Tabitha had done almost certainly fell outside the bounds of legality.

Turns out part of what I already knew was true; it just wasn't the whole story. Tabitha had gone over to Thad's house and found Dr. Davenport dead in his office. As she walked around the body she saw the handle of a small folding hunting knife sticking out of his chest. Thad's knife. It had been a gift from Arthur to Thad when Thad graduated from Duke, the blade engraved with the words, *Be the man I know you can be.*

"I know it was stupid, but I just panicked. Before I really thought about what I was doing, I grabbed the knife from his chest, wiped it clean, and threw it into an urn in the hallway."

Thad had not been at a meeting in Richmond, as she had told me earlier. The truth was that she hadn't seen him since the night before. He'd come over to her place Sunday night and they'd fought.

"Arthur could be hard on his boys." Tabitha's hand shook as she wiped a tear from the corner of her eye; the massive diamond on her left ring finger caught the light as she moved. "He loved them, but often held them to an impossible standard, particularly Thad, being the firstborn and all."

Tabitha said the two had gotten into it yet again about Thad's being in pharmaceutical sales. Dr. Davenport felt like Thad had chosen the path of least resistance instead of rising to his potential and going to medical school like his brother.

Thad told Tabitha that Arthur was halfway into a bottle of Macallan when Thad got home Sunday night. "He started in about how it was so embarrassing when Thad walked in 'hawking his crap' in front of his colleagues. He said how much smarter and more motivated David is, and why can't he be more like him . . . he just went on and on.

"Thad has the patience of a saint. Obviously." She threw me a guilty look from under her lashes. "So he was pretty good about letting that kind of stuff roll off, but I guess it got to him that night because he started yelling back. Thad said it got bad—years of resentment started coming out, both of them yelling and screaming at each other.

"He came to my place around 7:45 as upset as I've ever seen him. He said he was going to show his father that he couldn't control him. He said he was going to tell his father that he didn't need him or his money anymore." Tabitha's face twisted in anguish. "I know it was wrong of me—and selfish—but all I could think about was the wedding and where we would get married. I mean, we have less than two weeks to go and the invitations have already gone out and—" Fresh tears sprang to her eyes and she wiped them away quickly. "Anyway. Then we fought. It was awful, we almost never fight. Thad got so angry, he left my place at just after nine and said he was going to stay with his brother."

I was rapt listening to this story and wondered how much of it Carl Haight knew. This certainly did not look good for Thad.

"So why did you go over to the house the next day?"

She took a deep breath. "Arthur and I had always gotten along really well, and I just thought if I could talk to him and get him to calm down, maybe he'd apologize to Thad and we could go on like none of it ever happened. But then I saw him lying there . . . with Thad's knife . . . I mean, of course I knew Thad would never—could never—but I just reacted out of protective instinct and now . . ." This was the most genuine emotion I'd ever seen from Tabitha in all the years I'd known her.

"I called you for help, but by the time you got there I was so freaked out by what I'd done, I couldn't even admit it to you, so I made up that stuff about the obituary."

"I had a feeling there was more to the story than just you wanting me to write the obit," I said.

She nodded. "I called you because you were able to

get to the truth of what happened to Jordan, even after the sheriff closed the case. I need you to do the same thing here, Riley. You're not one of those people who just accepts things at face value." She said this like it was both a compliment and an insult. "And despite the face value here, there is no way Thad killed his father. He doesn't have a violent bone in his body. You have to help us!"

"Does Thad know what you did?"

"No." She shook her head. "I didn't have time to tell him. I hoped to tell him on the drive over to the station, but they separated us." She dropped her face into her hands and took another deep, steadying breath. With her eyes still focused on the carpet below, she said, "I know I have to tell Carl, but once I do he probably won't even look for other suspects. He'll focus all his energy on Thad—and me."

She had a point there. Dr. Davenport was a wealthy man and Thad (and by extension, Tabitha) stood to inherit a lot of money after his death. When you added in the rocky personal relationship, the murder weapon or weapons being in Thad's possession, and the argument the night before he died, it didn't take much to see Thad and Tabitha as lead suspects.

Tabitha stared at me and I could feel the weight of her desperation. It was painful. Whatever the truth was, Tabitha believed to her core that her fiancé was innocent.

"I need your help, Riley."

"I'm not sure what I can do . . ."

"You're smart. You'll figure it out. You knew there was something off with Jordan's death and you were right. You have to know there's something off here, too. You're already writing the obituary, right?"

I nodded.

"So just use those interviews to look into who could

have wanted Arthur dead. Did he have any enemies? Any bad business dealings? Anyone else who would profit from his being out of the way? Or maybe it was one of his girl-friends—he always had plenty of those . . ."

"Listen," I said, thinking about the mounting evidence against Thad. "My job as a reporter is to uncover the truth. Are you prepared for the possibility that you might not like what I find out?"

"We have nothing to hide," she said firmly. "Just find out what really happened. Because whatever it was, I can promise you it had nothing to do with me or Thad."

Despite Thad's means, motive, and opportunity, I wasn't convinced that he had killed his father—at least there was enough doubt there for me to want to know more. And I'll admit there was a small part of me that was excited by the possibility of uncovering new information or a hidden sus-pect on this case. That would show everyone at the *Times* that I wasn't just a one-hit wonder, wouldn't it?

"Okay," I said. "I'll look into it. But I'm not doing this for you or Thad. I'm looking for the truth—whatever that might be. You know that, right?"

"Oh thank you, thank you, thank you!" Tabitha cried as she pulled me into an aggressive embrace that suggested she did not understand any such thing.

When I got home, Jay was asleep on my couch with a very comfortable Coltrane curled up at his feet. I texted him be-fore I met Tabitha to let him know I'd be a while. He wrote back saying simply: I'll wait.

I walked in quietly and set my purse and keys down on the sofa table and allowed myself a moment to indulge in the sight. Jay was what women of an older generation would call "a real catch." He was smart, successful, kind, funny—not to mention easy on the eyes. I tiptoed over to the couch where he lay sleeping and leaned over to kiss his perfect mocha-skinned forehead. His lashes fluttered open like Snow White.

"Hey."

"Hi," I said, and dipped my head again to kiss him. "Thanks for taking care of Coltrane."

"Aw, he took care of me—that dog has the soul of a philosopher." He smiled and propped himself up on his elbow. "How'd it go? Everything okay?"

"Oh yeah," I said, unsure of how much I could ethically tell him. I didn't want to lie to him, but since Tabitha had made me promise to keep what she told me off the record until she talked to Carl, I couldn't tell him about the conversation either. Plus, there was a tiny part of me that worried about what Jay would think if he knew I'd agreed to look into who else might have a reason to want Arthur Davenport dead. He'd seen a lot of bad guys in his time with the DEA, and because of that he tended to worry about safety more than someone else might. The last thing I wanted was for him to worry. So I did what any woman would do who wanted to avoid answering a question posed by a gorgeous man who just happened to be lying on her couch: I distracted him.

Hey Riley,

My name is Jenna B and I am going to be ur Personal Success Concierge™ over the next month and hopefully a lot longer than that—haha lol!

I am so excited to meet u! When I read ur profile I was like, "OMG. This girl and I could be frickin' twins!" It's like we've lived doubles lives—seriously. U grew up in a small town; I grew up in a small suburb. U were an English major in college; I am thinking about majoring in English if I decide to go back to school—plus, I read Pride and Prejudice at least once a year. How frickin' weird is that?

Anyway. I want to just lay out for u how this whole thing is going to work. Ur free trial comes with an unlimited number of emails over the next 30 days. (After that we can figure it out. There are plans.) But basically I'm here for u whatever u need. U can ask me questions and I'll try to provide guidance and give u my perspective and—[TRIGGER WARNING]— sometimes even challenge ur truths. Challenging truth is an important aspect of being a Personal Success Concierge™. More on that ltr.

Anyway. Just a little bit about me: I am a gifted encourager and I have had an overdeveloped sense of intuition from a very young age, according to my mom. I love to workout, meditate, eat clean (except when it comes to Cinnabon, u feel me?), practice yoga, and journal when I have the time. My secret dream is to star in a movie opposite Eddie Redmayne. I also hope to own a tiny house someday.

Would love to know more about what makes u u and what u hope to accomplish over the next 30. Write back when u can. Can't wait to dive in!

xx,
Jenna B
Personal Success Concierge™
Bestmillenniallife.com

Dear Jenna B,

Thank you for the nice letter. I thought I marked the box next to "Thanks but no thanks" on the initial form. Maybe there was some mistake? In any case, I am not in need of a Personal Success Concierge.

Best of luck getting that tiny house someday!
Riley Ellison

Hey Riley,

A lot of people r intimidated by the process at first, but no worries I got u, haha lol! Plus, did you not get the memo that it is FREE, as in 100% gratis??? That's like a huge savings. U'd b silly not to take advantage of it. In the wise words of Nike, "Just do it."

Anyway. I'll make it easy for u: Fill in the blank of this sentence: The thing I am most afraid of in the world is: _____

xx,
Jenna B
Personal Success Concierge™
Bestmillenniallife.com

Getting roped into situations against my will.

All best,
Riley

CHAPTER 7

J ay left the next morning before the sun came up. He said he wanted to go home and catch a shower before heading up to the DC office, where he'd been spending a lot of time lately. I got up, made coffee, and sat down to my laptop as I did every morning to read the obituaries. I looked through the obituary sections from eight newspapers habitually. It had become a way to center myself, a ritual like drinking coffee or going for a run. Maybe it was the perspective obituaries offered. Maybe it was the reminder that we are all just bouncing around on this planet for a short time. Or maybe it was just that I loved learning about people's stories. Reading about a life well lived filled me with a certain sense of peace and hopefulness, and was as good a way to start my day as anything else I'd found.

That day's selections included a taxi driver from Connecticut whose hobby was growing large vegetables; a grandmother from Denver who had never cut her hair, not once in her whole life, and it was down to her calves when she died at age eighty-seven; and a once-famous violinist who lived in a small village in the English countryside who died after a long battle with Parkinson's. After the disease robbed him of his ability to play, he offered free lessons to any child in his village who expressed a desire to learn.

And I read about a woman from a small town in Oregon who once a month on Thursdays for over twenty-three years made homemade lasagna, garlic bread, and a green salad, and dropped it off at the local fire station. When she passed, more than forty firefighters, past and present, attended her funeral. I'm not a particularly spiritual person, but I like to think Mrs. Edith Westerson was looking down that day and saw how many lives she touched with her simple kindness.

Full up on perspective for the day, I walked into the office at just after 8 a.m. Gerlach Spencer and Bruce Henderson actually stood up and applauded as I walked in.

"The intern's got skills," Henderson said, as I set my things down at my desk. "That was quite a scoop you got last night."

After I talked with Tabitha, I had logged an update to the story I'd written earlier, to reflect what Tabitha told me about the events leading up the Arthur Davenport's death. I had to attribute the information to an "anonymous source close to the family," but it was still a strong piece containing new information about a hot case. I'll admit I felt proud of it, even if the story had just landed in my lap.

"Thanks. And I'm not an intern," I said.

"Who's your anonymous source?" Spencer asked, leaning against the side of my cubicle. "It wouldn't be your buddy Carl down at the sheriff's office, now would it?"

"Are you unclear about the definition of anonymous?" I said, allowing a little bravado to creep into my voice.

"Just because you and the new sheriff are old friends, don't go thinking you're going to get all the crime stories around here," he warned. "This one shoulda been mine."

I felt the stinging sensation in the base of my throat that always accompanied confrontation. I could feel the color creeping up my neck as I looked at Spencer, desperately trying to think of some witty retort. When the silence stretched on a moment too long, he said, "Oh, relax, kiddo. I'm only razzing you."

I couldn't tell if he had really been joking around, or if he had wanted to warn me for real but saw how freaked out I got and backtracked. Sometimes in a newsroom things could get competitive. I'd heard enough of Granddaddy's stories to know that.

I managed to laugh it off, and Spencer went back to his desk. I took a few minutes to get it together before what was sure to be my next uncomfortable conversation of the day: telling Flick I'd been assigned the Davenport obit. My stomach churned with dread at the thought of it. I didn't like to have any conversation with Hal Flick, let alone one in which I'd be telling him I'd gone over his head to get a plum assignment.

I hovered at his open office door. "Knock, knock."

He grunted an acknowledgment.

I guess I was more nervous than I thought because when I spoke my voice sounded preposterously close to Helena Bonham Carter's Bellatrix Lestrange—which is to say, comically aggressive (and inexplicably tinged with a British accent). "I was just coming by to tell you that Kay assigned me the obit for Arthur Davenport."

He looked at me with the same expression he might have while looking at a talking oven mitt.

"I already have a file with a list of contacts and other stuff, so should I just get started on that and run it past you when I have a draft?"

More blank staring.

"Flick, did you hear me?"

"I heard you. But I'm writing the Davenport obit."

"I'm sorry?"

"You're forgiven."

"Wait, what?"

"You said you were sorry so I forgave you. That's how these things work." Flick gave me his steely-eyed glare but behind his eyes I swear I saw a flash of something else.

"I was asked directly to write this obituary by a member of his family, Flick. It's mine."

"Dr. Arthur Davenport was a prominent member of Tuttle Corner. The whole county will want to read about him, especially given the way he died. You've written one obit in your life. You are not qualified to write this one."

I glared back at him. I should have known Flick would try to take this away from me. "Kay gave it to me," I said, defiantly. "Ask her."

"Ask me what?" Kay appeared in the doorway to Flick's office.

I hadn't known she'd been walking past when I used her name or else I might not have been so cavalier about it. The truth was, I didn't know what she was going to say. She might very well reverse course if Flick's objection was strong enough.

"Riley says she's writing the Davenport obit," Flick said. "C'mon, Jackson. The kid's a cub. She doesn't have the experience—"

"How am I ever supposed to get experience if you never let me do anything?" All that was missing was a foot stomp and a guttural "ugh" sound and I could have won the Oscar for best dramatic performance in the role of a self-indulgent teenager.

Kay ignored us both. "Riley's going to take this one," she said. "Flick, I want you to help her. Give her the benefit of your experience. We need to train new blood around here."

He started to object, but Kay talked over him. "You won't live forever and when it comes time for the *Times* to write your obit, it's probably gonna be Riley who does it, so teach her well." She winked at me and blew down the hall to put out the next fire.

The look on Flick's face said *Over my dead body,* which was kind of ironic given the situation.

"I'll get you a draft soon," I said, trying, and failing, to keep the smugness out of my voice.

"You know this isn't some sort of eulogy obit like the one you wrote for Jordan. This is a news story, as in real journalism. You're going to need to cover the good, the bad, and the ugly. Think you can handle that?"

"Yes." But I knew I wouldn't convince him with just talk—there was too much water under our particular bridge. I'd have to prove myself through my work.

He stood up the way old men do, leading with his head and shoulders, and then slowly straightened out. He lumbered around to his antiquated army-green file cabinet and pulled out a manila folder. "This is the advance file we have on Davenport. You know that research I've had you doing that you hate so much? Well, it's times like this that stuff comes in handy."

I took the file without saying anything. I felt a bit chastened. I had assumed Flick was just having me doing that research because he didn't like me.

I went back to my desk and began to work my way through the folder, making notes in the margins. One of the advantages of working for a weekly paper as opposed to a daily was that we could take more time with our stories. At a daily newspaper, a reporter had maybe four or five hours to write an obit. At the *Times,* I was grateful that we usually had at least a few days. Especially in this case where the cause of death was murder—and an unsolved one at that.

I was just about to pick up the phone to check on Tabitha, when Kay Jackson's voice called out from her office, "Ellison, can you come in here a sec?"

I'd never been called into Kay's office before. It made me a little nervous. "What's up?"

"Sit down. Close the door."

Uh-oh. My nervousness instantly upgraded to dread.

"Mayor Lancett just called," Kay said. "She wanted to thank us for the excellent reporting in the Davenport case."

I felt relieved. That was a good thing, right? I mean, I doubt it was every day that the mayor called to thank the newspaper for something! But my joy was short-lived . . .

"Then she started talking about how tourism plays a big part in the economy of Tuttle Corner and how the perception of multiple murders in our town could have a disastrous effect on local businesses, etcetera, etcetera. And how the town was still healing after 'that nasty business' with Sheriff Tackett."

I wasn't sure I understood what Kay was telling me.

"She didn't come out and say it, but my guess is this little phone call was a not-so-subtle suggestion to tone down our coverage of the Davenport murder."

"What?" I said, shocked. The mayor wanted to censor our newspaper because it might mean James Madison's Fish Shack gets a few less reservations this summer? That was ridiculous—and unethical.

Kay rushed in to reassure me. "Listen, I don't want you to worry, we don't answer to the mayor. Our responsibility is to our readers and to the truth."

"Okay," I said, still surprised at the mayor's subtle directive. "So what do we do?"

"We do what we always do. But you will need to be extra

careful, Riley. Every detail, every quote, every line has to be one hundred percent accurate, and one hundred percent verifiable."

I braced myself for her to ask who my anonymous source was. I wasn't going to tell her—not until Tabitha said I could. I may have been a journalist for only a month, but that was long enough to know that you never betray a source. Not to mention a friend. (Or a frenemy, as the case may be.)

"I understand that sometimes you need to print information from an anonymous source, but it's not ideal. Next story we publish on this, I'd like to be able to go on record with an attributable source."

I exhaled, relieved I didn't have to refuse her any information.

Kay exhaled too. She was tough as nails, but I could tell the mayor's phone call had rattled her cage a bit. She confirmed my suspicion when she smiled at me and said, "Hell of a time for Holman to be out at sea, huh?"

CHAPTER 8

Tabitha lived in a condo complex just off the main square that was no more than a three-minute walk from the *Times* offices. The complex consisted of a series of eight row houses in the Victorian style, each painted a different color, with wrought-iron roof cresting and bright white gingerbread scrollwork. The effect was charming, if a little Stepford. In fact, some residents threw a fit when the units were built, calling them an aesthetic insult to the architectural integrity of Tuttle Corner. I thought that was a little dramatic—they were cute, maybe a bit planned, but cute nonetheless. Grant St. Simon, Tabitha's father, built the complex and let his daughter live there rent-free.

Tabitha lived in the blue condo on the west end of the complex. She hadn't answered any of my calls or texts, so I decided to pop over to see if I could catch her at home. I saw her car out front and felt a wave of relief. But no one answered when I knocked. I knocked again, this time harder. "Tabitha? Are you home?" I waited for a response. "I really need to talk to you."

I knocked some more, and waited some more. As I was about to shout even louder and beg her to open up, the door to the townhouse next to Tabitha's swung open, and Millie Hedron peeked her head out.

"Oh hi, Miss Hedron," I said. "I'm sorry if I woke you."

Millie was still in her robe.

She waved a dismissive hand. "I've been up for hours with all the action around here."

"Action?"

She nodded and pulled the sides of her robe together. "Carl Haight came and took Tabitha down to the station about two hours ago. And boy-howdy can that girl scream."

"What?"

"Mm-hmm," she lowered her voice to a conspiratorial whisper. "He and Butter marched right up here, pounded on her door loud enough to wake the whole neighborhood. I couldn't hear everything Carl said, but—" she looked from left to right, "I have a feeling this has to do with Thad being arrested for his daddy's murder."

I was truly shocked. Had Carl figured out that Tabitha was the anonymous source from my piece? Had Tabitha told him what she did? I needed to find out—and quickly.

"I'm sorry, Miss Hedron, but I have to go," I said, already halfway down the walk. "Sorry I woke you!"

"You didn't, remember?" She called after me, but I couldn't stop to respond. I turned the corner and sped off toward the sheriff's office.

"I'm sorry, Riley," Gail said. "I can't let you see her. Rules are rules."

"Can I at least talk to Carl? Please?"

"I don't know." Gail looked over her shoulder toward his office. "He's been up half the night. I'm not sure now would be the best time—"

"I'll just be a minute! Thanks," I said without waiting for her response. When I got to Carl's door, I paused, took a deep breath, and readied myself. I wasn't sure what he had on Tabitha but I knew one thing for sure: I was not here to make her situation worse by giving away information she had shared anonymously.

"Sheriff Haight?" I said as I peeked my head into his office.

Carl had dark circles under his eyes and a two-day stubble on his chin. He looked like he hadn't been home in a while. "No comment for the press, Riley. We'll have something for you soon—but not yet."

"That's not why I'm here," I said. "I heard you're holding Tabitha—"

"No comment."

"Just tell me what she's charged with and I'll go away. I promise."

He looked at me, his lids heavy from exhaustion. We'd known each other long enough for him to know I was going to keep asking until I got some sort of answer—one way or another.

"Fine," he said, waving me inside. "She hasn't been charged with anything. I'm holding her for assaulting a police officer."

"What?" This was not what I was expecting to hear.

"We went to her house to ask her a couple of questions, in part based on your story in the *Times*, and she just got mad as a hornet. She ordered us to leave and when we wouldn't, she pushed Butter and he fell backward off her front step onto a little garden ornament thing she had setting out. An angel, I think. Those wings were awful sharp. Poor Butter had to have five stitches in his backside."

An involuntary giggle bubbled to the surface.

"It's not funny, Riley. Tabitha needs to control herself. Butter coulda been seriously hurt. And I need all the deputies I've got right now."

"I'm sorry. It's not funny, you're right." I dropped into

the chair in front of his desk. I felt badly for him; he was clearly exhausted and overwhelmed. He'd only been in the position of acting-sheriff for a couple of weeks and a murder case like this had to be incredibly stressful. I felt a kinship with him in that moment: we were both new to our jobs and both in just a little bit over our heads. "Have you been home since this all happened?"

"Just once to change my clothes and kiss Lisa and the baby."

"You know, I'm writing Dr. Davenport's obit for the *Times*. I'll be conducting interviews with the people who knew him best. If you want access to any of my notes, I'm happy to share."

I thought this sort of open communication could help us both. After all, in a small town people were far more likely to talk to an obituary writer than the law. And if Carl would open up and let me in on where things were in the investigation, it would certainly help me keep printing stories that had accurate, attributable information, like Kay wanted.

"Thanks," he said, but his lack of enthusiasm gave me pause.

"Unless you think you already have your man?"

"Riley—"

"Do you? Do you think Thad Davenport killed his father? Because from what I've heard it seems like there's room for doubt—"

He held up a hand to stop me. "I'm talking here friend-to-friend, okay? No chance of this ending up in the paper?"

I hesitated before nodding. On one hand, I wanted to know what he was going to say. But on the other, I'd already been warned about too many "off-the-record" moments.

"All right," I said, figuring if he gave me something

newsworthy, I could set about finding another source to confirm it for publication.

"It's not looking good for Thad," Carl said. "Between the knife and the drugs, it almost doesn't matter what the official cause of death was, because either way Thad had means and opportunity. As for motive," he paused, and I knew what he was going to say before he said it. My stomach churned with guilt. "The story in the paper from your *anonymous* source supplied plenty of motive."

"Carl, I—"

"It wasn't all that. The family bank account was motive enough, but the details you reported on didn't do him any favors. Tabitha's in a heap of trouble too."

So either Tabitha had told Carl everything, or he had figured it out on his own. I felt slightly relieved even though I didn't know what it would mean for Tabitha moving forward. My mother always said the truth will set you free, although I guess in this case it had had the opposite effect, given that Tab was being held in the county jail.

He went on. "And Thad's brother, David, can't confirm Thad's alibi because he was working late at the hospital. So what am I supposed to do here? I have a guy who fought with the victim, stood to gain financially from his demise, has no verifiable alibi, and had access to the murder weapon..."

"Then why don't you seem convinced?"

Carl again rubbed his forehead, and I could practically feel his headache from across the room. "It doesn't matter what I think. I'm paid to follow the evidence, and so far it is leading straight to Thad Davenport. Do you know the kind of pressure the mayor is putting on me to wrap this up ASAP?"

"I heard."

"That Toby calls over here every hour asking if we've set the charges yet." Carl looked like a man being squeezed between two heavy books. He leaned forward and lowered his voice to a whisper. "Honestly, my gut is telling me there's more to the story here."

I had the same gut feeling, despite the evidence. "What if I do some digging around? I have to talk to people for the obit anyway."

Carl was quiet for a long moment. And then he took out a slip of paper from his desk and wrote his personal cell number on it. He slid it over to me the way people made job offers in old movies. The implication, if I was reading him right, was that he wanted my input, just not officially. That was good enough for me, so I grabbed the slip of paper and went on my way.

CHAPTER 9

I was a little rankled by how hard Mayor Lancett's office was pushing Carl and the newspaper to close out the Davenport case. I guess I understood why she'd want it to go away, but shouldn't she be more interested in seeing that justice was served? In any event, I reminded myself that her agenda had nothing to do with mine. My job was to find out as much as I could about Arthur Davenport's life, and if the information I turned up just happened to shed light on who might have wanted to kill him, then so be it.

The first person I needed to talk to on both scores was Thad's brother, David. I got his number from Tabitha's file and texted to see if he could spare a few minutes. He texted right back that he had a break coming up soon and if I could get to the hospital right away, he'd be happy to talk to me.

I flew over to the hospital and ran inside, large iced mocha in hand. I wasn't four steps inside the building when I tripped over a cord running across the floor and promptly fell flat on my ass. My mocha went all over the place, the ice cubes making the sound of shattered glass and skittering across the highly polished floor. Several people gasped as all eyes in the place turned to me.

"I'm okay!" I called out as brightly as I could manage. I was wearing a yellow sundress, now covered in brown splatters, that I hoped provided ample coverage as I crawled around on hands and knees trying and mostly failing to pick up the ice cubes and put them back into my cup.

"I'll get that," a man wearing dark blue coveralls said as he walked up with a mop and one of those rolling buckets. "That was quite a fall. Are you sure you're not hurt?"

"Just my pride," I said, standing up and smiling weakly. "Sorry about the mess."

"Oh, it's nothing," the man said. "I'm sorry about having that cord there. I was just fixing to start working on the floor."

"Nope, it was my fault. I was rushing."

The man looked at me intently for a moment. I was starting to get uncomfortable when he said, "Are you by any chance that reporter from the *Times*? The one who busted Sheriff Tackett?"

This had happened a few times over the past month. Ours was a small town, and my picture had been in the paper after Holman and I had helped send the sheriff and county prosecutor to prison.

"That's me." I stuck my hand out to shake his. "Riley Ellison."

"Jack. Nice to meet you." He shook my hand. "If you're in a hurry, you can go on ahead. I'll get this taken care of."

I hated to leave him with the mess I'd made, but I didn't want to miss my opportunity to meet with David. "Thank you so much, Jack. I really appreciate your coming to my rescue!"

I made my way to the hospital cafeteria and scanned the room for a slightly younger version of Thad, which was what I expected David Davenport to look like. I was wrong.

"Riley?" A ridiculously handsome guy stood up from one of the small tables by the windows. He gave me a wide smile as he reached to shake my hand. "David Davenport. Sorry to make you come all the way down here, but this is my second home these days."

I could already tell this guy had more charisma in his right dimple than his brother had in his whole body. His eyes flicked down to the mocha-colored Rorschach on the front of my otherwise sunny dress.

"I, um, had a little spill," I said, feeling the heat creeping into my cheeks. And then I quickly changed the subject. "I'm so sorry about your father."

David ran a hand through his thick, dark hair as he sighed and looked to the left. The gesture was pure Thad, and it struck me that although the two didn't look alike at all, they definitely had similar mannerisms.

"Thanks. I'm still trying to make sense of what happened." He sat down across from me at the faux-wood table and dropped his hands into his lap. He looked young, incredibly attractive, and very tired. We got some of the fundamental questions out of the way, like where and when he was born, the basics of the family tree, and a general skeleton of his father's life before he married Thad and David's mother. I knew a lot of this already from the file, but it never hurt to get information firsthand. After we covered those topics, I wanted to get some deeper information about the relationship between father and son.

"Did your father's profession influence your decision to go into medicine?" I asked.

"Of course," he said quickly. "I grew up going to work with him, listening to him talk with his patients on the phone late at night. I was with him when people would stop us in the grocery store to thank him for taking care of someone they loved. I saw how what he did made a difference in people's lives. I knew I wanted to do something just as meaningful with my life."

It wasn't every day that you saw unabashed hero-wor-ship from a twenty-seven-year-old guy about his dad. "Will you go in to cardiology as well?"

"Not sure. I'm finishing up my first year of my internal medicine residency, and I have two more before I have to decide. I'm leaning toward it, but I just got off a Peds rota-tion and really liked that too. So I don't know, maybe pedi-atric cardiology?"

"Cool," I said and made like I was jotting something down. But really I was trying to think of another question. I wasn't expecting David Davenport to be so *interesting* given what I knew of his brother. Thad had always been nice to me when he came by the library to visit Tabitha, but he was chronically vanilla. Literally and figuratively. He had skin the color of a button mushroom, with ample dark hair covering his arms and occasionally sprouting out of the top of his collar. He wasn't necessarily unattractive, but I'd always assumed Tabitha's interest in him had as much to do with his family money as anything else. His brother on the other hand was dynamic and energetic and refresh-ingly un-hairy.

"Um, okay, so can you tell me about the kind of father Arthur was to you?"

He picked up his phone, which had been sitting face-down on the table, and checked the time.

"Oh, I'm sorry—do you have to go?" I asked.

"Nah, I have another few minutes. Do you mind if I grab a shake or something while we talk? Not sure when I'll get another break."

"Of course." I followed him over to the cafeteria line.

"You're from Tuttle, right?" he asked as we stood in line behind a man holding a large refillable coffee mug. "What year were you in school?"

"I graduated a year behind Tabitha."

"I was a few years ahead of you then."

"You didn't go to Tuttle, though." This wasn't a question. With a graduating class of eighty-seven people, I would have known anyone—or at least been able to recognize anyone—who was within a few years of my class.

David ordered a Green Monster shake from the woman working behind the counter. She blushed and he pretended not to notice, but something told me he knew exactly the effect he had on the opposite sex. "I went to Woodberry, over in Charlottesville."

That made sense. Woodberry was a fancy prep school about an hour from Tuttle Corner. It was known for strong academics, but an even stronger sports program. David, while clearly bright, was athletically built, with the thick neck of a football or rugby player. "Did Thad go there too?"

He paid for the shake, took his change, smiled at the pretty checkout girl again, and we walked back to the table. "No, he went through Tuttle schools. I don't think Woodberry was even on my parents' radar when Thad went through school." David's face changed at the mention of his older brother, who now stood accused of their father's murder. "You know, I just realized something," he said, a wistful look on his face.

"What?"

"I guess I'm an orphan now."

Technically that was true. I wasn't sure what to say, so I said nothing for a few moments, allowing David the space to sit with his realization. "Um, how long has your mom been gone?"

"She died when I was sixteen. Cancer," he said in the matter-of-fact way physicians have of talking about illness and death.

"Your father never remarried?"

"Nah," he said. "Got close a time or two but I don't think he was really interested in starting over after Mom passed. He used to joke, 'Marriage is a lot of work, and I already have a full-time job.'" David laughed. "But really, I think Dad was just a bit of a player, you know?"

The word *player* was not often applied to a sixty-year-old man and it struck me as odd. "Was he seeing anyone—I mean, just before he died?" I wasn't sure if I was asking as a part of my role as obituarist or crime reporter, or if it even mattered. Either way, David didn't look offended.

"Dad always had something going on," he said. "But he didn't usually talk to me too much about it, thank goodness." He smiled and gave me a wink.

With about five minutes left before he had to go back to work, I asked the one question that all good obit writers are supposed to try to get an answer to. "So, if you had to say, what was the one thing you learned from your father's life?"

David leaned forward, elbows resting on the table, his slate-blue eyes looking directly into mine, while he thought about how to answer this rather philosophical, cosmic question. Most people have to think about this one for a while. But David Davenport was not most people, and within a few seconds he said, "Life is short. Don't be an asshole."

It was an unexpected answer in both speed and wit, and it made me laugh.

He smiled. "It's funny, but I'm serious."

"No—I mean, I get it. . ." I said. I knew I needed to follow up on that, but I couldn't think of quite what to ask. *What was it about this guy that made me feel so flustered?* I again pretended to make notes in order to buy time to think.

"Riley?" He interrupted my thought.

"Yes?"

"Don't you want to ask me if I think my brother killed my father?"

That got my attention. "Do you?"

"Not a chance in hell. And you can quote me on that." There was no smile on his face when he spoke this time, no playful twinkle in his eye. He was dead serious and he wanted me to know it.

"What about the night of the murder," I said, my pen poised over my notebook. "Thad says he came to your house around nine."

"I wasn't home, but Thad has his own key. If he says he was there, he was there. It's just that I didn't see him."

His phone vibrated and he turned it over; his brow wrinkled at whatever was on the display. "Shoot—I have to run, I'm sorry." He looked up. "But maybe we could continue this conversation another time?"

"Sure. My deadline for the obit is Saturday."

"Oh," he said, "well, I'm going to be here until"—he turned over his wrist, which didn't have a watch on it—"forever." He smiled. "But maybe I could call you sometime?"

"Of course," I said. "You have my number. I'll be working on this right up until deadline if you think of anything else."

"Okay," he said. I was about to stick out my hand to shake his when he smiled and looked down at the ground. "What if I think of something else, like, totally unrelated?"

"Um, well, sure. You never know when one can include the odd tidbit in a piece . . ."

A pinkish hue appeared just under his high cheekbones. "Uh, I guess I'm really bad at this," he said and cleared his throat. "What I am trying to say—very awkwardly, obviously—is could I call you sometime? You know, not necessarily about this . . ."

My stomach flipped over. He was asking me out? I'd had no idea. I wasn't used to cute doctors asking me out. Or cute anybodies for that matter. Jay had asked me out online through Click.com, and the only other guy I'd dated before him was Ryan, who asked me out by passing me a note in tenth-grade Geometry. "Oh," I said, trying to play it off casually. "Oh . . . well, uh . . ." Casual wasn't really my thing.

"I'll take that as a no?"

"Gosh, David, that's so nice," I said quickly, not wanting to stretch out this hideous moment. "But I'm actually seeing someone."

"Aw, man." He smiled. "All the good ones are taken. Ah, well, it was worth a shot."

It was me who was fully blushing by this point. "Um, thanks," I said, tucking an errant hair behind my ear because I needed something to do other than stand there and look like an idiot.

We walked out of the cafeteria together without a word. I had parked out front, and there was one main corridor that led to the entrance. "Thanks for taking the time to talk with me," I said, which seemed somehow oddly formal. "Again, I'm sorry about your dad."

"Thanks." He flashed me his wide, confident smile, and I knew he'd be just fine after my rejection.

We said our goodbyes and he went up the elevators back into the bowels of the hospital. I headed out to the parking lot. But as I got into my car, I wasn't thinking about what he said about his father or his brother, or how I would incorporate his quotes into the obit. All I could think about was how odd it was for a good-looking, single doctor to hit on the woman writing his father's obituary *while* she was writing it. And, much to my own dismay, how flattered I was that I could turn the head of someone like David Davenport.

CHAPTER 10

Arthur Davenport's office was in a building adjacent to the hospital, so I figured as long as I was right there I'd pop over to see if his office manager could spare me a few minutes. Tabitha had told me that Arthur and Donna had worked together for years and that she knew more about his life than he did.

Donna was red-eyed and blotchy-cheeked when she came to the door. The office was closed for the day, but she and another woman were inside making phone calls and rescheduling patients with other physicians. She invited me right in when I told her I'd be writing Dr. Davenport's obituary for the *Times*.

"It's such a shock," she said as she let me inside. "Arthur... murdered? I still can't believe it..."

It was hard to see someone in this kind of pain, and it wasn't lost on me that this woman, who was not a blood relative, was clearly the most distraught of all the people I'd talked to thus far. She took me back to her office and sat me down in an old chair with peeling faux-leather on the armrest. We talked for almost twenty minutes and from what Donna had to say about him, you'd have thought Arthur Davenport hung the moon. She told me about how patients would travel for miles just to see him and how he was the hardest-working man she knew. I took copious notes and got more than a few quotes I could use for the obit. So I decided to veer off the obituary course for just a moment.

"Were there any patients who didn't like him? Anyone who might have wanted to harm him?"

Donna looked stricken. "Of course not! He was helping them all—in many cases, he had saved their lives! No, everyone loved him. I mean, on occasion, I suppose there was the odd . . ." she stopped herself.

"What?"

"Nothing," she said. "No—there wasn't anyone who would want to hurt Dr. Davenport." You could tell Donna would protect Arthur Davenport's reputation with her life, but I needed her to open up.

"The sheriff is going to be looking into all of this, you know."

She twisted the wedding ring on her left hand. "Arthur could be, um, well, it's just that for a very smart man sometimes he didn't always make the smartest choices."

I poised my pen over my notebook. "What do you mean?"

Her eyes darted toward the front of the office and she lowered her voice to a whisper, "Arthur liked the ladies."

This was the second time inside of an hour that I heard Arthur Davenport was a ladies' man. Love gone wrong is perhaps the oldest motive for murder in the book. I tried asking her the same question I'd asked David. "Was he seeing anyone before he died?"

She let out a snort. "Some*one*? Probably more like a few someones . . ."

"Can you give me any names?"

She shook her head, her face coloring. "No, no, I shouldn't have said anything. I'm sure it has no relation to . . . well, you know . . ." Her eyes grew misty again, and she dabbed at the corner of one with a crumpled tissue.

"Donna," I said, "the best thing you can do for Arthur now is to help us find out who did this to him. If you know something, you should speak up."

"I don't know," she said. She looked terribly uncomfortable, and the Southern girl inside me desperately wanted to rescue her from the situation, but my inner-reporter muzzled her and I waited in silence for Donna to continue. "You might want to, um, ask around about Arthur's past love life. There's a certain *someone* in town who was carrying a pretty heavy torch for him." She widened her eyes. "She thought they were destined to walk down the aisle, but I don't think he shared those same thoughts."

"Who?" I asked.

"That's all I'm going to say about that," she said and pursed her lips together.

I left it—for the moment—making a mental note to find out who this "certain someone" was at a later date. And then I switched gears. "I had a nice chat with David this morning."

"Oh, that David," she said with affection. "He's an ornery one."

Ornery wasn't exactly the word I would have chosen to describe him. I might have gone with *handsome, articulate, chiseled* . . .

"He was a little devil as a child—always getting into everything, real physical, like he never quite knew how to control himself. Gave his father fits as a little one," she said with a laugh. "But he always got away with it because he had that charm, you know? That scampy look in his eyes. No one could resist David when he looked at you with those eyes, least of all Arthur."

"And what about Thad?"

At the mention of Thad's name, she grew somber. "Thad was a different kind of boy," she explained. "He was much more serious. Always did the right thing, said the right thing—as opposed to David, who was a wild child. Thad wasn't like that. He was always polite, always well mannered. Much more serious, you know. More like his mother, I suppose."

"Do you think he could have done this to his father?"

Donna's eyes flashed. "Of course not!" It was an automatic response. "Thad would never hurt his father. He worshipped him—both the boys did."

That was the second person that morning to tell me there was no way Thad killed his father. Third, if you counted Tabitha. Strange that the evidence painted such a different picture.

"Artie—Arthur," she corrected herself, "was a big personality. He wasn't a saint, he was a man just like any other, but he was an excellent doctor and a caring father to those boys. I don't know who would could have . . . have . . . " This brought on a fresh wave of tears.

Poor Donna had had enough for one day. "Thank you for talking with me. You've been so helpful."

She stood and took my hand. "Thank you, dear," she said warmly. "I'll look forward to reading the obituary on Sunday. It'll be such a comfort to us all."

CHAPTER 11

When I got back to the *Times* office I was not-so-secretly proud that I'd been able to get two key interviews done in the short amount of time since I'd been given the assignment. Even Flick would have to acknowledge my competency on this one. So after setting my stuff down in my cubicle, I went to see him to receive my praise.

"How come you did the interviews without talking to me first?" Flick apparently did not find my research praiseworthy. "You heard Jackson. I am supposed to be giving you the benefit of my experience on this."

I hadn't expected him to throw me a parade, but I hadn't expected him to be angry with me either. "Yeah but c'mon, Flick. David? And his office manager? Obviously those two were going to included on the list."

"'Yeah-but' nothing—"

"I just thought that—"

"I know what you 'just thought,' Riley," Flick said. "You *just think* you know it all and that you don't need any help from anybody, but I'm here to tell you, kid, that isn't the case."

The familiar brew of humiliation and anger swirled inside my gut. I took a deep breath and forced myself to calm down before speaking. "Flick," I said using my most controlled voice, "I think if you look at my notes, you'll see that I did a pretty good job with the questions."

"Did you ask David if his father ever talked about moving away from Tuttle Corner? Or what he would have wanted to do if he hadn't been a cardiologist? And how about Donna—did you think to ask her if he ever got frustrated with his patients or staff?"

"No, but I—"

"Did you think to ask about any negative aspects of his life, or was it all softball stuff designed to make them feel better?"

I felt my cheeks grow hot. "Not exactly, but I did ask David what he learned from his father's life." That ought to shut him up for a second.

He fixed a challenging stare on me. "And what did he tell you?"

"Life is short. Don't be an asshole."

Flick looked at me like he was trying to figure out if I was quoting David or offering him advice. After a beat, he must have realized it was a quote. (Well, it actually worked on both levels.) And then Flick did something I had not seen him do in over six years. He started laughing—I mean, really laughing. His whole demeanor changed—the lines etched into his face from time and experience rearranged themselves; his shoulders, usually squared for battle, relaxed; his eyes crinkled at the edges. It was like looking at a whole different person. It took me completely off guard and I wasn't sure how to react, so I pulled a Holman and just looked at him like he was an anthropological curiosity.

As his laughter died down, he settled himself into his ancient rolling chair—the one he'd brought with him years ago from when he worked up in Washington, D.C. "That's a helluva line. I'll give you that."

Still unsure if it was safe to let my own guard down, I
sat too—but cautiously so, perched on the edge of the chair
across from him.

"So what did that mean?" he said, the trace of laughter
still in his voice.

"What?"

"When David said that. What did he mean?"

I looked at him, blank.

"Did he mean that he learned not to be an asshole because his dad was one, or because he wasn't one?"

Damn. It was an excellent question, and one I hadn't
thought to ask. Flick read it on my face like a neon sign. I
braced myself for the lashing I was about to get. But again,
he went another direction.

"Riley," he said in a softer, gentler tone than before.
"You're doing a good job. You're trying, I can see that. But
you're new to this and I've been around a long time. You
could learn a thing or two from me, you know?"

I regarded him carefully. Was he playing some sort of
game? To soften me up before delivering a death blow?
But the tenderness in his voice suggested not. It felt like a
genuine offer of guidance and direction, two things I could
really use. "Okay," I said.

He smiled and looked at me with such warmth it
almost took my breath away. "Okay then. Let's get to work."

I spent the next hour in Flick's office going over my
notes, talking through the interviews with David and
Donna, and formulating a plan of action for what I'd do
next. It was a strange thing to be working side by side with
the same man for whom I'd had such contempt over the
past few years. Flick had been my granddaddy's best friend
and colleague for more than forty years. I'd grown up calling him Uncle Hal, but everything changed when Grand-

dad died. The sheriff had ruled his death a suicide, even though Granddad wasn't remotely suicidal and didn't even own the gun he supposedly shot himself with. I'd begged Flick as a reporter—not to mention his friend—to help me look into it further. I'd brought him all sorts of information about inconsistencies that didn't add up, but Flick had shut me down, refused to help, wouldn't even discuss it with me. He told me to let it go. There was a part of me that would never forgive Hal Flick for giving up on my granddaddy the way he did.

I was walking out of his office with a revised question list in my hands when Flick said to my back, "Albert would have been proud of you, you know."

I stilled. It had been five years since Flick had spoken my granddaddy's name to me. Afraid to break the spell with any sudden movements, I made a little half turn toward him. "You think?"

"I know," he said. "He loved this beat, and he'd be real happy to see you here keeping it alive."

I should have let it go, let the moment be so that we might have been able to return to the subject another time. But hearing Flick say Granddaddy's name was like being given a drop of water after a long hike in the desert. I wanted more. "Flick, you don't really think he killed himself, do you?"

"Ah, geez, not this again," he said sharply. It felt like being smacked in the face.

"Forget it." I turned to leave.

"Riley—" I heard him call my name, but I was already halfway down the hall, my pulse pounding in the base of my throat with no one to blame but myself. I knew as well as anyone that leopards don't change their spots.

Hey Riley,

U have totally been on my mind and I've been wondering how ur doing. Did u listen to that guided meditation on how to be more assertive that I sent u the link for? I think it'll really help u with that whole "against your will" thing ur worried about.

If ur wanting a more intense kind of strategy, u should totally check out Bestmillenniallife.com's YOU'RE NOT THE BOSS OF ME app available in the App Store for Android and iOS. It's only $2.99 and it gives u daily affirmations that will totally teach u how to learn to stand up for urself in the workplace. It seriously changed my life! Before YOU'RE NOT THE BOSS OF ME, I used to say yes to everything—babysitting, dogsitting, housesitting. Now I have gained the confidence to say no to any kind of sitting except the kind I want to do on the couch—haha lol!

Anyway. I see from ur file that you've recently started a new job. That must be thrilling! Tell me all about it!

xx,
Jenna B
Personal Success Concierge™
Bestmillenniallife.com

Dear Jenna,

I have not had a chance to listen to the podcast yet—obviously, or else I would have found a way to let you know I really don't need your services. Maybe I should check out the app (haha lol, as you say).

➤

All best,
Riley

Dear Riley,

U r frickin' hilarious! U crack me up! Seriously, I have tears of laughter rolling down my cheeks now.

So tell me about ur job . . .

xx,
Jenna B
Personal Success Concierge™
Bestmillenniallife.com

Dear Jenna,

I wasn't trying to be funny, but I guess it's good to know I made you laugh.

My job is not going that well at the moment, if I'm being honest. I'm feeling a little overwhelmed. Plus, I'm afraid if I screw up, I'll not only lose my job but it could end up having serious consequences for a friend.

All best,
Riley

Hey Riley,

UGH. That sounds heavy. Here's a quote that always inspires

➤

me when I'm feeling overwhelmed: "I cheated on my fears, broke up with my doubts, got engaged to my faith, and now I'm married to my dreams." I'm not sure who said it because I saw it as a meme on Pinterest, but I'm pretty sure it was someone famous. And I like it because I feel like it works on so many levels. Hope it inspires u as much as it does me!

xx,
Jenna B
Personal Success Concierge™
Bestmillenniallife.com

CHAPTER 12

I arrived at Tuttle General for the second time that day. The plan was to see if I could find David to clarify a few things, and see if I could get one of his father's colleagues to talk to me about what he had been like to work with. I walked quickly through the lobby toward the elevators, but before I got there, a voice called out my name. A raspy Swedish-accented voice. *Damn.*

"Riley!"

I turned around slowly and plastered a static smile on my face. "Hey, Ridley."

Ridley floated up beside me and kissed me on both cheeks. She looked radiant, of course, her bright blond hair shining even brighter under the fluorescent lights—she was the very essence of health and vitality, a sharp contrast with the hospital setting of illness and death. She once again wore a belly-baring tank top and long cotton skirt, but today she wore a bright boho-chic kimono atop the whole outfit, which was so impossibly stylish that she looked like a maternity-store model as opposed to a real-life pregnant person. It made me want to puke.

"What are you doing here? You are not sick, I hope?" Ridley asked with a look of genuine concern on her flawless, not-even-kind-of-bloated face.

"Just here for work. Have to do some interviews for the

Davenport obit."

"I am here for a checkup." She pointed to the double doors just opposite the conference room: the Women's Health Associates office suite where Dr. Wilson, my—and Ridley's—OB/GYN worked. "Thirty-five weeks today." She put her hands on either side of her baby bump and swirled them, just as she'd done the other night.

Again, I had a niggling pang from somewhere deep within. It was hard to believe that thirty-five weeks ago I still thought Ryan and I had a future together. Maybe the feeling was nothing more than a physical manifestation of surprise. At least I hoped so.

"Well, hope you get a good report!" I said brightly. "See you—"

"Riley?" She interrupted me. *Double-damn.* "Would you like to have coffee with me sometime?"

"Oh, um, well, gee . . ." I was about as good at responding to being asked out by my ex-boyfriend's baby mama as I was by cute doctors.

She reached out a long, toned arm and touched my shoulder. "I'd like us to be friends." She flashed me the brilliant smile containing her perfectly proportioned teeth that fell into a straight line with just the barest hint of pink gum tissue peeking out from above. It was the kind of smile that made all mankind fall to its knees. But I was not all mankind, and I was not interested in being friends with Ridley. She was fine—a nice person, I'm sure—but she was having Ryan's baby, a distinction I used to believe would be mine, and so we did not need to be friends.

"Sure," I said in as noncommittal a way as possible. "Let's do that sometime! See you ar—"

She again interrupted my getaway, this time by pulling me into a tight hug. "Oh, thank you, Riley! I was so nervous to ask you, and Ryan said I shouldn't bother you—but I have not made any female friends since moving to Tuttle Corner and I think you and I have so much in common—I just know we are destined to be the best of friends!"

She was so tall that my head was at her breast level, and as she hugged me with more force than I felt was necessary, the side of my face smushed into her boobs—the only part of her that seemed to be swollen from pregnancy.

"Okay. All right," I said, as I pulled free. "That's good enough." I felt eyes on us and turned to see David Davenport coming off of the elevator, a look of bemusement on his handsome face.

"Hi," I waved him over. "Fancy seeing you here," I said, and then immediately regretted it. Not only did cute guys make me nervous, but inexplicably they made me talk like a seventy-year-old greeter at Wal-Mart.

"Hey," he said, but he wasn't looking at me. He was looking at Ridley. *Of course.*

"David," I said, making the obligatory introduction, "this is Ridley. Ridley, this is David Davenport."

Their eyes met and when they shook hands it was like a chemical reaction. Two beautiful people colliding, joining forces, their beauty shining out from around them in all directions, forming a sort of beauty-bubble that shielded them from the rest of the average-looking world.

"Nice to meet you," David said, and I could have sworn his voice was an octave lower than it had been this morning. His gaze was so intense it bordered on inappropriate. I mean, couldn't he see that this woman was pregnant?

"David," I said, trying to wrench his attention away from Ridley. "I have another couple of quick follow-up questions for the obit. Do you have a minute?"

The mention of time snapped him out of his trance. He

checked the clock on his phone. "You can walk me down to radiology—we can talk on the way." He then turned his attention back to Ridley and again lowered his voice. "Lovely to meet you, Ridley. I hope you don't mind me saying, but pregnancy suits you."

"You are too kind." Ridley lowered her eyes as if she felt self-conscious from his attention. *Whatever.* And then she looked at me. "I'll call you about that coffee, Riley. Maybe we can go later this week?"

"Sure, sure," I said, but was already taking David by the elbow and starting to walk down the hall. I would not be having coffee with Ridley, of that much I was sure.

Once we got far enough away, David said, "Who was that? She's incredible."

I refrained from rolling my eyes. "Ridley Nilsson. She's new to town."

"Is she married? I didn't see a ring. I mean, obviously she's about to have a baby, but . . ."

I hated it that Ridley was the kind of woman who could make men ask if she was taken at eight months pregnant. And I hated it how much I hated that. "Actually, do you know Ryan Sanford?"

"Yeah, his family has the farm and home store, right?"

I nodded. "The baby's his. They're not together though."

David stopped walking. Literally, this news stopped him in his tracks. "Really? So she's single?"

"Well, you could say she's double . . ."

He looked confused.

"Because she's pregnant. You know, she's incubating another human life?"

"Oh," he said, clearly not getting my joke. "Right. Hey, do you think I could have her number?"

Seriously? What was with this guy? First, he asks me

out this morning, and now—not even two hours later—he is asking me for another girl's phone number? What the hell?

"Yeah. Um, sure. I'll text it to you."

His eyes were sort of unfocused, no doubt calling up a vision of the Swedish siren in his mind.

"Anyway," I said louder than I probably needed to, "I wanted to clarify a couple of things. First, you said earlier that you're father had 'gotten close a few times' to remarrying—can you tell me to whom?"

"Oh, I was just sort of kidding," he said. "He was never officially engaged or anything like that."

"And you don't know if he was seeing anyone recently?"

David again checked his phone; he was concerned about time. "Dad didn't like to be alone, that's all I know. I don't know who he was with, but in the past nine years, Dad was rarely without female companionship."

That would have to be good enough for the time being. He was about to run off, so I asked him what he had meant when he said he learned not to be an asshole from his dad. "Did you say that because he was one, or because he wasn't?"

David laughed. "Good question. Um, I'd have to say a little bit of both. He was a good man, but I guess like everyone, he had his moments." We were approaching the hallway that led to the radiology department, and David stopped walking. He took a step closer, touched my elbow, and lowered his voice. "I was actually going to call you. I've come across some information that I think might be important."

"Like what?"

"Like, I've found something odd in Dad's files that might have something to do with why he was killed."

A beeping sound cut him off before he had a chance to

say more and he looked down at the pager attached to the waistband of his baby-blue scrubs. "I really gotta go now. I'll call you later, okay?"

Not okay. But what could I do. I stood there for a second with that sense of frustration you get when you're about to sneeze and something interrupts you. And then just before David walked through the swinging doors to radiology, he turned back around. I thought for one shining moment he was going to give me a clue as to what new information he'd come across, but instead he said, "Don't forget to text me Ridley's number, 'kay?"

CHAPTER 13

Franklin Steeler was an internal medicine doctor who had worked alongside Arthur Davenport for nearly ten years. I found him in his office doing paperwork, and when I said I'd like to chat with him about Dr. Davenport's obituary, he'd welcomed me right in. Steeler said he often referred his patients who needed a cardiology workup to Dr. Davenport.

"He was very thorough. My patients liked him, liked the way he treated them. I always felt comfortable sending them his way."

But, as he told me, there were a few notable exceptions. "Art was fond of the ladies, if you know what I mean," Dr. Steeler said as he waggled his eyebrows up and down. "After he lost Maribelle, I guess he sought comfort in the arms of other women. Uh, frequently."

Dr. Davenport really had a reputation around here. "Did it affect his work?" I asked, wondering what he meant about the "notable exceptions."

"Not really, but about a year ago, I referred him a patient of mine, a gentleman in his early forties who was having some unexplained chest pains. Arthur took him on—he always found room for one more patient no matter how busy he was—and I think ended up doing an angioplasty or maybe a stent, can't recall exactly, but in any case, during the course of visiting with the man and his wife during all those appointments . . ." Dr. Steeler again raised his eyebrows.

I couldn't quote eyebrow waggles; I was going to need him to say the words. "What happened during the course of all those appointments?"

He shifted in his chair, looking uncomfortable over revealing the worst of his departed colleague. "Arthur and Li—I mean, this woman—got to know each other and they started up a little *relationship*."

"And did the husband find out?"

Dr. Steeler nodded. "They weren't exactly discreet about it. Never could figure that out. Anyway, yeah, the husband caught them one day right in his own house and he just about lost his mind. He flew into a rage and ended up collapsing. The irony was, it was a good thing Arthur was there because he did CPR on him until the ambulance arrived."

I could hardly believe my ears. This was not only scandalous gossip—it provided another suspect who might have wanted Dr. Davenport dead. I wondered if this was the new information David had found out about.

"Can you tell me the name of this patient?" I asked, already knowing the answer.

"No chance. HIPAA and all that." But then he leaned in and lowered his voice. "But I'll bet if you ask around town you'll find someone who'll tell you. Like I said, they weren't very discreet about the whole thing."

I thanked him for talking to me and told him how helpful he'd been.

"I'll look for the obit in the paper. Sunday—is it?"

I nodded. Sunday it would be indeed.

CHAPTER 14

I f anyone in town would know with whom Dr. Davenport had had a scandalous affair, it would be Mrs. Eudora Winterthorne. Mrs. Winterthorne was the grand dame of Tuttle Corner. She was as "old as dirt," as she liked to say, but still had her perfectly manicured finger on the pulse of our town. And lucky for me, she just loved to gossip about other people's business, though she'd deny that with her dying breath.

I knocked on the large oak door to Villa 302 at Almond Terrace, the retirement community where Mrs. Winterthorne lived. She'd been widowed four years ago and decided to trade the big house she'd raised her family in for the maintenance-free living that Almond Terrace provided. She used a wheelchair because rheumatoid arthritis had ravaged her knees, but other than that Mrs. Winterthorne was in better shape than many people half her age.

"Well hey there, Riley," said Faye, Mrs. Winterthorne's nurse, as she opened the door. She leaned in to kiss my cheek. Faye was retired military, a twenty-year Army veteran who had served three tours in Desert Storm. She never married, had no children, and when she retired from service at the age of forty-eight, she took the position as Mrs. Winterthorne's personal caregiver. The two ended up being a perfect match, and in many ways behaved like an old married couple, griping and sniping at each other despite their deep bond.

I had called ahead to ask Faye if Eudora had time to visit with me to talk about Dr. Davenport's obituary, and she'd readily agreed. "It does her good to visit with people, especially when she can be useful," Faye said.

"Is that Riley?" I heard Mrs. Winterthorne's aged, velvety voice drift in from the other room. "Don't keep me in suspense, Faye. For heaven's sake, I can't roll up the steps myself!"

Faye rolled her eyes at me, not the least bit fazed by Mrs. Winterthorne's crabbiness. She led me down into the living room. "Come on in, sugar."

After the three of us chatted for a while and I caught them up on what my parents were up to, Mrs. Winterthorne got down to business.

"Now what is this about you wanting to know about Dr. Davenport's clandestine affairs?" She pursed her lips in judgment, but her eyes gleamed with excitement. "Surely, you're not going to print that in the obituary? One mustn't speak ill of the dead, you know."

"I'm just gathering information right now. Dr. Steeler couldn't tell me much, but I knew if anyone would know the real scoop about what went on, it'd be you."

"Oh, Riley, your mother taught you well. Trying to appeal to an old lady's vanity in order to squeeze some information out of her," she said, laughing.

I got nervous for a second that she wasn't going to open up, but then she said, "Well, you know I don't like to gossip," and I knew I was in luck.

Mrs. Winterthorne didn't take a breath for the next fifteen minutes. Turns out the married woman with whom Arthur Davenport had had the affair was Libby Nichols, the wife of Bennett Nichols, who was, as Dr. Steeler had said, forty-three years old.

"It raised more than a few eyebrows when those two got married," Eudora said. "Her just barely out of high school at the time and him nearly thirty. What with the Nicholses having so much, there were those who thought Libby was just in it for the money." It sounded from her tone that Mrs. Winterthorne herself had been of that opinion. "But, to their credit, they stayed married all these years, happily as far as we all knew."

"Until this business with Dr. Davenport?"

Mrs. Winterthorne nodded. "Several months back Bennett was having some minor health issues, according to his mama, Judy—do you know Judy and Jim Nichols? They live out on that farm down by Route K?"

"They own Nichols Insurance Group, right?" I knew this because when my poor Honda Fit had gotten blown up a few months ago, I had to file a claim with them. They'd been great about the whole thing, and actually made the process pretty painless.

"Jim built that business from the ground up and has done quite well. *Quite.* Anyway, Bennett went to see Arthur for his care, and of course brought his doting bride along on the visits. According to Judy, Libby took detailed notes about what tests he needed done and all that. Played the part of Florence Nightingale perfectly."

"So what happened?"

"I guess at some point, Libby got in touch with Arthur to ask him some 'follow-up questions'"—Mrs. Winterthorne made air quotes—"and supposedly she suggested he come out to her house to talk."

Faye sat on the arm of the sofa next to where Mrs. Winterthorne was parked. She shook her head and murmured,

"I mean, have you ever?"

"Never," Mrs. Winterthorne answered, lifting an eyebrow toward Faye.

"How long ago was that?" I asked.

"Let's see," she looked up as she thought. "According to Judy, they started up six months ago at least, but Bennett didn't find out until just recently."

She then went on to tell me essentially the same story, about Bennett walking in on the two of them, having a heart attack, and Dr. Davenport doing CPR until the ambulance arrived.

"How was the whole town not talking about something like this?" I asked, knowing the rumor mill in this town was one hundred percent functional.

A sly smile slid across Eudora's face. "That's just the thing," she said, "Bennett was adamant that word of this not get out. While he was recuperating in the hospital, he sent for Dr. Davenport. Judy never said, but I think Bennett must have threatened Arthur with something because right after that, I heard Arthur dropped Libby like a hot potato. Which did not set well with Libby, I might add."

Interesting. I wondered if that made Libby a suspect too?

Eudora went on. "He did tell his parents, which is how I heard about it. Judy is a dear friend—which reminds me—Faye, would you set a reminder for me to call her later and invite her for lunch at the clubhouse? I'd like to see how she's holding up."

"Sure thing," Faye said as she typed the reminder into her phone.

Mrs. Winterthorne turned back to me. "Poor Judy was just in knots about the whole thing, which is why she told me. She needed a sympathetic ear," she said. "My but how she dotes on that boy of hers . . . wait," she stopped herself mid-sentence, "is that why you're asking about this? Do you think this whole affair could have had something to do with Arthur's murder?"

"Do you?" I used the oldest trick in the book to get out of answering a question.

She paused for a moment. "I'll tell you one thing: I cannot imagine being able to forgive a person for an insult like that. And Bennett is a proud man."

"Do you think he could have wanted revenge? People have killed for less."

I noticed Faye frowning.

"What is it?" I asked, turning to her.

"It's probably nothing, but I'm in a King's Daughters circle with Donna Lopez—"

"Arthur's office manager," I said. "I just interviewed her earlier today."

Faye nodded. "Right. Well, I hadn't remembered it until just now, but at our meeting last week, she came in all upset. When we asked her what was wrong, she didn't get specific but said something along the lines of, 'It just burns me up to see people taking advantage of other people,' or something like that."

"Did she say if it had anything to do with work? Or was this a personal matter?"

Faye didn't know.

Mrs. Winterthorne, not to be out-gossiped, jumped in. "You know, Donna and Arthur were very close. After Maribelle passed, I think he leaned pretty heavily on her."

"Did they ever. . . ?" I asked, remembering Donna wore a wedding ring.

Mrs. Winterthorne shook her head vigorously. "Nothing like that," she said. "Donna is a good Christian and has been married to her husband Earl for eons. But I think she liked being needed by the Davenports. Donna and Earl weren't blessed with children, so Thad and David were like the boys she never had."

"Do you think she would have known about Arthur's affair with Libby?"

Both Faye and Mrs. Winterthorne nodded. Then Mrs. W said, "I think Donna Lopez knew just about everything there was to know about Arthur Davenport."

Very interesting. I definitely needed to get more information on this story. If nothing else, it opened the search for suspects in a couple of new directions. Maybe that would be enough to convince Carl to look somewhere other than just at Thad.

CHAPTER 15

J ay got back from the DC office early and texted to see if I wanted to meet up for a late lunch. We decided on Landry's General Store, which inexplicably had the best Cuban panini north of Havana, and a great little outdoor patio perfect for nice fall days. We sat outside at one of the round red powder-coated tables and I caught him up on my busy morning.

"Arthur was having an affair with a patient's wife?" Jay said between bites of his sandwich.

I nodded. "Apparently. And apparently that wasn't exactly new territory for him."

"What's the husband like?"

"Bennett Nichols?" I shrugged. "Haven't met him yet. But I plan to, I can tell you that for sure." I'd already decided I would try to go interview Libby and Bennett later that day. First, though, I wanted to talk to Carl and see if he knew about the affair. If he did, he sure hadn't mentioned it to me.

Jay set his sandwich down and looked at me, his face suddenly looking very serious.

"What?"

"Just . . ." he seemed to be struggling with what he wanted to say. "Just be careful. This Bennett guy could be dangerous."

"Oh, I'll be fine." I waved a dismissive hand.

"I'm serious, Riley."

"I'm just going to ask him some questions . . ."

"Do you want me to come with?"

I laughed. "What? Like as my muscle?"

Jay didn't laugh. His mouth flattened into a thin line. "I have experience interviewing combative suspects."

He was serious. He honestly thought I might take him up on his offer to come with me as I did my job, like he was some sort of bodyguard or something. It was both sweet and slightly offensive. "Um, no thanks. I'll be fine."

He looked at me for a long moment, and then shook his head. I guess he decided not to press it any further.

"Want to come over for dinner tonight?" I said, partially to smooth things over and partially because I liked eating meals with him.

"Sure," he said. "But why don't you come to my place. I have a new recipe for shrimp in arrabiata sauce that I've been wanting to try."

"Mmm," I said, leaning over to give him a kiss. "Sounds spicy."

He kissed me back and spicy took on a whole other meaning for a couple of blissful seconds until my cell phone vibrated on the table.

I reluctantly broke away. "This is Riley." It was Gail calling to tell me that Toby Lancett, the mayor's minion, and Tabitha had just been called into Carl's office and by the looks of it, something big was going down.

"Go." Jay nodded his head toward the exit before I even had a chance to say a word.

"But we're on for tonight?"

He nodded.

"I'll look forward to something hot," I said, and then as I

hoisted my bag onto my shoulder I added with a wink, "and the shrimp too."

⎯⎯⎯◆⎯⎯⎯

"Oh geez, Riley, this is not a good time," Carl said as I walked up to the door of his office, where a grim-looking Tabitha and a rather gleeful-looking Toby were sitting. Toby Lancett was short and stocky and wore athletic gear almost exclusively. Since he was perhaps the least athletic person I'd ever met, it was an odd choice. Today's ensemble was a kelly green Adidas jacket unzipped to reveal a snug-fitting white T-shirt with the words *Natural Born Baller* stamped across it in large block letters. I'm sure it wasn't what he was going for, but the effect was definitely less baller, more leprechaun.

"Well, if it isn't Tuttle Corner's newest Lois Lane," Toby said, his voice dripping with sarcasm.

I'd known Toby since I was knee-high to a grasshopper, as my granddaddy would have said, and he'd always been something of a loser. I remember the day he got caught shoplifting a king-size Twix bar from Landry's General Store. I'd been in there with my parents getting dinner and Toby, who was probably sixteen or seventeen—old enough to know better—just started bawling like a baby when Ruby caught him. He said he had hypoglycemia and needed it so he wouldn't faint. When that didn't go over so well with Ruby, he started threatening to sue her for harassment. That was the kind of kid he'd been. By all accounts the kind of adult he'd become wasn't much better, except now he had the mayor's backing.

"You'd better get your little pen and paper out, missy, because we've just had a confession in the Davenport case!"

I looked at Carl, who slid his eyes away from mine. Then I turned to Tabitha and a sick feeling bloomed in my gut. "Tell me you didn't . . ."

"Yes," she said as she threw back her shoulders and lifted her chin like a defiant ballerina. "I confessed to killing Dr. Davenport. I was angry about the way he mistreated Thad, and I wanted him out of the picture so Thad and I could inherit his fortune." Her caramel-colored eyes looked straight ahead the entire time she spoke.

"Tabitha," I said, a warning rising into my voice. "That isn't true. You know that isn't true. Carl, come on—"

Carl looked even more exhausted than he had before. "Riley," he said, "this is none of your concern. You need to go." He nodded at Gail, who had followed me into his office. She tried to put her arm around my shoulder and lead me out. I resisted.

"This is crazy," I said, "Tabitha—you don't have to do this."

"It's already done!" Toby looked like someone had just handed him an eight-pound plate of bacon. "Glad we could get this all wrapped up so neatly. Aunt Shaylene will be so pleased."

I ignored him. "Carl, you know she's just doing this to clear Thad's name."

"I am not," Tabitha said. "I did it. That's why I confessed. The guilt was too much for me." She said all of this without a trace of emotion, like it was from a script she'd memorized. There was no way Carl could believe this. No way anyone would believe this. And it occurred to me that that was probably her plan all along.

This theory was confirmed when, as soon as Toby turned his back, Tabitha bugged out her eyes at me and mouthed something unintelligible. I frowned at her so she'd know I had no idea what she was talking about.

"Riley," Tabitha said loudly. "I'm going to need you to

do something for me, since I'm indisposed for the foresee-able future." That was an interesting way to describe being locked up for first-degree murder, but okay.

Toby chimed in, "Better not have to do with a nail file and a birthday cake!" He belly-laughed at his own joke.

Tabitha's eyes bored into mine. "Can you call my wedding planner, *Libby Nichols*?"

That got my attention. I happened to know for a fact that Tabitha's wedding planner was a woman out of Richmond named Gloria, as I'd had to listen to Tabitha drone on and on about how thrilled she was to get in with Glorified Events, one of Virginia's most prestigious event planners.

"Call Libby and let her know there may be some trouble in paradise."

As I attempted to figure out what Tabitha was really trying to say to me, Toby piped up again.

"I'll say," he laughed. "You ready for a conjugal visit-honeymoon, sister?" He really was the worst.

I left the sheriff's office after promising Tabitha I'd get in touch with her "wedding planner" Libby Nichols. I figured she was trying to tell me to look more closely at Libby's involvement with Arthur Davenport. As it happened, that was pretty high on my priority list anyway.

I walked through Memorial Park on my way back to the office and thought about Tabitha taking the blame for Arthur's murder. It was the most selfless and romantic thing I'd ever seen her do. A tiny part of me was proud of her for sacrificing herself for the man she loved, but most of me was frustrated with her for being so shortsighted. Making a false confession was highly illegal.

I was about halfway through the park when I heard Toby calling my name. I sped up.

"Riley! Hey, Riley, wait up!" For a natural-born baller,

Toby was pretty damn slow.

"I've got to get back to work. What is it?" I hated to be rude to anyone, but Toby made it easy.

"I trust you're rushing back to the office to update the *Times* online with this latest development?"

"Something like that." I had way more information gathering to do before I wrote an update, but there was no sense in telling Toby that.

"Mayor Lancett would be most grateful if y'all could quickly report the news that the Davenport killer has been apprehended."

I stopped walking. "You don't seriously believe that Tabitha killed Arthur Davenport, do you?"

"She said she did." Toby didn't care one bit about what was true or what wasn't, as long as the scandal was put to bed.

"Well, I don't believe it for a minute." I started to walk toward the office at a pace I was certain he couldn't keep up with for long.

"You have a duty to report the news of Tuttle Corner," he said, chasing me as fast as his stubby legs would allow. "The mayor will be very disappointed if you don't!"

CHAPTER 16

I went back to the office, grabbed the Davenport file, and was about to Google Libby Nichols's phone number when I noticed I had a new voicemail from a number I didn't recognize.

Hey, Riley, it's David Davenport. I heard about Tabitha's confession and I'm shocked. Going to try to get by the sheriff's office to convince Carl Haight that there's about as much chance of Tabitha having killed my father as the man on the moon. I'm going to tell Carl about that new information I found, too. I don't know if it's relevant, but Dad had been involved with a biotech company called Invigor8— spelled with the number eight at the end. They hired him as a consultant on a new biologic they're developing. He left the study suddenly and I just thought it might be worth looking into what exactly happened. I have access to some of his files and I'm going to look through them. I'll let you know what I find out. All right, this is officially the world's longest voicemail—but I won't be available for a few hours so I wanted you to know. Anyway, thanks. And don't forget to send me—

I pressed End before he could finish that sentence.

I was still holding my phone when it rang and I nearly jumped out of my chair. "Hey," I said, without even looking at who it was. I assumed it was David calling me back.

A woman's tentative voice came across the line. "Is this Riley Ellison?"

I sat up straighter. "It is."

"And are you the one writing Arthur Davenport's obituary?"

"Yes . . ."

"Okay, good." The woman exhaled audibly. "My name is Susan Pettis and I was a patient of Dr. Davenport's and I'm just torn up about him been killed." She pronounced it *kilt*.

"What can I do for you, Ms. Pettis?"

"Susan, please, um, I'd been a patient of his on about seventeen years." The way she spoke in halted clips told me she was working her way up to something. "My regular doctor over in Henrico sent me over to see Dr. Davenport because I was too tired for a forty-six-year-old woman. Couldn't hardly walk down the street without needing to sit down. Anyway, Dr. Davenport really listened to me. He didn't make me feel like I was a complainer or nothing, he believed me and did all kind of tests. Found out I had three arteries blocked up like clogged drains. He had to go in and Roto-Rooter them out, 'course they don't call it that over there in the hospital," she added with a nervous laugh.

"He took good care of you then," I said.

"Saved my life. Told me those arteries were over ninety percent blocked from all the years of cheeseburgers and french fries. He said if he wouldn't have gone in and cleared 'em out, I'da been dead inside of a month. I credit that man with my life."

I was quiet as I jotted down this information. "What

would you like people to know about Arthur Davenport, Susan? I assume that's why you called."

"Yeah," she said, and then hesitated before speaking
again. "I just feel so bad about what happened to him, and I
wanted to make sure that it got into the paper that he was a
fine and decent man, a smart man, who listened to people."
She paused and I sensed something else was coming. "And
anyway, there's one other thing. I told the sheriff, but he
didn't sound too interested."

"Yes?"

"Last Wednesday, I came into town—had to get the
mower fixed and Tuttle has the closest shop," she explained.
"I saw Dr. Davenport standing on the corner of Plantation
and Somerset Drive around 3 p.m. He was talking, or what
looked to me like arguing, with another man. The man's
arms were flailing and he was red in the face. And then the
other man pushed Dr. Davenport with two hands right in
the chest."

"Do you know who the man was?"

"Never seen him before."

"Can you describe him?"

"Let's see, he was white, tall, and bald. And he was probably in his middle forties, if I had to guess."

I wrote all of this down. "Was he wearing a uniform or
anything distinctive?"

"No—he just looked like a regular guy. After I saw him
push Dr. Davenport, I pulled my car over in that direction—
you know, to see if the doc needed help or anything. I told
you, I owe that man my life. But when I got close enough
to see, Dr. Davenport had started walking back toward the
street in the other direction, and the man, the bald guy, had
his phone out and looked like he was texting somebody or
something."

"Can you remember anything else?"

"Only thing I can remember is he had a big tattoo on his left forearm. Couldn't see what the design was, but I saw the black ink against his skin. But that's all. Other than that, he just looked regular."

I took Susan's full name and contact information and thanked her for the call. The picture of Arthur Davenport as a hard-working, caring medical professional was coming clearer into view with each interview. Everyone I'd spoken to, without exception, had nothing but respect for him as a doctor. And yet he'd been murdered. That probably meant it was something in his personal life that motivated the killing. So far, I knew he had a rocky relationship with his oldest son. He'd had an affair with a married woman, and had possibly been threatened by her husband. And he'd been seen arguing with someone on the street the day before his death. None of these things screamed motive for murder, but all of the sudden I was desperate to find out if Bennett Nichols was tall, bald, and/or tattooed.

CHAPTER 17

The Nicholses lived in a large plantation-style home set way back off of a long paved private road. The landscaping alone probably cost more than I'd make in a lifetime at the newspaper. It was dark by the time I got there, but only just. I was awfully close to the dinner hour and wasn't expected, but I had a feeling the element of surprise might just work in my favor in this situation.

I rang the doorbell and waited a full minute with no answer. I rang it again and heard some noises from inside, so I knew someone was home. When she finally opened the door, I could see what the delay had been. Libby Nichols appeared to either have just rolled out of bed or out of a bottle of vodka. Or maybe both.

She was dressed in cutoff jean shorts and a black, long-sleeved thermal top unbuttoned far enough to see two inches of cleavage. Her long blond hair looked like it hadn't seen a brush in days—actual bed head, not the sexified version in shampoo ads. But despite the crazy hair, the wrinkled clothes, and the sour expression, you could see that Libby Nichols was a beautiful woman.

I introduced myself and asked if she and her husband had time to answer a few questions for an article I was writing for the *Times*.

"All right," she said. "But you'll have to excuse me, I'm

not feeling my best today."

Eager to take her up on her offer before she changed her mind, I followed her into the grand living room, which was decorated in soft grays and creams with lots of shiny, mirrored surfaces to reflect the light from the large picture windows along the back wall. It was very "tastefully done," as Mrs. Winterthorne would have said, but it smacked of a professional decorator.

A man I assumed to be Bennett Nichols sat in a large black leather recliner and barely looked at me when I walked in. His attention was on the massive flat-screen TV that hung over the fireplace. He was playing a video game, some shoot 'em up kind with glossy soldiers in beige uniforms hurling grenades into burned-out buildings. On the side table next to him was a fifth of Wild Turkey, three-quarters empty, and an ashtray containing the remnants of a joint. He wore a red Washington Nationals baseball hat, turned backward, under which poked out a thicket of dark brown hair. Not bald. I did a quick scan of his forearms too. No tattoos that I could see.

"What can we do for you?" Bennett said, without taking his eyes off his game.

I took a deep breath. I knew what I was doing was a little risky, but I also didn't want to waste a trip out here. I took out a notepad and said brightly, "I'm writing the obituary for Dr. Arthur Davenport and I heard you were a patient of his. I wondered if you had any stories or recollections about him that I could use in the obit?"

I heard a pinging sound that paused the game as he lowered his controller and looked at me. "Is this some kind of joke?"

"No," I said, playing dumb. "I've already spoken to a few of his other patients, but they were women. I wanted to get a man's take on him and I heard through the grapevine that you were one of his patients." I opened my eyes wider, presenting the very picture of innocence.

"That man," Bennett said through gritted teeth, "was a snake in the grass. You can print that if you want."

"Really? How so?"

"You want to know about that dirty son of a bitch—I'll tell you all you need to know," Bennett hissed.

Jackpot! I flipped to a new page in my notebook. But Libby interrupted before he could continue. "Aw, Benny's just pissed off 'cause Artie had a little thing for me," she said as she walked over and perched on the side of Bennett's recliner.

"Babe, you smell like rotten milk," Bennett said to Libby and crinkled his nose.

Her face colored. She turned into him and whispered, "I told you I wasn't feeling well today."

"Well, you stink," he said before turning back to me. "Anyways, Dr. Davenport was a first-class asshole."

"The truth is," Libby stood up and moved to the sofa, "Dr. Davenport took good care of Benny while he was sick, but he got a little too attached to me." She attempted a demure smile. "The two of them ended up having a little bit of a scuffle over it all, but it was fine. In the end, Artie knew I was taken."

"A scuffle?"

"Yeah, caught him trying to get his hands on my wife," Bennett said, his anger rising again. "I would have kicked his ass too, but I have a heart condition—which of course he knew."

"My hero," Libby cooed, and it was hard to tell if she was being sarcastic or not.

This was not the same story I got from Dr. Steeler and

Mrs. Winterthorne. "Um," I said, trying to think of a good follow-up question, "Do you have any idea who might have wanted him dead?"

"Duh—me," Bennett said.

The shock on my face must have shown because Libby jumped in quickly. "Wanting someone dead and killing them are two different things, you know. We were home together all night on Monday, if that's what you're getting around to asking."

Bennett's eyes left the TV and snapped to me. "Is that what you're after? 'Cause the sheriff's already been here. We didn't have anything to do with that scumbag dying— not that I'm sorry to see him dead. I won't lie about that." Between the flared nostrils and the hard-set jaw, Bennett looked like a man working awfully hard to control his temper.

"Can anyone else vouch for your whereabouts on Monday night at about 11 p.m.?"

"Seems like those are sheriff questions, not obituary-writer questions," Bennett said, a challenge in his low voice.

"Oh, didn't I mention?" I said. "I'm also a crime reporter for the *Times*."

His face went from surprise to anger in about three seconds flat. Libby's response was a little more controlled. "I think it's time for you to go," she said with a smile that did not reach her eyes. "Let me show you out."

Libby walked slowly as I followed her outside onto the driveway and the motion-sensor lights came on. Standing beneath the lights I could see dark circles under her eyes.

"Listen," she said, her tone more conciliatory now that we were outside, "the truth is that Arthur was crushing on me pretty hard. Benny gets upset about it, understandably. When we'd go in for appointments, Artie would stare at me and make inappropriate comments. And then one day he called me and said he had some news about Benny that he wanted to discuss with me in private. I thought it was a little weird, but I was worried about my husband so I agreed to meet with him—actually invited him out here to the house because my car was in the shop. But when he got here, he had only one thing on his mind."

I was pretty sure Libby was lying, but she had a confessional way of talking that drew me in. I didn't necessarily believe her, but I was still interested.

"He got a little handsy. I would've had no problem kicking him out—but then Benny walked in and just went ape-shit. He got himself so worked up his heart went into overdrive and he passed out right on our kitchen floor. Artie had to do CPR on him till the ambulance came. It was crazy."

"Sounds like it."

"Word got out, as it always does in this town, and people were saying Artie and I were in bed when Benny walked in. None of that's true. But it didn't stop the gossip. I actually blame Benny's mom for a lot of it. She never liked me—thought I was just after Benny's money—so I think she almost wanted it to be true, you know?" Libby's angelic face looked sad as she talked, the poor persecuted hot girl.

"So you and Arthur didn't have a relationship then?"

She nodded toward the house. "That man doesn't let me out of his sight. When would I have time enough for an affair?"

Fair enough, but it didn't really answer the question.

"Look at me," she said sweeping a hand down her long, lean frame. "Ever since I married Benny, people have been trying to figure out why. They can't accept that I love him even though he's a little bit older, even though he's a little bit possessive. And so they talk, they make up gossip—but the truth is, Riley, I love my husband. Dr. Davenport thought he could get in between that and he couldn't. But none of that has anything to do with how or why that man was killed."

"So, do you have any theories on who might have wanted to hurt Arthur?"

Libby scratched the side of her cheek. "You know," she said, as if the thought had just popped into her head, "now that you mention it, I remember Arthur mentioning an ex-girlfriend who'd threatened to kill him."

Well that certainly seemed relevant. Of course it also seemed a little too convenient for her to have "all of the sudden" remembered such information. But I played along. "Anyone I might know?"

"Depends," she said, a challenge in her eyes. "How familiar with local politics are you?"

I got a tingly feeling on the back of my neck.

"Does the name Mayor Shaylene Lancett ring a bell?" She crossed her arms and raised an eyebrow. " 'Cause I'm pretty sure at one point, Arthur was ringing hers."

CHAPTER 18

When I left the Nichols house, questions buzzed around my mind like fireflies in a jar. I wanted to know more about the relationship between Libby, Bennett, and Arthur, and if there was any truth to what Libby had just told me about Mayor Lancett. I knew better than to believe what she said without proof, but if she was telling the truth, it could shed a whole new light on the mayor's eagerness to get this case wrapped up.

The Nichols house was on the outer west edge of Tuttle Corner, pretty close to West Bay, where Jay lived. It was almost time for our date, so I thought I'd just head over that way. I was keyed up and wanted to talk things over with him—he might have some insight into what was really going on here. It'd be good to talk through all of this with someone so I could figure out what my next move was going to be.

I turned out of the Nichols driveway, and after a few seconds I noticed a gray BMW pull out behind me from one of the side roads. It was hard to tell, but it looked like it could be Jay's car. *What would Jay be doing out here?* I thought. At lunch I thought he said he had a meeting back at the Richmond office. I slowed down, hoping the car would catch up to where I could see if it was him—thinking that if it was, I could just follow him back to his place. But when I slowed down, the car slowed down too. So I sped up. And the car sped up too. A creepy feeling took hold.

It was dark and there were no lights on those rural county roads, so it was impossible for me to tell from my angle who it was, or even if it was a man or a woman. Since my entire knowledge base of what to do when being followed came from what I'd seen in movies, I did what I thought Reese Witherspoon would have done if someone were following her. I adjusted my mirror, sunk low in my seat, and pulled over to the side of the road so the car would have to pass me. I figured this would accomplish two things: one, I'd be able to see who was doing the following when it drove past, and two, it'd put an end to the whole thing because they would then no longer be behind me.

I trained my eyes on the rearview waiting for the car to speed past, but before it got to me, the car took a sudden left turn onto a gravel road that headed back toward town. *Huh?* So, again channeling my inner Reese, I whipped around and followed the car down the road. From this vantage point, I could now see that it was a man driving—at least it looked like a man, judging by the height and outline of the head; both details looked familiar to me. A prickly hot sensation crept up through my chest. *Was this Jay? Was Jay following me?*

I punched at his name in my Favorites section and waited for him to answer as I followed the gray BMW down the dirt road.

"Hey Riley," he said, his voice sounding perfectly casual.

"Hey. Just got done with work and I was thinking of heading over. What're you doing?"

Short pause. "Just driving home from work."

He sounded normal, but then again he'd been an undercover agent. He practically lied for a living. "Okay, cool.

Will you be home soon? I'm not far . . ."

"Uh, yeah." His voice was losing some of its coolness. "Shouldn't be too long."

"Uh-huh," I said. "How's the traffic on I-95?"

He paused, this time longer. "Um, you know . . ." In that moment I felt certain Jay was driving the car in front of me. And what was worse was that I was sure he knew that I knew it. It was time to end this.

I stepped on the accelerator until I got right up on the tail of the BMW and laid on the horn for about ten seconds. As expected, I heard the sound reverberate through the Bluetooth. My pulse raced. "You're following me?" I shouted.

"Riley, let me explain—"

"No need," I said, slamming on my brakes to turn around. "I think I understand perfectly."

———

There are a lot of good things about driving a used Nissan Cube. It gets good gas mileage; it's one of only three in Tuttle Corner, so I could always find it; and, after my beloved Honda Fit was blown up a few months ago, it was all I could afford with the insurance money. The downside of driving a used Cube was that it was not the best for outrunning a BMW.

After I turned around, Jay starting calling me repeatedly, which I completely ignored. I was livid. I knew he had been worried about me going out to the Nichols house, he'd said as much right to my face, and even though I told him I could handle it, it appeared as though he had appointed himself my security detail. It was beyond insulting.

Jay caught up to me right before I was going to turn from the gravel road back onto the main one and pulled his car in front of mine. I had no choice but to stop, my blood boiling at the gall of this man—who not only clearly didn't trust me, but who was now going to force me to talk to him when I so very obviously didn't want to. But with literally no place to go, I put my car into park. He got out and walked toward me. I craned my face to the passenger window, refusing, princess-like, to even look at him.

"Riley," he said through the glass. "Open up, let me explain."

I turned my shoulders even farther away from the window to make the point that I had no intention of speaking to him.

"C'mon . . ." His voice sounded as soft as one could sound when needing to project through a car window. "Please."

I didn't move.

He walked around the front of the car to the passenger side. So of course I turned my shoulders one hundred and eighty degrees the other way. He pivoted, midstep, and came back around to the driver side. The headlights from my car illuminated his path from one coast to the other. I switched them off and felt a surge of satisfaction when I heard him knock his knee on the Cube's left front bumper.

Now back at the driver's side window, he leaned his face close to the glass. "Okay, fine. Have it your way. I'll talk from here. You can listen."

I kept up my campaign of silence, arms folded tightly across my chest.

"I did go out to the Nichols house this afternoon, but I only did it to make sure you were okay."

At least he had the decency to not lie to me.

"I was worried about you. When I got back to the of-fice I ran Bennett Nichols's name through the system and found out he has a record of assault. The thought of you going out there alone ... well, it gnawed at me. So I thought I'd go out there and be nearby, you know, in case you needed me or something."

Bennett Nichols had a record for assault? I'd have to remember to check that out later, when I wasn't in a big old fight with my boyfriend.

"Why didn't you just call and tell me that?" I yelled through the window, still not looking at him.

"Because I didn't want to interfere, as crazy as that sounds." He put a hand up to the window. "Will you let me explain ... please?"

I hesitated and then rolled down the window. About three inches. "Talk." I said, my eyes focused straight ahead.

I heard him sigh, whether it was out of exasperation or relief I didn't know and didn't care. "Listen," he said, "I've seen people do some really messed-up things when they've felt threatened. My job ... well, let's just say it exposes me to the worst of human nature. I was worried about you, that's all. Maybe I overstepped—"

"Maybe?" I snapped

"I *did* overstep."

"You're damn right you did. Do you have any idea how insulting this is? Not to mention completely unprofessional!"

Jay hooked his fingers over the window (I briefly considered rolling it up). "I'm sorry. I acted out of instinct and it was a bad call ..."

I didn't know what to think. Was he really sorry or only sorry because I found out?

As if he could read my mind, he said, "Riley, I'm really sorry."

The intensity of his voice, almost begging me to forgive him, washed over me, dampening the remaining sparks of anger. "You should be," I said.

"I am. Honestly."

"You shouldn't have done that."

"I know. It was wrong. Let me make it up to you?"

I turned to look at him properly for the first time since he walked over. He certainly looked sorry. And sincere. And super cute. And like he might have a few interesting ideas about how to make it up to me if I rolled this window down a little farther. And so I did.

Hey Riley,

Can I just say that I think we might have an almost psychic connection! I was thinking about u at the exact minute ur email came through. Crazy!

Also crazy about ur man following u . . . I don't love that, I've gotta b honest. But if he says he's sorry then I guess it's fair to give him another chance. Fool me once, u know what I'm saying! But if he does it again, I think ur gonna need to invoke the wise words from Hamlet, Act III, Scene III, line 87, and tell him, "No."

I'm sending u a link to a Bestmillenniallife.com podcast available for $1.99 on iTunes. This one is called GIVE IT UP and it focuses on how to learn to let go and live a more present, now-centered existence. But whatever u do, make sure u get GIVE IT UP from Bestmillenniallife.com and not another company because apparently, there's another app with that same name that has quite a different message—haha lol!

Anyway. Give it a try and see if it helps—$1.99 is a pretty small investment* in ur mental well being, right? Or u could also share it with ur guy and see if it helps him. Sounds like the dude has some control issues.

xx,
Jenna B
Personal Success Concierge™
Bestmillenniallife.com

* I am obligated to tell you that the term "investment" here is used for promotional purposes only. Bestmillenniallife.com makes no claim that our products or services will directly result in any monetary gain. (Ugh, lawyers.)

Chapter 19

I woke up the next morning with Coltrane on my bed and Jay on my mind. After we'd made up, we decided to grab some dinner at Monroe's, a bar in West Bay, rather than go home and cook as we had planned. We had a good time at dinner, and by the end of the evening I'd almost forgotten about the way it had started. I hadn't stayed over at his place because Jay was working in the DC office again this morning and had to get up ridiculously early in order to make an early morning meeting. So instead of snuggling with Jay, I spent the night next to Coltrane, who—by the look of him, all coiled up like a large furry snake—was pretty happy with the way things worked out.

I was still a little bothered by what Jay did, but I was trying to let it go. After all, he'd apologized and I believed he meant it. And besides, he'd only followed me to make sure I was safe, so in a way that was a good thing. I rolled over and said to Coltrane, "A boyfriend who cares about your safety is better than one who doesn't, right, buddy?" He licked himself in response. I wasn't quite sure what to make of that.

Ready for some caffeine and a dose of perspective, I got up, made coffee, and went online to read the morning's obits. I read about a woman who died at the age of sixty-four after a long battle with breast cancer. It was filled with warrior imagery and metaphors about battles fought and ultimately lost—but interestingly, mourners were asked to make donations not to one of the many cancer charities, but to the Critter Connection, a nonprofit organization dedicated to the rescue and rehabilitation of guinea pigs. And then I read about the life and death of a Latino man living in New York City who started the first off-Broadway theater company to produce the work of Latino playwrights in English. His life had not been an easy one, according to his partner, but it had meant something to an entire community. Then there was the story of Galen McDougal, a former British MP who died at the age of ninety-two, a man described as "far too inquisitive for his own good" and "unembarrassable" by his friends and colleagues. He never married, had no children, but was said to have al-ways worked hard for his constituents—that was his legacy. That, and an infamous recording of him singing Rupert Holmes's "Piña Colada Song" at an office karaoke party back in 2004 that was referenced by three of the people in-terviewed in the obit. I guess you never know what people will remember you for once you're gone.

I thought about Arthur Davenport and what people would remember about his life now that he was gone. It was clear that he was what most of us are in the end: compli-cated. He was obviously a hard-working physician who had touched many people's lives through his work. But equally as obvious was that he also had some flaws that had got-ten him into trouble—how much trouble was the question on my mind. Could one of Arthur's many trysts been the reason he was murdered? There was the affair with Libby Nichols and the almost unbelievable implication about a relationship with the mayor.

It was almost unbelievable because up until a few years

ago, Shaylene Lancett was a single woman who owned a religious gift and book shop called Inviting Praise on the square in downtown Tuttle. Three years ago, she'd decided to run for mayor against Gary Dubois, who'd served as mayor for the three previous terms. Largely due to Mayor Dubois's unpopular push to move the Johnnycake Festival to the fall, Tuttle's citizens had voted Shaylene into office on a summer-or-bust corncake mandate. And so far, so good. She was generally considered a good mayor who didn't rock the proverbial boat too much.

Shaylene found love soon after taking office. She married Theo Gladstone just two years ago in a rather strange ceremony in Memorial Park. I knew this because my parents had been asked to play at the wedding (Shaylene and Theo's wedding song was "The Rainbow Connection"—which is also the name of my parents' band). I remember Mom telling me how the two of them met at special screening of the most recent Muppets movie during the summer family film series put on by the parks department. Shaylene and Theo were both of a certain age, both there alone, and both apparently huge Muppets fans. It was kismet. Their wedding had been Kermit-and-Piggy-themed down to the pink-and-green layer cake.

The idea that Shaylene Lancett was some sort of murderous ex-girlfriend of Arthur Davenport was more than a little peculiar. Had Shaylene and Arthur Davenport dated at some point? Was it before she married Theo, or could this be yet another affair? Or was this just something Libby Nichols made up to throw suspicion off herself and her husband? Those were all questions that needed answers. Lucky for me I had an entire day with which to chase them down. I knew my mom and Shaylene had kept in touch, so I texted Mom to see if she knew anything about Shaylene and Arthur. It was early, but I knew my mom never slept past seven. She called me about three seconds after I texted.

"Are you okay? Why are you asking about Shaylene and Arthur? What's happening, Riley?"

"Calm down, Mom," I said. "I'm writing Dr. Davenport's obit and I'm just fact checking a few things, that's all." That wasn't true, strictly speaking, but Mom had been nervous when I made the move to the newspaper and I didn't see any reason to worry her, especially while she was out of town.

"Oh. Well, if you're sure everything's okay . . ."

"Yes, Mom, I'm sure. What about Shaylene and Arthur?"

"Funny you mention it, because there was some sort of issue between them," she said. "I don't know exactly what it was, I just remember Shaylene telling me right before the wedding that they'd been close, but he'd done something unforgiveable."

That sounded ominous. "And she didn't say what?"

"No," my mom said. "I'd gone over to her house a few hours before the ceremony to go over some last-minute details and she was upset. She didn't want to talk about it. One thing I can tell you is that she's completely gaga over Theo. Can you imagine two people who love the Muppets that much finding each other?"

We chatted for a while longer about how things were going on their road trip, and then she put my dad on the phone, who spent at least six minutes singing the praises of Craisins. "Have you ever had one, Riley? It's like the raisin's bolder, tastier cousin! I can't believe I've lived fifty-six years without ever having had a Craisin. Now I've got bags of them stashed all over the place. I've got Craisins in the car, in my guitar case, in my dopp kit . . ."

I love my father very much but finally had to cut him off. This kind of talk could go on for a while. "Okay, love you guys! I'll see you when you get back, okay?"

After about ten "I love yous" and "We're so proud of yous" later I left for work with that feeling you get when you leave for the airport and you're sure you've forgotten something critical. I had my purse and my laptop, so it wasn't that... could it be somebody's birthday? I mentally scrolled through my mom, dad, Dr. H, Tabitha, Ryan ... nope ...

"You okay?" Flick walked up behind me and through the front door.

"I think so." Probably just a case of having too much on my mind, I thought. I set down my bag at my cubicle and followed Flick down the hall.

As we walked into his office he said, "You're not worried about Holman, are you?"

The question actually made me laugh. Of all the things I might currently be worried about, Holman wasn't one of them. "Uh, no."

He hesitated for a moment, and looked like he was working his way up to something. "Um, it's none of my business or anything, but you and Holman ... are you guys ... ?"

Before he could complete the thought I jumped in. "Oh gosh no!"

He flinched at my strong response.

"I don't mean to sound rude about it or anything," I said, color rushing to my cheeks, "but we are just friends. Co-workers. That's it."

"Okay, okay," he said. "Just wondering. It's none of my business, I was just worried about you." It was his turn to look embarrassed now. "Not that it's my place or anything, but I was concerned—or maybe just curious, I guess." Flick couldn't have looked more uncomfortable if he had been standing in the feminine hygiene aisle at Landry's.

I felt a sudden rush of affection for him that I hadn't felt in years. He reminded me so much of my granddaddy, even though they were opposites in many ways. Where Flick was gruff, Granddad had been even-tempered. The two of them frequently sparred over politics or sports or which was the best movie about real-life journalists. Granddad favored *All the President's Men*, while Flick argued for *Broadcast News*, but their constant back-and-forth was a testament to their deep respect and affection for each other.

"Flick," I said, unable to keep the question at bay. "Do you miss him?"

It only took him a half second to catch onto what I was talking about. He looked me dead in the eye. "Every single day."

We sat in silence with years of grief around us, filling his small office with emotions that neither one of us was particularly good at handling. I took a deep breath and asked the question that had haunted me for the past five years: "Why didn't you fight for him?"

Flick's eyes snapped up to mine, and I thought for a minute he was going to yell at me again. But he didn't. He sat with the question for a good ten seconds before he answered. "Albert was my best friend in the world, and I would have done anything for him. Anything." He paused, gathering his thoughts before speaking again. "And before he died, he asked me for something. He made me promise. And so I kept my promise even though it meant breaking your heart."

Tears blurred my vision; I blinked and one rolled down my cheek. "What do you mean?"

"He asked me to keep you safe."

"What?" I asked, confused. "Safe from what, from who?"

Flick shook his head. "I can't say anymore."

"But you have to!" I felt the desperation of five years of unanswered questions building inside my chest.

"If I told you, I wouldn't be keeping up my end of the deal." A sad, slow smile crossed his face. "But I want you to know that I've never given up on finding out what happened to Albert." And then he gave me a look that I felt in my bones. "And I never will."

If he was still trying to find out "what happened to Albert," that must mean he didn't think it was a suicide after all. I knew it! I started to say this just as Flick's phone rang and he picked it up. He nodded his head toward the door. I didn't want to leave. I wanted him to tell me what he was doing, what he knew, what his theories were.

He motioned with his free hand at the door. He wasn't going to talk to me—at least not at that moment. I'd have to try again later. I stood up and walked out of his office in a daze. *Why had Granddad asked Flick to protect me? And from what? And why had Flick kept this a secret until now?* It was obvious Flick didn't want to tell me, but eventually he'd have to. I'd find a way to make him. I wasn't a kid anymore, I was a full-grown woman—a reporter, no less—who could handle whatever secrets Flick was hiding. And more than that, I deserved to know the truth.

Chapter 20

I'd barely sat down at my desk when Kay Jackson called from down the hall, "Ellison, can I see you a minute?"

"Look out! Intern walking," Gerlach Spencer joked as I passed his desk on my way to Kay's office.

"Shut up, Spencer."

"I'm only joking, kiddo. I'm sure she just wants to give you an encouraging hug." He busted out laughing and gave Henderson a high-five over their shared cubicle wall. *Idiots*, I thought. There should be a law against forty-year-olds high-fiving.

I felt buzzy with nerves as I once again walked into my boss's office not knowing what she was going to say. Kay stood with her hands on her hips, her body language a nonverbal warning that I wasn't getting an encouraging hug.

"Did you tell Toby Lancett yesterday that you were not going to report on Tabitha St. Simon's confession to the Davenport murder because she is a friend of yours?"

The question hit me like a wrecking ball. "Of course not!" My denial came out in a high-pitch tone I barely recognized.

"Because that's what Toby told the mayor. And that's what she reamed my ass about for five straight minutes just now."

My pulse went into overdrive. "No, that's not what I—"

I started to say, but then I stopped myself. I had sort of said that to Toby, hadn't I? I mean, I didn't say I wasn't going to report the story, but I did say that I didn't believe Tabitha killed Arthur Davenport despite her confessing to the crime. "I mean, what I said was—"

She cut me off. "Did you know about Tabitha St. Simon's confession?"

I nodded, too scared to speak.

"When did it happen?"

"Late yesterday afternoon."

She stared at me without saying a word, but I could see her jaw flexing in anger. "Then why didn't you log an update?"

"I was going to—I just . . ."

The truth is I hadn't updated the story because I felt so sure that Tabitha's confession was fake, that it seemed silly to report on it. I hadn't exactly *not* written the article on purpose . . . it was more like it never even occurred to me. It just didn't seem like news. And then there was what happened with Jay: finding out he followed me, then our argument, then making up . . . it pushed all thoughts of Tabitha's confession from my mind. That had to be what I felt like I was forgetting this morning. If only I'd been able to figure it out before Kay had.

I tried explaining myself to Kay (minus the part about Jay of course), but with each word I said, she just looked angrier. When I finished my defense, such as it was, she muttered something under her breath before taking a deep breath. She blew it out slowly, as if she needed the time to control her reaction.

"You compromised the integrity of this paper, Riley. I'm not sure if you did this because you're inexperienced and don't understand how non-biased reporting is *literally* the

cornerstone of the American newspaper, or if you did it because you were trying to protect your friend."

"I wasn't trying to protect Tabitha, I swear! She's
not even really my friend. We're more like frenemies,
actually . . . she's always insulting me and barking orders
at me—" The look on Kay's face stopped my ramble.

"You screwed up," Kay said. "And I even warned you
about this. Do you have any idea how bad it is for the local
paper to be at odds with the mayor?"

"I'm sorry, Kay. I'm *so* sorry. I'll go write the story right
now. I have quotes and everything—I can have it to you in
twenty minutes."

"Nope." Kay shook her head before I even finished talking. "You're off the story. I'm giving it to Spencer. You can
keep the obit, but you're off the rest of it."

Her words were like a slap to the face, quick and painful. It was just one little mistake! And it wasn't even like I'd
misquoted someone or gotten any facts wrong—I just de-
layed reporting something that was clearly false for a few
hours . . . but even as the rationalizations were coming to
my mind, I knew that's just what they were: rationalizations
for my mistakes.

Kay stared at me, waiting for me to say something. I
don't know if she expected me to argue with her, to plead
my case, to beg for a second chance, but I didn't trust myself to speak. I was afraid if I opened my mouth I might
start crying, and I was not about to let that happen, so I just
nodded and walked out of her office as fast as I could.

"What—no trophy?" Spencer chided as I sped past his
desk with my head down, trying like hell to hold in my tears
until I got to the women's restroom. At least I knew no one
would bother me in there. I pushed open the door and as
soon as it swung shut, the tears fell.

Hey Riley,

OMFG. I cannot believe that ur boss freaked out because of one tiny mistake! See, this is my problem with Baby Boomer bosses: they are so JUDGEY. Like they never made a mistake before!

Anyway. Riley, I want u to focus on what I'm about to say because it is the absolute 1000% truth: Don't let ur boss make u feel you're some kind of screwup just because of one teeny misstep. U r doing the best u can and if ur boss can't see that then she is the one with the problem. She's probably afraid that ur going to take her job. I read somewhere that Baby Boomers' second biggest workplace fear is Millennials taking their jobs, behind losing their health insurance.

And remember, in the wise words of Queen Bey,* "Power is not given to you, you have to take it."

xx,
Jenna B.
Personal Success Concierge™
Bestmillenniallife.com

*The use of this quote does not constitute an endorsement of any kind by Beyoncé, who is not now nor has never been a paid spokesperson for Bestmillenniallife.com (but who I think we both know would totally slay as a Personal Success Concierge™—haha lol!).

Dear Jenna,

Thank you for the encouragement; I really needed that right now. However, as much as I love me some Beyoncé, I'm not

➤

sure that quote applies in this scenario. And actually, I think
my boss is from Gen X.

Anyway, thanks for being on my side.

All best,
Riley

Hey Riley,

Number 1 Rule of Life: Beyoncé always applies. And Gen Xers
are just as bad.

xx,
Jenna B
Personal Success Concierge™
Bestmillenniallife.com

Chapter 21

I waited until the redness in my eyes and cheeks had faded before going back to my desk. I resolved to focus on the obit and make sure there was no angle I didn't cover. At least I could still do that right. I'd be sure to check in with Flick and get his approval at every step so that by the time it got to Kay it would be beyond reproach. Maybe that would make up a tiny bit for my colossal error in judgment. But as soon as I opened the obit document on my laptop, my phone vibrated. It was a text from Carl's private number: Meet me at Tuttle Gen now. David Davenport has been poisoned.

I left the newsroom through the back door without telling anyone where I was heading. When I got to the hospital, the woman at the information desk stonewalled me, saying since I was neither David's family nor with the sheriff's office she could not tell me anything. Carl was nowhere to be found and not responding to my texts.

I took the elevator to the fifth floor and asked at the closest nurses station if they knew where David was, but the woman I spoke with had no information, or at least none she was willing to give out to a random girl wandering the halls with a notepad.

I decided to head back down to the information desk and see if I could sweet talk someone down there into giving me his room number. I had my doubts, but it was worth a try.

I went back to the elevator bank and when it opened, my old friend Jack the custodian was in there. "Back again?" he said with a smile.

"Yeah," I said and pushed the *L* button. "No coffee this time, though."

He laughed. "You working on a story or something?"

"I'm actually going to be writing Dr. Arthur Davenport's obituary for the *Times*." The door opened and we both headed in the direction of the lobby.

"Heard about that. Sad deal." He was quiet for a moment and then continued, "I've always been fascinated with obituaries."

"Really?"

"I've read them all my life," he said. "My sister and I wrote one for our mom a while back and it was harder than I thought it'd be."

I'd heard this a lot from people who wrote the death notices for their loved ones. It was a difficult thing to reduce an entire life to two or three newspaper inches, and many people toiled over it. I think that's why so many allow the funeral home directors to write it for them. When they're grieving, writing is often the last thing they want to do. That was one of the reasons I think the *Times* readers responded so positively to our running editorial obits. Many small newspapers had cut them altogether as budgets and readership declined, but in a small town we were sort of insulated from that. It was one of the many reasons I loved living in Tuttle Corner.

"If you wrote from the heart, I'm sure it touched the people who knew your mom," I said. It probably sounded trite, but it was all I could think to say; I was glad when Jack smiled like maybe the thought made him feel better.

"I hope so," he said. "She was a pretty special lady."

The information desk was unmanned as we approached. So much for my plan. "Hey," I turned to Jack, "you haven't heard anything about Dr. Davenport's son, David, being admitted have you?"

He nodded. "Just heard about it from Sheila down in the ER. Apparently, he was doing rounds and just passed out cold."

"Did she say why?"

"I heard someone say they think maybe it was food poisoning."

Oh. *Food* poisoning. Was that all this was?

"Do you know what floor he's on?"

"Maybe four? That's the internal medicine ward."

"Thanks again—see you around!"

"Not if I see you first," Jack said with a good-natured laugh as he took his yellow mop bucket and went on his way.

I rode the elevator back up to the fourth floor, got off, and saw Carl sitting in a chair near the end of the hallway.

"Please tell me David has food poisoning."

"What?" He looked at me like I was speaking Klingon. "No, David has poison-poisoning. As in someone tried to kill him."

Damn. Someone was hunting Davenports.

———

Like most rumors, the food poisoning one had a kernel of truth. So while David Davenport did not have food poisoning, he had most likely been poisoned by way of food. After drinking a protein shake for lunch he had passed out on the floor of the ER, where he was checking on patients. Luckily, since he was at the hospital, a quick-thinking nurse figured out what was going on and was able to get him the appropriate treatment.

"He's fortunate," Dr. Cavell said to us before opening the door to his room. "There was an enormous amount of digitalis in his system. If he'd been at home, he would have very likely died just like his father."

Dr. Cavell granted Carl and me a few minutes but warned us not to push David. Assuming his recovery went well, he'd probably be able to go home in a couple of days. Until then, he'd need to finish his course of treatment and, above all else, rest.

Carl opened the door and the sight caught me up short. David's skin looked almost gray. He looked so different from the vibrant guy I'd met yesterday.

His eyelids fluttered open as we approached his bedside. "Hey guys." His voice was weak, higher than normal.

Carl wasted no time in getting right to the questions. "Can you think of anyone who'd want to do this to you, David?"

David closed his eyes as he thought. "I really can't," he said, slowly opening his eyes back up. "But I mean first Dad and now me? What's going on here?" He sounded scared, and I had the feeling a guy like David Davenport didn't often sound scared.

I instinctively reached out for his hand and gave it a gentle squeeze.

"I hope you don't think my brother did this. Because there is no—"

"We don't." Carl cut in before David got too upset. "Thad was being held at the county jail when this happened, so unless he figured out how to bend the laws of time and space, there's no way he had anything to do with this."

David looked relieved.

"David," I said slowly, a thought coming to mind. "Did you have a chance to look through those files?" I remembered what he'd said on his voicemail.

He tried to shake his head but what resulted was more like a head roll from side to side.

"What files?" Carl asked. I filled him in on Arthur's relationship to Invigor8 and the drug they were developing. If he already knew this information, he didn't let on.

"You called it a biologic. What exactly is that?" Carl asked David.

"It's basically a type of medicine that uses living organisms—like plant or animal cells as opposed to chemicals like a traditional drug might."

"Okay," Carl said, making some notes in his pad. "And what was this drug for?"

"I don't know. It was real hush-hush. Dad had to sign a bunch of confidentiality documents because they were in the patent-development phase. But his relationship with Invigor8 had soured. At first he seemed excited about their new product, but then he told me a few weeks ago that he felt like they were trying to rush to market. Last week Dad told me he was going to sever his ties with them." He paused to catch his breath.

"All right. We'll check it out," Carl said, making notes in his notebook.

I had yet to ask Carl what he knew (or didn't know) about Arthur's relationship with Libby or Bennett Nichols, but since we were both there with David, I brought up the subject. "Did you know anything about a relationship your father had with a woman named Libby Nichols?"

David rolled his eyes. "Yeah, I knew."

"What do you know about it?"

"I think he was taking care of Libby's husband when the two of them started up."

"Did it end badly?" I asked.

"Do things with a married woman ever not end badly?" David gave me measured look. "I think her husband found out and freaked. But I don't know a lot about it. Dad didn't really tell me about that part of his life." His fading voice trailed off. I wanted to ask him about Shaylene Lancett too, but he was tired and it seemed like it was time for us to leave.

"All right," Carl said, taking a step toward the door. "You get some rest now. We'll be in touch."

After we closed David's door, Carl turned to me. "You can forget about the Bennett and Libby Nichols angle, Riley. Trust me."

"Why?"

"The Nicholses have airtight alibis for the time Arthur Davenport was killed. And before you go guessing that they are each other's alibi—let me inform you that that is not the case."

"Wait—what?" I thought Libby said she and Bennett were home alone at the time of the murder. "Did something change?"

"Let's just say that we have proof of Libby and Bennett's location on the night Arthur was killed, and it was nowhere near the Davenport estate."

"Where were they?"

"You're on a need-to-know basis and you don't need to know that."

"Fine," I said, irritated. "What do we do next?"

Carl sighed. "The mayor is hell-bent on the prosecutor filing charges against Thad PDQ, and if she hears that we're looking into something new, well, I'd rather not have to explain that till we know a little more. She and Toby are crawling all over me about this."

Even though I hadn't had a chance to verify it yet, I told Carl what Libby had said about the mayor. It seemed like important information for him to have, especially in light of the pressure her office was putting on him.

Carl sighed again, this time louder and longer. "If that's true—emphasis on *if*—we're going to need to know about it. It'll be tricky for me to ask those sorts of questions without garnering more heat"—and suddenly the reason Carl wanted me here became crystal clear. He needed me to look into the things he couldn't. "Do you think you can ask around about some of this more sensitive stuff—just to get a taste of whether this is just a bunch of smoke and no fire?"

I bit my pinky nail, a nervous habit I hadn't reverted to in years. It felt like I was at a crossroads. On one hand, I was off the story. Kay Jackson had been clear about that. On the other hand, I had come to the hospital knowing full well that I was violating the order my boss had given me because I also knew if this led to a break in the story, it'd be a huge scoop for the paper and a way to get me back into Kay's good graces. Of course, if she found out I disobeyed her, she'd be furious. Maybe so much so that she'd fire me? And losing this job was not an option—not after I'd left my job at the library and made such a big point about starting a new career. It would be the talk of the town, and I'd be Riley Bless Her Heart once again.

"Do you think you can do that for me?" Carl asked.

I stared back at him silently, trying to decide what I should do. What would Holman tell me? He'd probably say something annoyingly vague and Yoda-esque like, *"Your instincts, you must trust."* My instincts were being annoyingly quiet, so I thought about what Jenna B said. What was it—*Power isn't given to you, you have to take it.* Maybe she was right. This story felt like it was mine, and I wanted to take it back.

A feeling was building inside me as the moment stretched on. It was time to decide what kind of reporter I was going to be: the kind who took risks and followed my instincts, or the kind who obediently stayed inside the lines. I thought of Thad and Tabitha sitting in jail cells and David lying in a hospital bed. I thought of Holman and Granddaddy and their passion for telling the truth and then of Flick, who seemed strangely afraid of it. All of a sudden, it didn't seem like much of a choice. I decided to forget following the rules and forget being afraid. Breaking this story, even if it meant breaking a few rules, would be my chance to prove to Kay Jackson—and to myself, too—that I belonged at the *Times*.

CHAPTER 22

The first image that popped up when I typed "Invigor8" into my browser was a headshot of a middle-aged bald man with a large black tattoo of a bird on his forearm. An electric buzz zipped through my veins. How many big bald dudes with arm tattoos could there be running around Tuttle Corner, especially with connections to Invigor8? This had to be the guy Dr. Davenport's patient Susan described as having fought with Arthur on the street. The caption identified this man as Brandon Laytner, age forty-two.

I read article after article and learned a few key things. Invigor8 was a small-cap biotech startup headquartered on the western edge of Tuttle County. Brandon Laytner had started the company after he dropped out of Stanford's medical school, and it was still privately owned. He'd been considered "one to watch" by many, and as a result there were dozens of articles in which he was quoted as saying his biopharma tech would revolutionize the pharmaceutical industry. Each article was filled with bravado-laden quotes from him that were increasingly confident, bordering on delusional. *He was going to change the world. He was going to cure cancer. He was going to be the best there ever was.* Brandon Laytner was the Muhammad Ali of biopharmaceutical startups. The product that he and everyone else thought was going to make him rich and famous a few years back was some sort of biologic for the treatment of breast cancer, but it failed in its phase-three trial and those dreams quickly evaporated.

After that Laytner went into a deep depression. Several articles noted how he went from courting press attention to a relatively reclusive existence. He went through an expensive divorce, moved from Richmond back to Tuttle County to be near his parents, and basically went into hiding. Or so it seemed.

After suspending operations for over a year and a half, he'd hired back a few key members of his former staff, and went back to work developing a new biologic. This time, however, he kept a much lower profile and avoided talking specifics with the press. From what I read, I could tell only that the drug he was developing had application in cardiac care management, but I couldn't tell exactly what its function might be.

This had to be the drug Dr. Davenport was consulting on—but I needed confirmation. Since Mrs. Winterthorne and Faye had been so sure Donna Lopez knew everything there was to know about Arthur, I decided to call her up and see if she could shed any light on his involvement with Invigor8. She confirmed that, yes, he had been involved in the patent-development process for a new drug Invigor8 was developing.

"Had been?" I asked.

"Just last week Arthur quit the study. Walked away from some good money, too."

"Do you know why?"

"Not really. I just know that Arthur was supposed to read through their research data and give his opinion on the efficacy and safety from a cardiac standpoint. He had binders full of research he was going through. Then last week, real suddenly, he told me to box them all up—he was done with it. Said not to throw it away because of confidentiality, that someone from the company would be coming over to the office to collect it."

I asked her if she knew how Invigor8 felt about him leaving the study.

"The head of the company, Brandon something-or-other, came to the clinic himself demanding to see Arthur."

"Was he upset?" I asked, thinking of Susan seeing Dr. Davenport arguing with a bald man on the street.

"Oh yes. He said he couldn't accept that Dr. Davenport didn't want to continue on the project. He wouldn't even take back the boxes of research files. He said he knew Arthur would change his mind. I had to lug them back into the storage closet myself."

"When did he come by? What day?"

"Must have been late last week." She thought for another second. "Yes, it was a week ago Tuesday—I remember because Arthur spends all day on Tuesdays in the cath lab. I think Mr. Laytner thought I was fibbing. I even took him back to Arthur's office to show him it was empty." She was quiet for a moment and then it sounded like she pressed her mouth right into the phone to say, "Do you think that man could have had something to do with all of this?"

I didn't want to start the rumor mill going any more than I probably already had so I said, "I'm just trying to gather as much information about Dr. Davenport's life as I can. You never know when something is going to be relevant."

"That makes sense," she said thoughtfully. "You know, now that you say that, I think there is something else I should mention. Something I didn't think was important before, but now I'm not so sure."

I had a feeling I knew what she was going to say, and I was right. Donna told me the same basic story about Libby and Bennett Nichols that I'd heard from the others.

"How did Libby take it when he ended things?"

"Ended things?"

"Yeah, when he broke it off."

"I didn't know he had," she said. "I mean, it wasn't like he told me everything, but as far as I knew, Arthur and Libby were still seeing each other right up till the very end."

It was close to noon by the time I got off the phone with Donna, and Coltrane, who was enjoying having me home during the day, nosed the bell I had hung on the front door to let me know he wanted out. I had taught him to do this in a single twenty-minute training session involving repetition of the phrase "ring the bell" and a handful of Pup-Peronis. As a former police dog, he was such a smart boy. I often thought that if I had the time, I could probably teach him to go get the paper, make my morning coffee, and do my laundry.

In addition to being smart, Coltrane was a big dog and got cranky if he didn't get his exercise, so I slipped on my shoes and leashed him up. The air had the beginnings of a fall chill, and I could tell by the extra spring in Coltrane's step that he appreciated the lower temperatures and decreased humidity as much as I did. Summers were long in Tuttle Corner and the fall was short—but boy was it nice.

As Coltrane and I walked around my block, I noticed how many houses had already set out their pumpkins and hay bales. The Washingtons had three of those huge inflatable Halloween figures set up on their lawn, and as we passed by the last of them, an at least twenty-foot-tall pumpkin-head guy who looked like the character from *The*

Nightmare Before Christmas flashed and made thunder sounds, scaring poor Coltrane half to death.

Fallen leaves covered the fading green lawns, while some of the more colorful ones clung to their branches. I loved fall; it was my favorite time of year. I'd been so busy lately, I hadn't even realized how quickly October was slipping by. Halloween would be here soon, and then after that the other holidays would fall into place one after the next after the next. I wondered if Jay and I would spend Christmas together, or if he'd travel back to Massachusetts to see his family. My parents would love to take him with us to the Christmas Eve service at the Unitarian church. They have this lovely tradition of handing out candles to everyone, turning down all the lights in the sanctuary, and as the light spreads slowly throughout the room candle to candle, everyone sings "Silent Night." It's beautiful, and something I look forward to every year. I felt a fizz of excitement at the thought of having Jay there with us this year; I was in the middle of this thought when Ryan called my name from the front porch of Missy Gellerman's house.

"Hey Riles!" He trotted out to the sidewalk to meet us and immediately crouched down to give C some love. Coltrane whined and licked Ryan's face—and I had a feeling if it were socially acceptable, Ryan would have done the same. Those two were like peanut butter and jelly. A few times over the past month, Ryan had asked if he could take Coltrane to work at his parents' store. I'd always agreed— even though I knew Ryan had been partially using it as an excuse to come over and see me—because Coltrane loved the wide-open spaces out there. I didn't want to begrudge my dog a fun day just because my ex had delusions of us getting back together.

"Someone is sure happy to see you."

He stood up, maybe a little closer to me than he needed to be, and said, "Glad to see you too, sugar."

I suppressed a smile. "What're you doing here?"

In his UVA T-shirt and long board shorts, Ryan looked just as he had in college. He was tall, over six feet, with sandy brown hair, gorgeous blue eyes, and the kind of lopsided smile that could charm you into any number of bad decisions. Virtually every memory of mine over the past seven years had something to do with Ryan Sanford, and yet we'd hardly talked since he moved back to Tuttle. It had been hard, he had not only been my boyfriend but pretty much my only friend for the past several years. After everything that happened between us, I needed some space to move on and, despite what he said, he did too.

"I'm buying this place." Ryan jerked a thumb toward Missy's house.

So much for space. *"What?"*

"Yeah, Missy's moving to Asheville to be near her kids, so she's selling. And I've always loved this area, so I thought, why the hell not?" His handsome, optimistic grin belied the obvious problem here: this house backed up to mine. Only my six-foot privacy fence separated the backyards.

"Are you serious?"

"Yeah, why?"

I made some sort of glottal sound that I felt he should understand.

"What?"

"Ryan, this house is literally in my backyard."

"So?"

I wasn't sure if he really didn't get how inappropriate that was, or if he was just being obtuse. So I asked him exactly that.

"I don't even know what *obtuse* is. I bought this house because it's in a great neighborhood, it has an awesome yard, and there's a separate apartment in the basement. I'm going to live down there and give Ridley and our little dudette the upstairs."

"Ridley is going to live here too?" My eyes nearly popped out of my head.

"Yeah," Ryan said, still looking like he couldn't understand why this would bother me. "We decided it'd be best for the baby to have us all live together—even though we're not, you know, a traditional family."

There was so much in what he just said that evoked emotion, not the least of which was that Ryan was making mature and responsible decisions to take care of his family. Old habits die hard, so a sliver of me felt proud of him, but the majority of me was straight-up pissed that he was going to make me take a front row seat to watch his new life unfold.

"Don't you think it's going to be a little weird living so close to me?"

"Nah," he said. "We're cool. And Ridley loves you."

I was speechless. That is not hyperbole. I honest-to-goodness could not find the words to respond to this information, so I simply turned around and walked back toward my house.

"I don't know why you're so upset about this," he called after me. "It'll be fun! You'll see!"

Hey Riley,

So I have to admit that I don't know that much about owning real estate because due to a small misunderstanding with a Victoria's Secret credit card, I am apparently considered "high risk" by lenders—haha lol! But I can totally understand what ur saying about how weird it is for ur ex to move in his baby mama drama right behind ur house! In the wise words of Selena Gomez, "That is not okay."

But here is the part of the process when I have to [TRIGGER WARNING] challenge ur truth: Why do u think this upsets u so much? I mean, I need u to really think about it. If ur truly over Ryan then why does it matter where he lives? Could there be some unresolved issues hiding inside ur reaction to his home purchase? Do we need to examine them?

PS: This is why I plan to buy a tiny house as soon as my credit clears up. U can just move it when u need a change of scenery! Plus, they are so freaking ADORABLE! I am obsessed with that show on HGTV. U should totally check it out.

xx,
Jenna B
Personal Success Concierge™
Bestmilleniallife.com

Dear Jenna,

That was a remarkably lucid response (until the tiny house stuff). I hope you won't be offended that I am going to choose to completely ignore it. I have a lot going on right now and I just can't deal with having those "unresolved issues" challenged at this time.

➤

PS: I have too many books to ever live in a tiny house. Plus, my dog is huge.

All best,
Riley

Dear Jenna,

Okay, you've made your point, you can stop sending me pictures of tiny houses with big bookshelves and even bigger dogs. (But, to be fair, I think that last one with the Great Dane reading Shakespeare was photoshopped.)

All best,
Riley

CHAPTER 23

On my way back to the *Times* I decided to stop into the sheriff's office to see what the latest was with Tabitha. I also wanted to see what, if any, progress Carl had made on figuring out who had poisoned David. It still didn't make any sense to me. Surely that and his father's murder were related, but I couldn't see how. If Libby or Bennett Nichols had anything to do with Arthur's death, why would they have a problem with David? Or if the CEO of Invigor8 had snapped in a fit of rage over Dr. Davenport pulling out of the drug trial, what would any of that have to do with his son?

I walked into the sheriff's department and Gail smiled at me. "Hey," she said, looking up from the file she was holding. "He's in his office. Thad's being released in a few minutes."

"Really?"

"Prosecutor hasn't filed charges yet, so he's free to go, but can't leave town."

"And Tabitha?"

Gail lowered her voice. "Between you, me, and the fence post, I think Carl's just gonna let her walk on this one if she'll recant."

"Cool," I said, looking around the station. "Is Gerlach Spencer here by any chance?"

I had seen that Spencer had written a piece online about Tabitha's confession and a few other updated details about the story, so I knew he was on it. I had to be careful. If he saw me catting around here, he'd tell Kay for sure. The obit was my cover story, though, and a pretty good one at that. After all, I could easily be here to interview Dr. Davenport's eldest son for the obituary.

"Haven't seen him since this morning. You can go on back to Carl's office if you want."

Through the glass to his office I saw Tiffany Peters, the county coroner, and wondered if that meant that the report had come back from the Richmond ME. I hovered just outside Carl's door and waited for someone to notice me.

"Hey, Riley!" Tiffany said. "You're so sweet to come down here to hear my report!" She gave me a beauty-queen smile as I walked in the office.

"Okay if I listen in?" I looked at Carl.

He nodded and I noted again how tired he looked—even worse than before; the skin on his cheeks had started to get those red splotches. Not like chickenpox, more like gin blossoms, but I knew Carl didn't drink. It had to have been the stress.

"As I was saying," Tiffany said, reading from a sheet of paper. "The autopsy report found congestion of the brain, lungs, and kidneys. And while no identifiable tablets were found, analysis of blood, stomach contents, and liver revealed digitalis concentrations well above therapeutic levels. Myocardial and coronary artery diseases were excluded—that means he didn't have any kind of underlying heart condition that he would have needed digitalis for.

"There was a single puncture wound on the left side of the abdomen, measuring two by three millimeters, with clean and clear edges and little blood loss, indicating the insult was inflicted post-mortem." Tiffany looked up. "That means he was stabbed after he died."

"But what's the point of stabbing someone after they're dead?" I asked.

No one ventured a guess.

I continued. "And do we know anything about the timing of all of this? I mean, if Thad left his father—drunk but alive at 7:30 p.m.—do we know anything about when Arthur actually ingested the poison?"

"Great question." Tiffany flipped to another page in the report. "According to this, Arthur had acute digitalis toxicity, which means the drug was likely introduced into the system fairly rapidly. The Digoxigon pills are point-twenty-five milligrams each, so assuming the killer crushed up the pills and put them into the whiskey, the time it took to take effect would really depend on how much of the stuff he or she used."

I nodded, thinking this through. "So would it have been possible that the scotch was laced with the pills long before Thad was there, and even though Arthur was drinking it, he just hadn't taken in a lethal amount yet?"

"It's possible. This is one of the things the prosecutor is going to have to look at," Carl said. "There are still a lot of unanswered questions."

"Does the Davenport estate have any security cameras that might have caught if anyone else came or went from the house that night?" I asked.

"The property has cameras, but apparently they haven't been used since Mrs. Davenport passed away. Arthur told Jim over at Command Security that he didn't need any protection beyond the twenty-two he kept in the front closet." Clearly, Arthur had been wrong about that.

Carl stood up and put his hat on. "Thanks for coming by

with this report, Tiffany. I appreciate you rushing it over."

"There's one other thing that showed up that I want to point out," she paused, holding us hostage to the moment just a beat longer than necessary. "There were traces of crushed tobacco leaves ground into the rug around where Arthur's body was found. The forensic team also found them in the entry and the hallway leading into Arthur's office."

"Tobacco leaves?" I asked. "Like from a cigarette?"

Carl shook his head. "No, that'd be nicotine."

"Right," Tiffany said. "What we found were actual raw tobacco leaves. Did Arthur ever do any tobacco farming?"

"Not that I know of," Carl said.

"I'd have a hard time believing a cardiologist would have had anything to do with a tobacco farm. Half of his patients' problems were caused by smoking," I added.

"All right," Carl said, looking at the clock on his wall. "I've got to get going on Thad's paperwork. Thanks again for getting this to me."

"My pleasure!" Tiffany said, and it was clear that she meant it.

———•—•———

A short while later, I stood just outside the steps to the sheriff's office with Thad, Tabitha, and a still grim-faced Carl Haight. As Gail predicted, Carl had decided to let Tabitha's fake confession slide with the understanding that she was not to interfere in the investigation again.

"No more dramatics," he said and pointed a finger at her. "I understand this is an emotional situation, but you need to take a step back and let me do my job. If I have any more trouble from you, I won't be so nice next time."

"I promise," Tabitha said, and she even had the decency to look contrite.

"Thad, you're also free to go, but don't leave town," Carl continued. "The prosecutor hasn't decided to file charges yet, but she still has that option."

Thad squinted up at Carl, the sun bouncing off of his pale skin, made even more so by spending two days in the clink. He extended a hand to Carl, which I thought was pretty big of him considering. "Thank you," he said.

It took me a minute to realize he was thanking him for letting Tabitha off the hook.

As soon as Carl walked back inside, Tabitha turned to me. "Spill."

"What?"

"The autopsy report. It's public record anyway. You might as well tell us what was in it and save us the trouble of hunting it down. It's really the least you can do."

"The least I can do? What're you talking—" I stopped myself. On her best day Tabitha was suspicious and snappish; with all the stress she was under at that moment, it was probably wise not to argue with her. So I chose the path of least resistance and told them everything Tiffany Peters had just shared with Carl and me.

"Your dad didn't have anything to do with tobacco farming, did he?" I asked Thad.

"No, never."

"That's what I thought."

Tabitha jumped in. "So that means the killer must live or work on a tobacco farm. Okay. So here's a list of things we need to do." She ticked off each item on her fingers as she talked. "Number one, we need to get a listing of all the tobacco farms in the area. Two, we need to find out if anyone involved in those farms had a connection to Arthur. Three, Thad, you and I need to get over to City Hall and apply for our marriage license—it's good for thirty days.

Four, Riley, you—"

"You can't be serious," Thad interrupted her.

"What?"

"We can't get married in ten days."

Tabitha couldn't have looked more surprised if she'd been smacked across the face by Cookie Monster. "Huh?"

That was my cue. "Seems like you kids have some things to talk about, so I'm just gonna head—"

"No, Riley, stay." Tabitha put her hand on her tiny hip (which she'd been working on with Gregor, her trainer, in order to look good in her wedding dress). "Thad, what are you talking about?"

"Listen, I'm not saying call it off or anything—just postpone. With everything that's happened . . ."

Thad kept talking and I, desperate to avoid being a part of this awkward and personal conversation, took a step back and looked around—anywhere but at the two of them. My head was swiveled toward the square when something there caught my attention. It was stupid Gerlach Spencer with his stupid messenger bag slung across his stupid chest walking out of the *Times* office and toward the sheriff's office.

"Don't you agree, Riley?" Tabitha's voice snapped my attention back to the moment.

"What?"

"I said, don't you agree that Arthur would have wanted us to get married? That he wouldn't want his death to come between us?"

"I . . . um . . ."

Spencer would be close enough to see me soon. I needed to get out of there—*fast*.

"I gotta go," I said already turning to dash down the back alley behind the sheriff's office. "I'm sure you'll figure out what's best!"

In my haste to flee the scene, I rounded the corner and almost mowed into Ridley, who had been walking up Forsythe. I threw up a silent prayer that I hadn't actually knocked her over (knocking down my ex's pregnant girlfriend would *so* be the talk of the town) as I snuck a glance behind me. Spencer was about fifty yards back; he looked like he was on the phone. I wondered if he'd seen me.

"Hi!" I said, grabbing Ridley by the elbow and leading her off in the opposite direction. "What are you out here doing? Going shopping? Meeting Ryan for lunch?" It may have been the first time I'd ever initiated conversation with Ridley.

"I was just heading to see you actually," she said. "I heard what happened to that handsome friend of yours— David? I want to help."

Help? What the hell was she talking about? "Um, I'm not sure what you can do. Maybe you could bring him some flowers or something?"

"I already went to go see him."

"You did?" They met for like two minutes. Now she was visiting him in the hospital? Why was this woman suddenly *everywhere*?

"David and I, we made a . . . connection," she said, taking a moment before settling on the right word. "He told me what he told you about his father's death maybe having to do with that Invigor8 company. He says you are investigating. Let me help you."

We walked along Forsythe, which runs parallel to the park along the back of the municipal buildings that frame the east edge of Memorial Park. I glanced through the open spaces between buildings and saw Spencer entering the sheriff's office. He'd find out Thad and Tabitha had been released and probably get a copy of the autopsy report, too. *Damn*. That meant he'd be onto the tobacco-leaves lead as well. But he didn't know about the Invigor8 connection—that tip came from David. At least I had that lead all to myself. Or almost all to myself, I thought as I looked at Ridley.

"I will go with you," she said firmly.

"I'm sorry—you'll go with me where?"

"I will go with you to go talk to this CEO man. I will find out if he was involved in doing these terrible things to David and his father." And then, without a hint of irony or self-consciousness, she added, "I am very good at getting men to talk to me."

I thought about stupid Spencer inside the sheriff's office getting all the information that I had, and about how he'd probably have the story online in a couple of hours. If I had any hope of getting a scoop, I'd have to look into the leads he didn't have. That meant two things: Arthur's complicated love life and Invigor8. I looked at Ridley again, in all her six-foot-goddess glory, and thought, *Maybe she's just the edge you need?* I made the decision in an instant. It was time, for once, for me to reap the benefits of Ridley's particular brand of magic.

CHAPTER 24

On the drive over to Invigor8, I gave Ridley strict instructions that I was to do all the talking once we got there.

"We will be like Thelma and Louise," she gushed.

"No. We will not. They died in a fiery crash after committing serious crimes. We are only going there to ask some questions and find out the nature of his relationship with Arthur Davenport, okay? I don't want you bringing up David or, heaven forbid, making any kind of accusation about him being involved in murder or poisoning or anything like that, okay?"

I had visions of an angry Brandon Laytner calling the newspaper to complain about the baseless accusations from "the beautiful reporter and her shorter, plainer sidekick." Kay Jackson would fire me faster than a jackrabbit on roller skates.

"I understand," Ridley agreed. "I am there only to, uh, grease the wheels?"

As painful as it was, I had to give Ridley credit for unapologetically owning her beauty and being willing to exploit her sex appeal for the greater good. It seemed, at least in that moment, terribly modern to me.

"So . . ." I said, after a few silent minutes in the car. "I hear we're going to be neighbors."

"Yes," she said, and at first I couldn't tell if she thought that was a good or a bad thing. "We'll see. Ryan thinks we will live all together as a family, but I'm not sure this is best."

I knew it was probably crossing some sort of line, but my curiosity got the better of me. "How come?"

"He has made it clear that he isn't in love with me." She sounded both regretful and resolved at the same time, and I felt a little sorry for her for the first time since I'd met her. "He loves the baby, of course, and he wants to be close to us both."

It was none of my business, and the right thing to do was to change the subject. I didn't do the right thing. "But what do you want?"

She answered without pause. "To be happy, of course. I'd like us to be together—Ryan and the baby and me—but," she shrugged, "I won't sit around waiting for someone who is in love with someone else."

My eyes were on the road, but I could feel Ridley looking at me. Was she talking about me? Was she seriously telling me that Ryan was still in love with me and that was the reason they couldn't be together as a family? My stomach suddenly felt like it was churning cement. I didn't say anything, hoping that would be the end of it.

It wasn't.

"Riley," Ridley said. "I can see this makes you uncomfortable, but I'm not telling you anything you don't already know."

My cheeks felt like they were on fire. "Listen, Ryan probably just wants what he can't have. He—"

"No," she said, firmly but without any rancor. "Even in Colorado when he and I were dating, he loved you. I knew it then, and I should have stayed away. But what's the expression? The heart wants what the heart wants."

"Ridley—"

"It is okay," she said evenly. "I know the truth. I am okay with it. I was a good distraction for Ryan while he was trying to get himself together, but his heart was always here with you." She swirled her hands around her baby bump. "But now things are complicated."

"They certainly are," I said under my breath. Thankfully, at that exact moment we pulled up in front of the Invigor8 offices.

———

When we walked inside unannounced and without an appointment, the receptionist tried to turn us away. But Ridley would not be denied, and after several minutes of going back and forth with the receptionist at an increasing volume, Brandon Laytner himself came out of his office to see what the issue was. He took one look at Ridley and ushered us right into his office. I'm not even sure he heard me say I was with the *Times*. Or honestly, if he even knew I was there.

Brandon Laytner was true to his picture—large, bald, and extremely scary looking. His office was comically manly, right down to all the framed photos on the walls of him with his various kills. Brandon and a dead bear, Brandon and a dead elk, Brandon and two other dudes holding up a very large, very dead fish. He was like the living embodiment of Gaston from *Beauty and the Beast*—at least six-foot-four and looked like he was made of raw steel. He wore a pink button-down that stretched across his broad chest, with the cuffs rolled up so you could just see the bottom of a tattoo peeking out.

"May I see your tattoo?" Ridley asked as she flashed her best thousand-watt smile.

Brandon rolled back his sleeve. "It's a phoenix rising

from the ashes. It symbolizes rebirth, perseverance, and fortitude."

I almost laughed out loud; it was obvious he was trying to be the most masculine version of himself in front of Ridley, and I found it deeply amusing.

If Ridley found his act laughable, she didn't show it. Instead, she used his interest to our advantage. She leaned in and reached for his arm, gently holding his forearm under the guise of getting a better look. "Very nice, Brandon. May I call you Brandon?"

"Of course. Ridley, right?"

"Yes."

"When are you due?" He asked, nodding to her belly.

"Soon," she said in a noncommittal way, then smiled at him again.

"If you don't mind me saying, you really have that whole pregnant-woman-glow thing going on."

"Thank you."

"Your husband is a lucky man."

I almost puked right there. I could not believe this was happening. *Again.* Another man falling head over heels for Ridley.

She demurred, and then held up her bare left hand. "No husband. I am—how do you say?—doing it solo."

Since I knew Ridley spoke perfect English, I could see what was going on here; she was playing the hot and helpless foreigner. I wasn't sure how I felt about that, but since her efforts seemed to be working, I didn't jump in and call her on it. There'd be time for that later. Before Brandon got down on one knee and proposed marriage, I cleared my throat.

"I'm sorry," he turned to me for the first time. "Your name, again?"

"Riley."

"That's cute. Ridley/Riley. You two are like double trouble." His condescending laugh crawled underneath my skin.

"You've built up quite a company here," I said, changing the subject. "I'd love to know more about what you guys do."

Brandon puffed up like a proud papa. "Invigor8 is on the cutting edge of the biomedical engineering industry. We are small, nimble, and are about to change the *freaking world* with our latest development." Understated he was not.

"And what is that?" Ridley lifted an eyebrow in a flirty *impress me* sort of gesture.

Brandon looked to the open door and then lowered his voice. "I'm not at liberty to discuss details, but let's just say that Invigor8 is not only about to revolutionize the pharmaceutical industry, but the tobacco industry as well."

"Tobacco?" I said, my heartbeat ticking up.

He nodded. "We're still in the patent-development phase, so I can't say too much, but we have made some incredibly exciting advances in biopharming, specifically with tobacco. If everything goes as planned, Invigor8 will become a household name."

"What is biopharming?" Ridley asked.

"Yeah, it's sort of a play on words—*farm* with an *f* and *pharmaceuticals* with a *ph*. But it's basically bioengineering plants to create drugs that are more effective, cheaper, and safer for patients. In our case, we're working with tobacco plants. This is Virginia after all."

"What kind of drug are you creating?"

"Can't say. Top secret. But the whole world will know soon. And believe me, you'll be impressed." He winked at

Ridley, who to her credit did her best to look interested.

Clearly, Brandon Laytner had a massive ego, unnatural confidence, and an unusually thick neck. And his rocky relationship with Arthur Davenport gave me pause. If this drug under development was so revolutionary, why would Dr. Davenport quit the study so suddenly? Was it possible he noticed some problems in the research? Would that have been enough of a motive for Brandon to want Dr. Davenport silenced permanently?

"Mr. Laytner," I said, and then waited for him to wrench his eyes away from Ridley. "I was wondering if you could tell me about your company's relationship with Arthur Davenport?"

"Nasty business, him getting killed like that," he said without the slightest bit of emotion. "I was shocked to hear the news."

"How well did you know him?"

"Not well," Brandon said. "We'd only worked together a few months, but I had a lot of respect for the man."

He was answering my questions, but only just. I dug deeper. "Do you know his children?"

Brandon looked a little surprised by the question, but shook his head. "Never met them. Like I said, we'd only been working together a few months and even then it was mostly through email." If he was lying, I couldn't tell.

"How long had Arthur been working for Invigor8 before he died?" I wanted to test the waters to see how forthcoming Laytner would be. He didn't know that I already knew that Arthur had severed ties. Would he try to cover that up? Or would he come clean and tell me the reason?

"Let's see," he said, his eyes floating over to Ridley then back to me. "I first talked to Artie about coming on board last spring, maybe in April?"

I paused to see if he was going to go on or if I'd have to prod. When he spent the next twenty seconds staring at Ridley, I knew I was going to have to prod. "And how were things going? As far as his work was concerned?"

"What did you say you were writing about again?"

"I'm just gathering some background information on Dr. Davenport for the *Times*," I said, vaguely.

"Look, are you fishing around for information on why Arthur quit the study? 'Cause I'll tell you straight up. It didn't have anything to do with Invigor8, or me, or with our new drug. Arthur quit because he had a conflict of interest with one of our investors."

Ridley, who had been good and silent up until that moment, jumped into the conversation. "What does this mean, 'conflict of interest'?"

Maybe it was her slight Swedish accent, or maybe it was her act from before, but Brandon began a long, boring mansplanation of what the term 'conflict of interest' means. "A conflict of interest is when the goals of two different people involved in the deal are incompatible. In business—"

"I know what the words mean, Brandon." She said smoothly as she crossed one long leg over another, gently putting him in his place. "I was asking what this conflict was about, specifically."

"Of course." He had the decency to look chastened for a second, but quickly recovered. "The conflict was of a personal nature. Let's call it a difference of opinion with one of our key investors."

"Can you elaborate on that?" I asked.

"No, I'm afraid not."

"Can you tell me who this key investor is?"

"Sorry."

"Can you tell me the nature of their disagreement?"

"No."

"How did Dr. Davenport's exit affect your study?"

"How do you think?" Brandon's face darkened.

"So is it fair to say you were angry with him for leaving you high and dry?"

"Angry doesn't begin to cover it," he said. "I was planning to sue him for breach of contract."

"But he was killed before you could do that?"

"Yes."

"Some people would say that's a pretty strong motive for murder . . ." I knew I was dangerously close to crossing the line, but I didn't care. I was onto something, I could feel it. And I now had Brandon's full attention.

"Listen," he said in a low, controlled voice. "I didn't have anything to do with Arthur's death. Him quitting the study was going to be a huge pain in the ass, and of course I was mad about it, but not mad enough to kill. What we have is going to be so big, I'll have doctors lined up around the block to get in on it." Brandon clenched his jaw again and I could see a little vein in his forehead begin to bulge out. Clearly, I'd hit a nerve.

Ridley jumped in to break the tension. "I'm sorry," she said. "We are just trying to get at the truth. Our boss is expecting us to come up with something or else we will get in very much trouble."

"I understand," he said, leaning forward in his chair. "All I'm saying is that the guy had a lot of irons in the fire, if you know what I mean. Maybe he pissed off someone else—someone who isn't as civilized as I am."

The way he said the word *civilized* gave me chills. There was something about Brandon Laytner that set me on edge. I felt certain that he wasn't the type of person you'd want to cross.

"One last question, Mr. Laytner," I said before he could kick us out. "Were you arguing with Arthur Davenport on the Wednesday before his death—on the corner of Plantation and Somerset Drive around 3 p.m.?"

His face went blank. "No. Why? Did someone say I was?" He whipped out his phone, tapped it a few times, and then held it up to me, display facing out. "Look. Wednesday 3 p.m. I had a meeting with my accountant, Ross Childers. You can call him to verify if you want."

I would definitely do that, but I could tell by the confidence with which he'd said it, the meeting would check out. Was it possible Arthur was arguing with another big bald tattooed guy? Or Did Susan Pettis just get it entirely wrong?

"Well, I need to get back to work," Brandon said, suddenly standing up. Apparently the interview was over. "But if you have any other questions, feel free to call me anytime," he said, handing Ridley a card. "All my numbers are on there. Home, cell, office. Call anytime. Seriously."

Yeah, Brandon, we all get how seriously you'd like Ridley to call you.

Ridley took the card and rewarded him with a big smile and a long, lingering handshake. I thought he might die of happiness.

But as soon as we were out of the office and back in my car, she wiped the doe-eyed look off of her face and shuddered. "That guy is a creep."

"He sure is."

"So what do you think?"

I had to admit it felt good that Ridley was so interested in what I had to say. She was one of the only people who seemed to actually be interested in my theories. I was feeling warmer toward her by the minute, and wasn't entirely happy about it.

"I can't say for sure. I need to do some more digging around."

"But I was helpful?" There was something so sincere and hopeful in her voice, it tugged at my heart. I did not want to be yet another person who falls at the feet of the all-mighty Ridley. I was trying really hard not to like her, but she was making it tough.

"Yes, Ridley," I said begrudgingly. "You were very helpful."

CHAPTER 25

I dropped Ridley off at Ryan's parents' house and drove back to the office. I couldn't stop thinking about Brandon Laytner and how he casually threw out there that his supposed new wonder drug was tobacco-based. And tobacco leaves were found at the scene of the murder. There had to be a connection there. Could the leaves have come from Arthur himself? Or were they evidence left by his killer? As much as I wanted to explore these questions further, as I walked in to the *Times* office, I was reminded by stupid Spencer that my current assignment had nothing to do with murder, suspicious CEOs, or tobacco leaves.

"No hard feelings about the Davenport story, eh?"

"Nope," I said, biting back a torrent of hard feelings.

"It wasn't personal, you just messed up. Your loss was my gain, amiright?" He held up a hand to give me a high-five.

I glared at him and used every ounce of self-control I had in my body to not smack his hand into his own forehead. My angry reaction seemed only to amuse him.

"You're too easy, intern. I was just kidding," he laughed. "Sorry Kay took you off the story. Hey, if you want to, we can kind of work together on it? Like share sources, theories, that kind of thing."

I could not believe what I was hearing. He wanted me

to help him? Was he on crack? "That's okay. I've got my hands full with the obit." I turned away to illustrate just how busy I was.

"I was just offering since Holman's gone. I thought maybe you'd like to see what it's like to work with a reporter who isn't certifiably insane. That goofy Canuck puts the 'eh' in crazy, know what I'm saying?" He laughed again, this time harder.

My anger spiked. I'd had it. It was one thing to condescend to me, but to insult Holman was taking it too far. Holman was a great reporter and a stellar human being, albeit a little quirky, but to hear him disparaged by this overgrown frat boy made my blood boil. I was about to let that nationalistic son-of-a-bitch have it when he started laughing again.

"Geez, you should see your face right now," he said. "You need to learn to take a joke, kiddo. *Relax*."

I didn't consider myself overly sensitive, but if there is one thing that really lit my fire, it was people telling me to relax. I used to get that kind of thing all the time in college. It was usually some random guy who just told some off-color joke that I didn't laugh at. *Relax*, they'd say, *lighten up*. It made me want to punch them in the throat. So far I had never resorted to actual violence, but Gerlach Spencer might be my first victim.

"You know—" I started to say, but his phone rang (he had a "Who Let the Dogs Out" ringtone) and he cut me off by answering it. "Oh yeah?" he said, looking right at me. For a minute I thought it was someone calling to tell him I'd been out working on the story. I froze, waiting. But then after a few silent seconds he said, "Be right there." He lowered his phone and gave me a self-satisfied smirk. "That was one of my sources calling with a tip on a lead in the Davenport story."

"Who?" I asked. "What'd they say?"

"I thought you didn't want to work on the story with me?" He snorted out a gruff laugh. "Guess you'll just have to wait to read about it online like everybody else."

Hey Riley,

Okay, so it sounds like this Kreplach guy is a total
nothingburger. But I have something that I think is perfect for
this situation! Bestmillenniallife.com just launched their BURN
BABY BURN app for iPhone and Android. It's available in the
App store for a one-time fee of $4.99, but trust me when I say
it's totally worth it!

The app allows u to choose from a drop-down menu of
frustrations typical in Millennial life and then provides u with
customizable responses. Example: Next time this Spencer
dude calls u an intern, u simply find "underestimate" on the
drop-down menu, select "co-worker," select "male," select "age-
range 35+" and the app will instantly generate a burn like this
one: "Whatever, you pimple-hunting kebab basket."

The beauty of the BURN BABY BURN app is that although
the burns are totally random, people from older generations
will think they are Millennial code for something and spend
forever wondering—or better yet, Googling— what it means.
How hilarious is that? There is seriously nothing funnier than
an old person trying to figure out slang on the internet! It was
actually developed by some guy in IT as a joke against his
parents, but the people up the food chain at BML.com loved
it so much they totally monetized it. Turns out, it's one of our
biggest sellers. Anyway, in the wise words of Ryan Gosling,
"Hey girl, you need this."

xx,
Jenna B.
Personal Success Concierge™
Bestmillenniallife.com

CHAPTER 26

Fuming, I went back to my desk to focus on a couple of my more mundane stories: a write-up on the progress of the new roundabout at the corner of Fifth and Towns and a piece on last week's ice cream social at the Methodist Church. Once I got through those, I decided to focus on the obit. I knew I needed to knock that out of the park if I was going to impress Kay enough to be put back on the crime beat in the future. So I pulled up the draft of the obit I had and gave it a quick read. It was coming together, but was still missing something. I had the basic outline of his life covered well enough, his early life, family history, professional achievements—still, it felt dry and stale. I needed to do more showing and less telling, as my high school English comp teacher would have said. Dr. Davenport was by all accounts a good doctor who meant a lot to his patients. What I needed was a glimpse of him from that angle. Maybe I could start with a vignette, a story in which Arthur Davenport was doing something so characteristic of him that readers who knew him would nod their heads and smile, and make the readers who didn't know him wish they had.

I combed through page after page of notes, but I couldn't find that one ace-in-the-hole story that I was looking for. But the theme that kept emerging as I looked over what I'd learned about Dr. Davenport was that his work defined him. Nearly everyone I spoke to called him either a "workaholic" or said he was "unbelievably dedicated" or something along those lines. I thought back to Flick's advice about wanting to bring the deceased back to life, if only for a few paragraphs. Yes, it would have to be a story about his life as a physician, as someone who saved people's lives, that would open this obit. But I didn't have anything I could use yet. I picked up the phone and dialed Tuttle General.

Fred Kander had taken the position of hospital administrator four years ago, at the age of twenty-nine. Most people in Tuttle Corner were openly skeptical about a man his age being able to run the hospital that served four counties. But run it he had, and last year Kander had been credited with implementing several cost-saving strategies, while lowering readmission rates and extending primary-care volume.

When I explained that I was writing Arthur Davenport's obit, Fred said he'd be happy to talk to me.

"Losing Arthur," he said solemnly, "especially in this way, has been quite a shock to the entire Tuttle General family."

"I'm sure it has," I said. "Can you tell me a little bit about his place in the hospital system?"

"He consistently received the highest ratings from patients. In recent years, we've been focusing on collecting data about all aspects of the patient experience here, and when it came to bedside manner, Dr. Davenport consistently ranked near the top. His patients loved him. And not only that," he added, "but his complication and death rates were far below average."

"Meaning that most of his patients did well after their procedures?"

"All surgery involves risk, and even the best practitioners have patients whose outcomes are less than ideal—sometimes related to the procedure, sometimes because of other underlying conditions. But Dr. Davenport's patients did better, on balance, after their procedures than patients who saw other doctors. Even within our own system."

That was interesting. "Were any of his colleagues jealous? Did they feel threatened by Dr. Davenport's success rate and likability?"

Fred sounded surprised at the question. "If any of his colleagues had a problem with him for any reason, no one told me about it. Arthur was really looked up to around here. He mentored many of our younger physicians. He focused on his patients, on the work. He led by example. Always the first one in and the last one out. Just a great doctor overall."

"How did he handle it when the outcome wasn't good?" I asked.

"What do you mean?"

"I mean, how did Dr. Davenport handle those people who had complications or didn't survive? I would imagine that in thirty-plus years of practicing medicine, that scenario had to come up more than few times."

"Of course," Fred said, now a hint of defensiveness crept into his tone. "Cardiac patients are often very sick people, and no doctor is able to make every patient better."

"Right. So how did Dr. Davenport, specifically, handle those sorts of cases?"

"Always with the utmost compassion. He was invested in his patients' lives—he often attended their funerals or made donations in their names after they passed. It was quite touching."

Now there was a great angle! I needed a story about

that to open the obit. "Really? Tell me more about that."

"Just last month Arthur made a very generous donation in the name of one of his patients, the mother of one of
our employees, who died rather unexpectedly after a procedure. She was a lifelong smoker—from what Arthur said,
that was probably the root of her health issues. Anyway,
Arthur made a donation to the Foundation for a Smokefree
America in her name. He said he felt that was one way he
could bring meaning to her death."

"Can you share the name of the patient with me? I'd
love to talk to her family and maybe get a quote from them
for the piece."

"Sorry. The privacy laws around here are very strict, as
I'm sure you're aware."

Of course. HIPAA privacy regulations were really
cramping my style. And then the thought hit me like a
lightening bolt: I did have access to one place that kept
a listing of people in Tuttle County who died, the family
members they left behind, and even where they'd like con-
tributions sent to in their name. I was an obituary writer
after all. And it was time to hit up the morgue.

CHAPTER 27

I'm not sure what you're looking for." Flick stood over me, frowning.

Back in the day, the name for the storage room in most newspaper offices where they kept back issues was "the morgue." Nowadays, most of the information, at least in the recent past, could be accessed online. The *Times*, seeking to straddle the old world in which print journalism was a thriving part of the community and the new one in which technology ruled, had both. In the basement room that had been used for years as our morgue, you could still find eons of old print editions and files crammed with clippings and photos—plus, Kay Jackson had added a dedicated computer that could digitally access more recent content from the archives.

"I thought I might be able to find the patient of Dr. Davenport's that Kander mentioned if I searched the obits for women who died last month of a cardiac-related illness, and those that listed Foundation for a Smokefree America as their charity of choice."

"But you don't even know if this woman was from Tuttle County," said Flick. "The hospital draws from a four-county area."

I ignored him. This would be a great lead for Arthur's obit, and it was worth doing some research to find it. I typed in another barrage of search terms hoping the computer would bring up something useful.

"Besides, the obit often won't give the cause of death. Are you going to search every woman who has died in Tuttle over the past two months, call their families, and ask who their doctor was?"

I kept on looking. If Flick was going to be negative, I would just ignore him. I was able to isolate the death notices and obits for the month of September in Tuttle County. While it was true that this wasn't a comprehensive list of everyone who had died, it was probably pretty close.

After watching me click through story after story, Flick finally said, "There might be a smarter way to go about doing this."

"Flick," I said, my frustration finally getting the best of me. "You've been pushing me to dig deep, to work harder in the writing of this obit, and here I am doing that. I know you aren't a big fan of technology, but this is how people do research these days. This machine here," I tapped the side of the computer, "has all the information I need."

"You know what other machine has all the information you need?" He tapped the side of temple. "This one right here."

"You know who this woman is? Why didn't you say anything?"

"I wanted to teach you that you don't get answers to the questions you don't ask."

———◆———

Helen Wynette Krisanski, known to her friends and family as Heely, died suddenly during a stay at Tuttle General Hospital. She was sixty-seven years old.

Born and raised in Henrico County, Helen Krisanski grew up playing along the banks of the James River, and it was from there that her lifelong love of horticulture began. Fascinated by all things grown from the ground, Helen had a green thumb like no other. She always said it was fate when she met and married her husband, Charles Krisanski, because he had just inherited his family's farm and was looking for someone to help him run it. Heely and Charles remained partners in love and farming until his death in 2015.

Unable to keep up the farm herself, Heely moved to West Bay, VA, in early 2016 to be closer to her children. She quickly found work on an indigo farm, one of the first in the area. "Heely had a way with the indigo that none of the rest of us understood," said Craig Luetkemeyer, the owner of Luke's Farm, where Helen worked. "It was like those plants grew just for her. None of the rest of us could get 'em to do anything. But they just sprouted under her care."

Helen is survived by her son, Jonathan Krisanski, 42, and her daughter, Lauren McCarty, 38, both of West Bay, VA, and thousands of budding indigo plants.

Funeral services will be held at First Baptist in West Bay. In lieu of flowers, donations in Helen's name can be made to Farm Aid.

———

"But I thought Dr. Davenport made a donation in her name to the Foundation for a Smokefree America. Maybe it isn't her..." I said, crestfallen.

"The daughter, that Lauren McCarty, was the one I spoke with," Flick said. "As I recall, she said her mother'd been a lifelong smoker. I can't remember exactly all the details, but I'm sure she was a patient of Davenport's. I remember because Lauren talked about being in the waiting room after the procedure and watching Dr. Davenport walk out. Said his face was as white as a sheet."

We had come up to Flick's office, and now he lumbered over to his filing cabinet, pulled out a manila folder,
and took out a piece of paper with some scribbled notes.
"Daughter's phone number's on there," he said, offering it
to me. "I keep notes for at least a year."

I went back to my desk to call Lauren McCarty. She
didn't pick up, so I left a message for her that was purpose-
fully vague. I wanted her to call me back, and I thought if I
made her curious it improved the odds of that happening.

Since there wasn't much else I could do for the obit until I heard back from Ms. McCarty, I decided to do a quick
search of the tobacco farms in the area. I didn't think it
would yield much useful information, but I did it anyway. I
looked around to make sure stupid Spencer wasn't around.
Check. The coast was clear.

Born and raised in Virginia, I was aware of the com-
plexities surrounding tobacco production. It was a frequent
topic of conversation in schools and around dinner tables
in Tuttle County, and everyone had their opinion. But no
matter how people felt about our great State of Virginia
and its third-leading cash crop, there was one undeniable
fact: tobacco production was shrinking.

In 2004, the US government passed the Fair and Equi-
table Tobacco Reform Act, which ended a program that had
supported pricing quotas. This meant that tobacco farmers
could no longer count on a certain pricing or quota struc-
ture for selling their crops. As a result, the US Department
of Agriculture agreed to provide compensation to eligible
tobacco growers for this lost value. Some farmers ended
up taking the buyout, some didn't. Some started producing
other commodities or increased their existing non-tobacco
crops, others expanded their tobacco acreage as contract
volume picked up, and still others chose to close up shop.

The ones who chose to quit were mostly the elderly or folks who couldn't work the land, or didn't have anyone to leave it to. I'll never forget when Richie Scruggs, a kid who was in my class in second grade, came to school and announced he and his family would be moving to Florida because "the government took my daddy's farm away." That wasn't exactly what happened, of course, but I'm sure that's what it felt like.

My phone rang and I turned it over expecting to see Jay's number on the display, but it was Lauren McCarty. *That was fast,* I thought. I thanked her for returning the call and explained to her the reason for it.

There was silence on the other end of the line for longer than I expected, but I resisted the urge to prompt her. Granddaddy always said that ninety percent of obit interviews are positive—joyful even, because people get to relive special moments and talk about the departed. But they come with sadness too, when the finality of their loss eventually rises up like a wave to clobber them.

"Lauren?" I asked gently.

She sniffed and I could tell she had started crying.

"I'm so sorry to have upset you."

"No, it's okay, I'm fine," she said, and took in a deep breath. "I'm sorry. I still miss my mom, that's all."

"I'm so sorry for your loss. It sounds like your mother was a lovely woman."

I could hear a smile return to her voice. "She was. Mom was a born nurturer. That was her gift: she could make anything grow. And since she's been gone, well, I've just missed that in ways I didn't know I would."

"She worked on an indigo farm, is that right?' I asked, remembering the obit.

"Most recently, yes. She was a farmer all her life, though,"

Lauren said. "We grew up on my father's family farm out in the county, but after Dad passed away two years ago, Mom moved to Tuttle Corner to be closer to me and my brother John. He's had some hard times and Mom wanted to be there for him."

"That must have been nice to have her nearby."

"It was. She liked it too," Lauren said. "She found a job working out at Luke's Farm. It was a perfect fit because they'd been trying to diversify part of their acreage into indigo but had been struggling. Mom had the magic touch and got them sorted in no time."

"Oh yeah?"

"They'd been trying to take advantage of the new program for tobacco famers wanting to switch over, but it wasn't as easy as they thought it'd be."

"Did you say tobacco?"

"Yes, Luke's was a tobacco farm—well, still is mostly, but ever since the buyout, people have been trying to find ways to diversify their crops. Indigo grows in the same soil with the same equipment so it's a natural switch."

Interesting. I jotted down a note and then directed the conversation back to the issue at hand. "Can you tell me about your mom's experience with Dr. Davenport?"

Lauren paused a moment and I heard her take in a breath. "I don't blame him, if that's what you're asking."

"You don't?" I didn't know what she was referring to but I didn't want to let on.

"He told us that there was a chance Mom would have complications. Granted, he told us it was less than a one-percent chance, so you never really think it's going to happen—" She broke off again and I could tell she was struggling to keep her composure. "Dr. Davenport was very kind. I think in many ways he was as shocked as we were."

"Do you mind me asking what happened?"

"Mom had something called atherosclerosis—she was having some chest pain and shortness of breath, so my brother made her an appointment to see Dr. Davenport. He said she had a blockage and needed this procedure called a cardiac cathero ... or maybe it was an angio-something-or-other ... I can't remember exactly what it was called, but Dr. Davenport said it was like a Roto-Rooter for your heart."

I remembered Susan Pettis had described her procedure the same way.

"Anyways, during the procedure I guess some of the plaque in her artery broke off and traveled to her brain. Caused a stroke right on the spot and there wasn't anything anyone could do. When Dr. Davenport came out to tell us what had happened, he was pale and sweating. I knew as soon as I looked at him."

"I'm so sorry," I said. "That must have been a terrible shock."

"It was." Then she added after a moment, "I guess it was just her time."

I still hadn't come across any information to use in the obit, so I tried to steer the conversation back to Dr. Davenport without seeming insensitive. "I heard from his colleagues that Dr. Davenport sometimes attended the funerals of his patients or made donations in their name. Was that the case for you?"

"He did both, actually," Lauren said. "He came to the church service and made a donation to the Foundation for a Smokefree America in Mom's name."

I noticed her words didn't match her tone. Instead of sounding touched or grateful, she sounded—for the first time in our conversation—bitter. "Was that not a good thing?"

"Well," she said, "as someone who grew up farming tobacco, the Foundation for a Smokefree America wasn't exactly the best choice of places to make a donation in her name. It felt like adding insult to injury, if you want to know the truth."

This was not the heartwarming anecdote I wanted to open the obit. Far from making Arthur sound like a caring doctor, it made him seem insensitive. But it was interesting, and, I reminded myself, I wasn't writing a eulogy. This obit was supposed to be an objective look at who Arthur Davenport was. The good, the bad, and the ugly, as Flick had said. I took Lauren's full contact information and thanked her for her time.

"You're welcome," she said, sounding weary. "At least she's with Daddy now. That was always her favorite place— right next to him."

CHAPTER 28

I was about to leave for the day when the bell on the front door chimed to signal that someone had walked in. People are in and out of our newsroom all day, so I didn't think twice about it until a sickening cloud of men's cologne wafted over and assaulted my nasal passages. That smell could only belong to one person. A second after the smell hit, I heard Toby's nasal, high-pitched voice ring out. "Hey, hey, newsroom!"

I quickly closed my browser and stuffed the obit file into my bag. I could tell he was getting closer by the concentration of stink heading my way.

"Hey there, Riley!"

"Hello," I said without looking up.

"What's the matter, Buttercup? You mad at ol' Toby?" He leaned against my cubicle wall, so his OOTD (Outfit of the Day) was in full view. He wore brand-spanking-new white men's high-top basketball shoes, with navy knit pants and a bright orange long-sleeved shirt in a technical fabric that fit snuggly across his belly, leaving little to the imagination. Today's shirt message: *Beware of My Game.* As I looked up at him, all I could think was how I'd never be able to un-know that Toby had an outie. Ew.

"I'm not mad," I said, pretending to straighten some papers on my desk. "Just busy."

"Aw, don't do me like that," he said in a tone of voice best described as insulted-baby. "Tell Toby what you're working on?"

"Not the Davenport story, thanks to you."

This made him laugh, which made his shirt rise up a few inches, which exposed a strip of hairy belly skin directly at eye level. I looked away as fast as my eyeballs would allow.

"You're writing Artie's obituary, aren't you?" He peeked around for evidence. "He was a good man, Arthur was. Aunt Shaylene says that's why we've got to close the books on this case. Bring his killer to justice."

"Mm-hmm," I said, still averting my eyes from the aggressively pale patch of skin.

"Now personally, I think it was Thad that done it," he lowered his voice to a whisper. "Thad always did have kind of a serial killer vibe about him, don't you think?"

"As a matter of fact, I don't," I said, standing up. "But I suppose it doesn't matter what I think. You've made sure of that."

Toby laughed again and his shirt, which had been struggling to stay on the lower part of his stomach, hit the tipping point and suddenly sprung up like a roller shade, zipping upward so that only the words *Beware of My . . .* were visible. The effect was: *Beware of My Big, Hairy Belly.*

"Now would you look at what you did there," he said, grabbing his shirt by the hem and pulling it back down. "You made my shirt go all haywire!" He laughed some more, but this time had the forethought to hold his shirt down. "All's I did was bring it to your boss's attention that you might have a little too much bias in this case."

I started to spit back a retort but stopped myself before I said anything I'd regret. "See you later, Toby. If you're looking for Kay, she's in her office." I turned and walked toward the door, but the little pest followed me down the corridor.

"Actually, it's you I came looking for."

"Oh yeah? What for—you want to get me fired this time?"

"I was . . . I mean, Aunt Shaylene, was wondering if you might like to interview her for the obituary."

This stopped me. "Mayor Lancett wants to be quoted in Arthur Davenport's obit?"

"The thing is, those two were close friends growing up, you know. And she's so broken up about his untimely demise. She thought it might be nice to be recorded in the local newspaper as having attested to his fine character."

I'll admit I was surprised. I'd thought Libby Nichols was just spreading rumors when she hinted that Arthur and the mayor had something going on, but now I wondered if she might have been right. "Okay. . ." I said.

"Can you come by first thing tomorrow?" Toby asked. "She'll save you fifteen minutes."

I agreed, and Toby and I walked out of the *Times* office together just as Jared Rayburn, the owner of My Secret Garden flower shop, was walking in carrying a huge arrangement of orange roses with fiery red tips.

We said hello and I held the door open for him. Jared was a member of my father's poetry group and although he was a sweet guy, he wasn't exactly what you'd call talkative. Jared was in many ways a study in contradictions: He was five-foot eight, built like a ballet dancer, a card-carrying member of the NRA, owned a flower shop, wrote poetry, and founded the local chapter of the Brigade of the American Revolution reenactment society. Oh, and rumor had it that he used to work in the CIA. I don't know if that was true or not, but I'd often thought Jared would make a fascinating subject of a biography.

"Who's the lucky duck?" Toby said, eyeing the flowers. Jared glanced down and squinted as he read the name on the envelope. "Looks like it's you, Riley."

"Those are for me?"

"A rose by any other name. . ." He shrugged, and handed me the low, square vase containing the gorgeous arrangement.

It may not have been my most feminist moment, but I'll admit there was something of an inner-swoon at the thought of Jay sending flowers to make up for acting like an overprotective goon the other day. It wasn't like roses changed anything exactly, but between the apology and the flowers, I was feeling pretty good about him. Plus, they were *soooo* pretty!

"Thanks!" I squealed.

"Sheesh, what'd your man do?" Toby asked, raising an eyebrow. "Or maybe I should ask what'd *you* do?" He snorted out a salacious laugh.

"Shut up, Toby," I said, irritated he was sullying my moment. "Some men are just romantic."

"Whatevs," he said. "Don't be late tomorrow morning!"

With Toby gone, I dipped my head to inhale the flowers' sweet scent. *Heavenly.* I plucked the card from the little pitchfork and gently opened it, my belly swirling with anticipation. It wasn't every day a girl got roses! At least not this girl. Ryan would bring me a rose once a year on our anniversary—but it was usually the gas station variety inside one of those green plastic tubes, not a professionally delivered arrangement like this one. This looked like something out of a movie. With what was surely a goofy smile plastered on my face, I pulled out the card and read the note contained within:

Meeting you brightened my day, hope these brighten yours ... xo, Brandon Laytner

What. The. Hell. I looked at the back of the envelope and sure enough, in tiny slanted letters it said: *Ridley.* A rose by any other name indeed.

CHAPTER 29

I stuffed the card back into the envelope and tried not to bite Mr. Gradin's head off when he passed me on the way to my car and said, "Isn't someone a lucky lady?"

I gritted my teeth and faked a cheerful tone. "She sure is!"

She sure is. Fricking Ridley. *Again.* Did that woman's allure know no bounds? I made the quick drive home and then, as if the universe was testing how much it would take to get a good Southern girl to lose her shit, I pulled up to my house to find none other than the Fantastic Miss Ridley sitting on my porch swing.

"Ryan and I had a big fight," she said as I walked up to my front door. "I didn't have anywhere else to go." Her eyes landed then on the flowers. "Those are beautiful, by the way."

"Glad you like them." I thrust the vase into her hands and got out my keys. "They're for you."

She opened the card, read it, rolled her eyes, and flicked it down on my entry table. "Ryan was mad that I went with you to talk to Brandon. He said it wasn't a smart decision."

I hadn't thought of it before but maybe he was right. Had it been irresponsible of me to involve Ridley in all of this? She didn't work for the newspaper (despite what Brandon thought) and she was pregnant, after all. I glanced at the roses and felt a pang of guilt for using her as eye candy. But then I remembered it was Ridley who came to me looking for a way to help—not the other way around.

"Does he know about your 'connection' with David?" I tried to keep the sarcasm out of my voice. "I mean, could he have been jealous?"

"I doubt it," she said as she nestled into my overstuffed sofa. Coltrane sat in front of her, panting, waiting for more of her attention. *Traitor.* I stayed standing in a subtle form of protest. Although, to be fair, I also got her a glass of lemonade, so as protests go, it was pretty weak.

"Sometimes I think he can be a bit controlling," she said. "Like he knows what's best all the time."

This I could relate to. I had spent much of the past year thinking through all the ways Ryan had controlled the narrative of our seven years together. We ate at the restaurants he liked best, we went to the movies he wanted to see, and I even went to the college he wanted to go to. Don't get me wrong, I was a willing participant, but that was one of the reasons we were able to be together as long as we were. I handed Ryan control over my life, which felt really good at the time because he didn't over-think, he didn't ruminate, and he did what seemed like a good idea at the time—and when I was with him, I did that too. It worked out great until he decided it would be a good idea to move on without me. If there is one lesson I learned going through heartbreak hell over Ryan, it was that I'd never abdicate again. It might not always be smooth sailing, but I was the captain of my own ship and I'd sink or swim by my own hand.

But I didn't want to talk about any of this with Ridley. I still had a complicated sense of loyalty to Ryan and talking about him with his baby mama just didn't feel right. It felt like a betrayal.

"So," I said. "Maybe you should go talk it out with him? You know, clear the air?" That was my not-so-subtle way of trying to get her perfect butt off my sofa.

But she had other ideas. She turned on her side, laid her head down on my fuzzy ivory throw pillow, and closed her eyes. "Later," she said in a sleepy voice. "I'm too tired to move now—this baby is stealing all my energy. Would you mind if I took just a little cat nap?" And then she fell asleep before I could answer.

Being the sucker that I am, I covered her with a blanket and quietly took my laptop and insubordinate dog into the bedroom. Then I texted Ryan and told her Ridley was at my place so he wouldn't worry. As I closed the door, I could hear Ridley snoring like an eight-hundred-pound grizzly bear with a head cold. It was the first time I'd smiled since I got home.

———————

I was sitting on my bed working on a story about the up-coming K–5 spelling bee when my phone rang. It was Jay. I knew it wasn't rational, but I was a little mad at him for *not* having sent me flowers. It makes about as much sense as being mad at someone in real life when they do something bad to you in a dream—but I couldn't help it. I had been so touched when I thought he sent me those flowers as an apology that when I realized he hadn't, it felt like a slight.

"Hey," he said. "How was your day?"

"Actually, it could have been better," I said. He was driving home after working in DC all day and I knew that I-95 would be a parking lot, so I took my time filling him in about Kay's decision to take me off the story, David being poisoned, and my visit with Brandon Laytner. I left out the part about Ridley coming with me, and of course the flowers.

"Tabitha confessed to killing Arthur Davenport?" Jay was as shocked as I had been.

"Yes, but she only did it to try to clear Thad's name. Obviously, no one believed her."

"Geez," Jay said, "that's the most selfless thing I've ever seen Tabitha do. But crazy stupid." He was quiet for a moment and then asked. "Why didn't you report it?"

I felt a surge of defensiveness. "Why would I report a fake confession?"

"Well, whether or not it's fake isn't really your call . . ."

I felt stung even though I knew he was right. "I know that, it was just . . . it was . . ." The adolescent in me wanted to say that part of the reason I had forgotten to report it was because I was so thrown off that he'd been following me, but I knew that wasn't exactly fair. "I just screwed up. That's all."

"Maybe it's for the best, anyway."

"What do you mean?"

"It's just that this is such a complex story and you're, you know, still new. Maybe it's better to cut your teeth on a less dangerous story."

That spark of anger I had felt after I found out he'd followed me reignited. "I just made one tiny mistake and other than that, I think I've been handling the story just fine."

"Oh, I know," he said quickly. "But it's not like an unsolved murder is exactly an appropriate assignment for a junior reporter."

"Wow. I didn't realize you had so little faith in me."

"I didn't mean it like that, I was just—"

"Just saying you think it's a *good* thing that I was essentially demoted."

"Riley, no, that's not what I meant—"

"Then what did you mean?"

He hesitated. "I mean, it's just that some of the stuff you're doing can be dangerous, even for the most experienced reporter. Plus, I gotta be honest, some of it sounds more like a job for law enforcement than the press."

A tight feeling rose up the length of my throat. All the frustrations from the past couple of days—Kay Jackson and stupid Spencer and Holman being gone and Ryan and Ridley and the flowers that Jay didn't send me—all came knock-knock-knocking at my door. "So, you think I should just stay in the office and what? Only write articles about puppies and rainbows?"

"What?" Jay said, his confusion obvious. "No, Riley, all I'm saying is that you're not a cop. Interviewing suspects, sussing out alibis—that seems more like something the sheriff should be doing, not you."

"I'm fact checking, Jay. Which is, by the way, maybe the most important aspect of my job. I'm a reporter, remember?"

"Yeah, but . . . c'mon."

"C'mon what?" I asked, but didn't give him a chance to answer. "You know what, I'm going to just go."

"No, honey—I think we've just gotten way off track here—"

"Yeah, I think so too," I said, a second before hanging up on him.

CHAPTER 30

I wanted to scream or slam a door or something, but with Ridley asleep on my couch I couldn't do any of that. So I scribbled her a note, got into my car, and started driving without any real idea of where I was heading. Jay called back several times but I didn't pick up. There was no point in talking to him when I was this angry.

Without really thinking about where I was going, I found myself back at the Nichols house. And this time when I pulled down the long drive, the blue truck was gone and the only car parked in the gravel driveway was a giant Mercedes, steel gray with the license plate: *LIBEE1*.

"What do you want now?" Libby said when she opened the door. Now wearing skinny jeans, a tight T-shirt, and a long Kendra Scott necklace, she looked every bit the Real Housewife, right down to her snotty attitude.

"Where were you and your husband when Arthur was killed?" If she wasn't going to bother with pleasantries, neither was I.

"None of your business." She held onto the edge of the massive arched wooden door as she spoke, and I wondered how long before she closed it in my face.

"I'm just trying to figure out who killed Arthur Davenport. I'd think you'd want to do the same, since the two of you were so *close*."

She glared at me and then instead of closing the door, she swung it open, inviting me inside. She said nothing, but sauntered back toward the kitchen where, sitting on the massive white marble island, sat a half-empty glass of white wine.

"Chardonnay?"

I shook my head.

She picked up her glass, took a sip, and motioned for me to sit down on one of the upholstered swivel stools lined up in front of the island. I took a seat, waiting for her to answer my question.

"Bennett didn't kill Arthur, if that's what you're thinking."

"Bennett isn't the only one with a reason to want him dead."

A laugh gurgled up from deep within her chest. "Are you saying you think *I* killed Arthur?"

"The way I heard it, you weren't too happy when he broke things off."

She rolled her eyes. "He didn't break anything off, genius. We just wanted people to think we were over. The truth is, we were far from it."

I had suspected as much ever since I talked to Donna, but I was glad to have confirmation from Libby herself. "That's not what you told me last night."

"Listen," she said after another sip of wine. "Arthur and I were more than just a fling. We cared about each other ... a lot." She paused, took another sip, and then slowly set the wine glass down. "I was going to leave Bennett." Her big eyes were moist with emotion, and in that moment I had no idea if she was acting. If I were a betting woman, I'd say no—but it was hard to tell, since almost everything this woman had told me since I met her had been a lie.

"So what happened?"

"What happened was I fell in love with Artie and he fell in love with me. We didn't plan it, it just happened. And we were finally ready to come out and be together—you know—in public and all. But then Bennett came home and found us that day."

"So Bennett knew?"

She nodded. "I told him I was in love with Arthur and I was going to leave him. And that's when he had his heart attack, or whatever it was."

"And that was, what, about two weeks before Arthur was killed?"

"About."

"And so how are you so sure he wasn't the one who killed Arthur? Sounds like one hell of a motive to me."

She laughed again, but this time with no humor at all— it was one big thrusty *ha*. With her eyes glued to mine, she pulled up the left sleeve of her T-shirt. As the fabric moved away, I saw a purplish discoloration that wrapped around her arm just under the shoulder. She turned a half-turn to the right and I could see three slots of unmarred skin be-tween each swath of purple. Finger marks. Someone had grabbed Libby around the shoulder, hard.

"It's not that Bennett wasn't mad enough to kill some-body that night, he just had a different somebody in mind."

I felt sick to my stomach.

"Sheriff Haight and Butter were out here Thursday night right around the time Arthur died," she said.

"I'm so sorry, Libby . . ."

She rolled her sleeve back down. "Wasn't the first time. Won't be the last if he has his way."

I fought the impulse to ask her why she stayed with a man who hurt her, but stopped myself. I'd volunteered at a women's shelter in college and knew that sort of question didn't have a simple answer—and besides, it wasn't any of my business.

"Was Bennett arrested?"

Libby shook her head. "I called the sheriff because I honestly didn't know what Benny was going to do that night. I'd've preferred to have handled it myself, but he came home from work on Monday pissed as hell. I still don't know what happened, because after his heart attack and in the hospital he was all 'I love you, baby,' and 'I forgive you.' Begged me not to go, said he'd change, said he'd find a way to fix our marriage."

She took another long sip of wine, emptying her glass. "I didn't want him to have another freaking heart attack, so I just told him we'd figure things out. I wasn't planning on staying long, just until he got stronger."

"What did Arthur have to say about that?"

"He wanted me to come live with him right away, like while Bennett was still in the hospital." She pulled off the cork and poured another glass of wine for herself. Again she looked at me, nodding her head in offer.

I shook my head. "So why didn't you?"

"Bennett and I have been together for fourteen years—basically my whole adult life. Our relationship is complicated. And as much as everyone would like to think it isn't true, I did love him at one point. I didn't feel like it was right to leave him when he was so sick like that."

"So what happened after he was released from the hospital?"

"He came home and after a few days, he started going into the office again, getting his strength back. I was planning to wait till he was back up to speed before telling him it was over. And then, like I said, on Monday he came home from work all amped up. Screaming about how I'd screwed

him over in more ways than I knew, how I'd ruined everything. He got drunk—I shoulda left then, I just knew what
was coming—but I didn't. I always wanted to believe better
of him than he deserved." She paused. "Anyway, then he
came after me. I got free and ran to the bedroom, grabbed
the gun I keep in my nightstand, called 911, and waited
with that gun trained on the door until they got here."

I knew there was some question I was supposed to ask,
but I honestly couldn't think of what to say. All I could do
was picture a scared and hurt Libby Nichols hiding in her
bedroom waiting to see if she was going to have to shoot
her husband to save her own life.

"What happened when the sheriff got here?"

"By then Benny had calmed down some. Carl took him
outside in cuffs and would have taken him down to the
office, but I said I didn't want to press charges."

"How come?" I asked the question gently.

"It wouldn't do any good—probably just make him
madder. Right now I'm just trying to keep him calm and
happy long enough for me to figure a few things out. And
then, I'm so outta here."

For the first time since I'd met the woman, I knew without a shadow of a doubt that Libby Nichols was telling
me the truth.

She walked me back to the front door. Just before I left
something caught my eye—it was a framed picture sitting
on her entry table. It looked familiar. I took a step closer. It
was the same photograph that I'd seen hanging in Brandon
Laytner's office. Bennett, Brandon, and another man who
looked vaguely familiar, all in hats and sunglasses, on a
boat holding up a huge swordfish.

"What?" Libby asked, noticing my reaction.

"Is this Bennett and Brandon Laytner?"

"Yeah. They've been friends since high school. Why?"

"No reason," I said, unable to pinpoint why this surprised me so much. I guess it made sense. Both of them were about the same age and grew up here; it stood to reason they'd be friends. "I just met him the other day."

"He's a real treat, huh?"

"Yeah," I said, my mind spinning out questions faster than I could catch them. "Did you know Arthur was consulting for Brandon's company?"

She nodded. "He was, but he quit. I told him he didn't want any part of anything that Brandon and Bennett were involved in—"

"Did you say Bennett was involved in Invigor8?"

"He's one of the principal investors. Why?"

So *that* must have been the real reason Arthur quit the study, and the mysterious "conflict of interest" Brandon was referring to earlier. It all made much more sense now. And, to my mind, made Bennett Nichols look guiltier than ever.

I thanked Libby again for her time. Not really knowing what else to say, I said, "Take care of yourself."

She gave me a wicked smile and said, "Oh girl, you can count on that."

CHAPTER 31

When I left the Nichols house, I couldn't get that bruise out of my mind. I had instantly disliked Bennett Nichols when I'd met him—and that was before I realized he was the kind of chickenshit coward who hits women. I couldn't imagine what Libby had been through during their fourteen-year relationship, and I hoped she was serious when she said she was planning to leave him.

All of a sudden my anger at Jay seemed unimportant. I wanted to hold him and have him hold me back. I still disagreed with him, but it had been childish of me to hang up on him. He didn't deserve that. One of my biggest mistakes with Ryan had been my habit of retreating when things got tough. It was one of the things that made our relationship go sideways, and I was determined not to make the same mistake again. So I drove toward Jay's place and practiced an apology for my behavior—one that did not let him off the hook but took responsibility for my part in the argument.

I pulled up to Jay's Victorian-style apartment complex and saw his car in the parking lot. After giving myself a quick once-over in the dim light of the driver's side sun visor, I walked up the two flights of stairs to door number 208 and knocked.

But it wasn't Jay who answered. "Oh," a tall, thin woman said. "You're not the pizza guy."

My surprise quickly turned to shock, which quickly turned to paralysis. All of my earlier thoughts about not retreating when things got tough evaporated into a puff of smoke. Another woman had just answered my boyfriend's door and my every instinct was to turn and run away as fast as I could. But I felt like I was frozen in a block of ice. I think I managed to spit out the word, "No."

The woman looked at me, the obvious question on her face: *Who are you then?* And I felt sure the same question was on my own face.

"Do you need some cash, Ginny?" I heard Jay's voice call out from inside the apartment. It felt like an electric shock to my system. I think I winced.

"No, it's not the pizza," she called over her shoulder, and then turned her pretty face back to me. "Can I help you?"

I didn't trust myself to speak, so I just shook my head no, as I took in the woman standing inside my boyfriend's apartment. She wore an ivory silk blouse with black, cropped, wide-leg pants over slouchy leather boots that looked like they cost more than all my shoes put together. I couldn't tell how old she was, but if I had to guess I'd ballpark her in her midthirties maybe. She gave off a chic, sophisticated vibe with her shiny black shoulder-length hair, big brown eyes, and the most perfect eyebrows I'd ever seen. Seriously, they were flawless. They had to have been filled in with something . . . what was it . . . gel, powder, pencil . . . no one could have eyebrows that were that naturally thick and impeccably arched.

I remained entranced by her mesmerizing brows until she wrinkled them. She looked confused now, and a little worried. The last thing I wanted her to do was to call Jay over here, so I forced myself to speak. "Wrong apartment. Sorry." My voice came out cracked and thin.

Ginny smiled and it lit up her whole face. "No problem," she said. "Have a good night."

She closed the door and I immediately flattened myself against the wall, my breath ragged. *What had I just walked in on?* I raced down the stairs, my mind a jumbled mess as I struggled to take stock of the situation. Okay. So Jay has an attractive woman I've never seen before in his apartment and they are ordering a pizza. Okay. *Don't panic.* What could be the possible explanations for that? 1. She could be his sister (nope, he's an only child like me). 2. She could be his friend (he's never mentioned a friend named Ginny before). 3. She could be his co-worker. 4. She could be his date.

Number 4 was the most painful option, but I felt like it was in many ways the one that made the most sense. We had been seeing each other for a couple of months and as I thought back, I guess we had never explicitly said that we weren't going to see other people . . . I just assumed that since we had been spending so much time together, neither of us would want to see anyone else. But maybe it was just me who didn't want to see anyone else.

My mind started spooling. Maybe he'd been seeing other people this whole time. We probably hung out three nights a week or so; maybe he had other dates on those other nights and just didn't mention them. My neurosis spun downhill like a rolling stone. Maybe dating just one person at a time isn't even how things work anymore. I had to face the fact that I didn't really know a lot about modern dating. Ryan and I got together when we were teenagers, so technically, this was my first full-adult relationship. Maybe social norms had changed in the past seven years. Maybe I was old-fashioned to think that just because we were hanging out a few times a week, we were "exclusive." I had so many questions. I needed answers. I know I probably should have just asked Jay, but I decided to hit up another source instead.

Hey Riley,

To answer ur question, the norm for Milllennial dating is ur either just hooking up or ur in a serious (exclusive) relationship. There's not a lot of in between these days. And usually if it's the latter, u have already talked about it. Why do u ask?

xx,
Jenna B.
Personal Success Concierge™
Bestmillenniallife.com

Dear Jenna,

If you don't know why I'm asking, you might want to tune up that "overdeveloped sense of intuition" of yours.

All best,
Riley

Hey Riley,

I am intuiting from ur tone that this is about u and ur man. I'm so sorry.

PS: Let's not turn on each other.   ➤

xx,
Jenna B.
Personal Success Concierge™
Bestmillenniallife.com

Dear Jenna,

I'm sorry I lashed out. I'm just really confused right now. I think
my boyfriend is seeing someone and I don't have anyone to
blame but myself because I never even asked him if we were
exclusive. I just assumed. What an idiot.

All best,
Riley

Hey Riley,

This totally reminds me of that time Kourtney caught Scott
with that skank from the Valley a few years ago—do u
remember that? And he said he didn't do anything wrong
because they'd never said they were exclusive? Well, I
think the court of public opinion settled that one, firmly on
Kourtney's side, of course!

Same situation. This is not ur fault, Riley. U r a romantic and
u assumed ur man was too. But turns out he is just a regular
dude. Harsh.

xx,
Jenna B
Personal Success Concierge™
Bestmillenniallife.com

Dear Jenna,

That is maybe the most depressing thing about this whole
situation: "turns out he is just a regular dude."
PS: Who are Kourtney and Scott?

All best,
Riley

Hey Riley,

I hope ur kidding. If not, I am going to need to revoke ur
Millennial card, haha, lol!

xx,
Jenna B
Personal Success Concierge™
Bestmillenniallife.com

Dear Jenna,

I'm going to sleep now. I know I'm going to have to talk to Jay
about this eventually, but not while he's on a date. Ugh. I can't
even type that without feeling sick.

All best,
Riley

Hey Riley,

➤

Try some peppermint tea. It'll help with the nausea. And if u pour a little Tito's in there, it'll help with the broken heart. And remember the wise words of T. Swift, the queen of breakups, "If somebody hurts you, it's okay to cry a river, just remember to build a bridge to get over it."

xx,
Jenna B
Personal Success Concierge™
Bestmillenniallife.com

Chapter 32

The phone ringing in the middle of the night with bad news is a cliché, but it's a cliché for a reason. So when my phone rang at 2:47 a.m. I knew it was not going to be good.

"Riley, can you come to Tuttle Gen?" It was Thad.

I sat straight up in bed. "What is it? Is it David?"

"No, it's Tabitha," he said. "She's okay, but she's had an accident and is asking for you. Third floor, room 302."

I drove to the hospital as fast as I could and parked in one of the four empty spaces in the lot closest to the door. Given that it was almost 3 a.m., there weren't many people around. I locked my car and literally ran inside, zipping past two men on a smoke break at the requisite twenty feet from the hospital building.

"Hey Riley, you okay?" One of the men called out to me.

I turned around and in the dark I could barely make out Jack and another man sitting on a bench, the orange tips of their cigarettes like two floating pinpricks of light.

"Oh, hi Jack," I said, but didn't stop moving. I didn't have time to chitchat. "I'm fine, a friend of mine has had an accident."

"Oh, I'm sorry. Hope she's okay!"

"Thanks." I gave him a backward wave as I approached the front doors and hurried toward the elevators. I'd never been to the hospital at this time and it felt spooky. The halls were dark, and although I saw the occasional person working, the place felt empty. I reached her room and knocked on the door, holding my breath, afraid of what I might find on the other side.

"Geez, *finally*," Tabitha said as I walked in.

Her impatience reassured me that whatever happened wasn't life-threatening, but the sight of her lying in the hospital bed in the context of everything that had happened over the past three days was more than a little disturbing. "What happened? Are you okay?"

"Of course I'm not okay," she said. "I'm going to have to wear a freaking boot under my wedding dress!"

"Thanks for coming, Riley," Thad said. He sat in a chair next to Tabitha's bed and held her hand tight in his. "Babe, I keep telling you—don't worry about the wedding."

"I'm not pushing anything back," she said firmly. "In nine days, we are getting married if I have to be rolled down the aisle in this bed."

He put his hands up in surrender. I had a feeling that was going to be a familiar gesture for the rest of their relationship.

"Just tell me what happened," I said.

Tabitha took in a big breath. "I've come across some new information, and in the course of gathering this information, I . . ." she paused. "I made an error in judgment that caused some physical harm, so I will need you to pick up where I left off."

Thad made a scoffing sound and Tabitha shot him the evil eye before continuing. "Carl is clearly overwhelmed and time is of the essence here, so I decided to do some research and drive around to all the tobacco farms in the area. You know, knock on doors, talk to the owners, fish for information—that sort of thing."

I was aghast. "Tabitha, that is really dangerous!"

She waved me off. "Thad came with me. Besides, I've taken Krav Maga for six years and carry a can of pepper spray everywhere I go. No one is going to mess with me."

"And yet here you lie in a hospital bed," Thad said. You could tell he was more scared than angry.

"You know it has nothing to do with that," Tabitha said with a sweetness not typical for her.

"Go on," I said, anxious to find out how we ended up where we were.

"I visited three farms in the area and was able to talk to the owners at all of them. I dug around for information—did they spend much time in Tuttle Corner? Did they see a cardiologist? I asked them any question I could think of that would prove a connection between them and the Davenports. They all ended up with a big fat zero. The fourth farm is owned by someone named Dwayne Statler, who was out of town when Arthur was killed. I never was able to get ahold of the owner of the fifth farm, so I went to the county registrar and found out it was someone named Charles Krisanski."

"Krisanski?" I asked, a gnawing feeling starting in my stomach.

"Yeah, do you know him?"

"Maybe. Go on."

"I dug a little deeper and soon found out why I couldn't get a hold of Charles Krisanski."

I cut in. "Because he's dead."

"How did you know that?"

"Finish your story and I'll tell you."

"Okay, so Charles Krisanski died two years ago after an industrial accident on his farm. After his death, the farm reverted to his wife, who is the next of kin. But when I started looking into it—"

"She's dead too," I said.

"If you already knew all of this, why didn't you tell me! You could have saved me a lot of trouble," Tabitha hissed.

"Finish your story."

"Well anyway, it was odd, so I decided to go over there, this time on my own. I was expecting to see barren land or an empty plot, but when I got there, it looked like operations were in full swing. There was a big section that looked freshly farmed, with live plants and equipment, areas roped off with twine, and little green budding plants. Someone is working that land despite the fact that both the owners are deceased."

"I told her not to go—" Thad said.

She talked over him. "I was just planning to drive by, but when I saw the land was in use, I decided to poke around. There was a weird-looking building sitting on the back of the property. It was metal siding two-thirds of the way up and then the top was all glass, which is what made it look like a greenhouse. I tried the doors but they were locked and so—"

Thad made another exasperated sound.

"Maybe it wasn't the best idea I ever had, but I found a ladder leaning up against the side of the building and I climbed up just high enough so I could peek inside—"

Thad, unable to take her slow buildup, jumped in with the rest. "She fell off the goddamn ladder, hit the side of her head on the way down, and landed on her ankle with enough force to shoot the bone right out the side of her skin." His voice trembled with restrained emotion. "She blacked out after the fall and because she was out there by herself she lay there for who-knows-how-long. When she came to, thankfully, she was able to reach her phone and call me. I raced out to get her because I knew I could make it faster than the ambulance."

Tabitha had tears in her eyes now. She looked distraught at how pained Thad was over her accident, but she tried to brush over it with her trademark confidence. "I'm gonna be fine," she said. "I admit it wasn't my finest hour, but the important thing is, Riley, you need to look into this farm and see who is using it. Something is off here."

"Why didn't you just tell Carl all of this instead of going out there yourself?" I asked, shocked that she'd be so reckless.

"Exactly," Thad muttered through gritted teeth.

"Calm down, you two," Tabitha said. "I was going to, and I will. But you know he is going to have to do everything by the book and that'll take forever. I just thought if I could figure out who was working the land, I could . . . expedite the process a little." She had the nerve to smile at us. "By the way, how did you know the Krisanskis?"

I explained to Thad and Tabitha everything I'd learned about Helen Krisanski's death and her connection to Dr. Davenport.

Tabitha, who had to be either in serious pain or majorly medicated, looked as excited as I'd ever seen her. "Maybe the daughter had a grudge against Arthur? Maybe she blamed him for her mom's death?"

I thought about this but rejected the idea pretty quickly. Lauren had sounded more sad than angry when we spoke about Arthur earlier in the day. She didn't seem to be hiding anything, and certainly not something as big as having killed the man I was interviewing her about. But I did agree that it was strange someone was using the Krisanski farm, given she had specifically told me they weren't.

"I don't think so," I said, rising to leave. "But I'll touch base with her again and let you know what I find out."

I needed to talk to Carl about all of this, and preferably before my meeting with the mayor. I told them I'd take it from there and ordered Tabitha to rest, which was laughable since Tabitha had never taken an order from anybody in her life, least of all me.

Thad stood up to walk me out, but before we got to the door Tabitha said, "Hurry, Riley."

At first I thought she was saying that because of the wedding, but when I looked at her she flicked her eyes to Thad. Suddenly her mania made more sense to me. Someone was threatening Thad's family and she was worried he could be next. All of this sleuthing around was to protect the man she loved.

And, okay, maybe a little bit to protect her wedding, too.

Chapter 33

The sun was rising as I drove home from the hospital. I'd get home just in time to take Coltrane out for his morning walk, shower, and change before heading to meet Mayor Lancett. I called out to Coltrane when I walked inside, expecting him to come bounding to the door like always. But he didn't.

"Coltrane!" I called again, tossing my purse and keys onto the entry table. "Come on, buddy. Let's get you outside."

Again, nothing. This wasn't normal; it was too quiet. All of the sudden everything around me seemed sharpened into high definition. I stood still, looking around at every surface of my house. *Where was Coltrane? Was someone here?* There was no broken window—I could see all the way to the back of the kitchen where the deadbolt was firmly slid into place. Coltrane slept in my room with me, usually on the bed. I wondered if it was possible he was still asleep. Maybe all the excitement last night with the phone call and all had made him extra tired.

I crept down the hallway, carefully and quietly, and peeked through my bedroom door, which stood open. No Coltrane. But there was something new there. A plain white piece of paper sitting on my bed. *On. My. Bed.*

Trembling, I picked up the paper and read: *DAVENPORT*

DESERVED TO DIE. YOU DON'T. STOP PLAYING SHERIFF.

Gravity shifted around me like a slipping transmission and I had to steady myself to stay upright. Someone had been in my bedroom. Could they still be in my house? Where was Coltrane? I was paralyzed with panic. I'm not sure how long I stood there immobilized by fear, but it was a faint scratching noise that brought me back to life. It was coming from the back door. *Coltrane.*

I ran to the door and almost collapsed with relief when I saw my dog standing on his hind legs looking through the glass on the back door. I threw open the deadbolt and let him inside.

Coltrane nearly mauled me, sniffing every inch of me like he was trying to make sure I was all right. He jumped on me and licked my face, soft whines escaping from him every few seconds. I ran my hands through his fur to make sure he was unharmed and nuzzled into his neck, telling him, "It's okay, it's okay."

My heart was beating too fast and I struggled to think what I should do. Someone had been in my home. In my bedroom. Near my dog. I texted Carl's private number and told him I needed to talk to him ASAP.

Ten minutes later, he stood in my living room, the note now resting inside of a plastic evidence bag. Carl's face was an implacable mask as I told him about Tabitha's field trip to the Krisanski farm, my talk with Libby Nichols, my conversation with Brandon Laytner, and my upcoming meeting with the mayor.

"You've done something to spook our killer. Problem is, we don't know which of the many things you've done has him or her nervous."

I thought I detected a note of irritation in his voice. I ignored it.

"My money is on Brandon Laytner. There's something off about that guy. And the connection to the tobacco leaves and Bennett Nichols is a little too coincidental for me."

"I'll go talk to him this morning. Ask him his whereabouts the night Davenport was killed, and earlier today for that matter."

"And he also may have a reason to want David out of the way," I said, connections taking shape in my mind. "David said he was going to look at the Invigor8 files in Arthur's office. Maybe somehow Brandon found out about that? If he already killed once to protect his new wonder drug, it isn't such a stretch to think he'd do it again."

"That's right," Carl agreed. "And that's exactly why you need to take a step back from this."

"Oh, no, no, no, Carl," I said, standing up. "You are not about to protect me off this story." I'd worked hard to chase these leads, leads that stupid Spencer didn't even have, and I was not about to let all that hard work go to waste, especially now that I was obviously getting close to the truth.

"Listen, you've been threatened very directly here." He brandished the bag. "I can't take a chance of anyone else getting hurt on this."

"No one is going to get hurt. We can use this—don't you see? The murderer is clearly watching me—we can use that to bait him out into the open. It's perfect."

But he was shaking his head before I even finished my sentence. "Absolutely not. The Tuttle County sheriff's department does not bait killers, Riley. And certainly not with civilians."

"But this is an *opportunity*," I said, trying to appeal to his desire to solve the case. "This is as close as we've come to figuring out who's behind all of this. We have their attention. Let's use that!" I wished so badly Holman was there—he'd totally let me be used as bait.

"No way," Carl said, and I could see from the firm set of his jaw that he was not going to waver on this. His phone vibrated and he looked down to check it. "This is Butter. I've got to take it."

He stepped outside, giving me a chance to think about what I needed to do next. Carl was kidding himself if he thought I was going to step aside on this investigation, but he had been right about one thing: something I'd done recently had won me the attention of the killer. I needed to figure out what it was and then do it again—this time with a plan.

Carl came back inside and explained the call had been from Butter saying that Lindsey Davis, the prosecutor, wanted to meet with him this morning regarding the charges against Thad. He said in light of present circumstances, he was going to request that Ms. Davis not file any charges just yet. And then he said, "Stay away from this case, Riley. I'm dead serious. Whoever killed Arthur Davenport isn't playing around. I appreciate you helping me out, but we'll take it from here."

"I think you're being ridiculous."

"I know you do, and I know you're thinking about blowing me off and investigating on your own. I also need you to know that if I get wind that you're still asking around on this, I'll have no choice but to tell Kay Jackson what you're doing."

He was going to rat me out to my boss? Frustration, like a roaring river, coursed through my veins. "Now you're threatening me too, Carl? *Nice.*"

"I'm just trying to keep you safe," he said, his voice softer now. "And if you won't stay away to save your life, I figure just maybe you'll stay away to save your job."

CHAPTER 34

I had never been the kind of girl who punched walls, but that's exactly what I felt like doing after Carl Haight left my house. Not only did he cut me off from working with him, but now if I looked into the case any further, he'd tell Kay, who would almost certainly fire me. It was an unfair dirty trick and of course Carl knew that.

But there was no way I was going to stop. There was too much at stake and I was too close. I'd just have to be smarter about it. It was Friday morning, which meant that I could still use writing the obit as my cover for a little while longer. I'd met my other deadlines for the week, but that only meant I'd soon be getting new assignments. My time was running out on the Davenport story. I knew I'd have to make the next twenty-four hours count.

After formulating a loose plan of what I wanted to get accomplished that day, I texted Ryan to see if he could take Coltrane with him to work. Of course, he came right over.

"Drop him off about six tonight?" Ryan asked after he loaded a very excited Coltrane into the back of his pickup.

"Sounds good," I said. "Thanks again. I've got a long day ahead and I think he'll have more fun with you than here all alone." *And he will be safe*, I thought. I couldn't tell Ryan about the note for fear of getting yet another lecture from yet another man trying to "keep me safe."

"He can chase squirrels while I inventory the hay bales," he said, and then gave me an appraising look. "You sure you're okay?"

"I'm fine."

"Because you know. . ."—he dug his hands into the pockets of his shorts—"even though, we're not, you know . . . anymore, you can still talk to me. I'll always be here for you."

"Thanks," I said. Given the events of the past twenty-four hours, he couldn't know how much his words meant to me. And I wasn't sure I wanted him to.

He took a step toward me and then stopped himself, like he just remembered he wasn't allowed to do that anymore. Platonic friendship was uncharted territory for Ryan and me, and neither of us knew quite what it was supposed to look like. He reached out and grabbed my hand. "You know I'd do anything for you, don't you?"

"I do." I squeezed back.

We stood like that for a few moments like that, a strange current between us made up of one part shared history and one part pure chemistry. Thankfully, before either of us moved a muscle, Coltrane let out an impatient bark.

Ryan laughed. "Okay, guess the boss says it's time to go."

"Thanks again, Ryan," I said, and waved goodbye as they pulled out of the driveway.

The mayor's shop, Inviting Praise, was just two doors down from Rosalee's Tavern, and since I still had about a half an hour until my meeting with the mayor, I ducked into Rosalee's for a quick bite. The café was crowded, as it always was in the mornings, but I spied a small table over by the window.

"Bonjour, Mademoiselle," Rosalee greeted me as I stepped inside. Rosalee was French, and her accent made everything she said sound sophisticated and sexy.

Tuttle isn't known for being overly accepting of new-comers, but for some reason when Rosalee moved down here from DC and opened her now-eponymous restaurant, the town immediately adopted her as its token exotic for-eigner. Everyone ate at Rosalee's, and I suspected it was as much for the café's charming owner as the food. "Bon *app*," she trilled as she escorted me to my table and dropped a menu into my hands.

I looked over the menu even though I always got the same thing for breakfast. My eyes were skimming the *des patisseries* section when a nearby voice said, "Let me guess—an almond croissant?"

It was Jay. My stomach flipped over and I felt an im-mediate flush to my face. "Hi," I managed to say without throwing up. Which was quite an accomplishment given how freaked out I was.

"I hoped you'd be here," he said. "Can I sit?"

I nodded and he slid into the chair across from me. I hadn't entirely decided what I was going to say to him about the status of our relationship. I was pretty sure I wasn't interested in a relationship in which we both could date other people—but I was also pretty sure I didn't want to give him an ultimatum.

"Listen, Jay—" I started to say.

"Wait, can I just say something first?" He scooted for-ward in his chair and lowered his voice. "I'm sorry, Riley. I'm *so* sorry. I shouldn't have second-guessed you. That was out of line and I apologize. I haven't been myself lately . . ."

"Thank you," I said, "But—"

"Can you forgive me?" His dark eyes were full of hope. He had no idea that what I was upset about was much big-ger than our tiff the night before.

I wasn't ready to have this conversation, but I knew that now was the time whether I was ready or not. "I came by your apartment last night"—I paused for a millisecond, and in that instant Jay must have put the pieces together because at first he looked surprised, then guilty as I finished the thought—"and a woman answered the door. She thought I was the pizza delivery guy."

He didn't deny it, and what was left of my hope crumbled into dust. I think up until that moment, I thought that maybe I'd been wrong, that it hadn't been what it looked like. But his face was dripping with pity and I knew there had been no misunderstanding.

"It's fine," I said, sitting up straighter. "I mean, whatever. I was just, um, surprised that's all."

"Riley . . ."

"It's fine. I mean, it's fine for some people . . . but as much as I'd like to pretend that I'm laid back enough to have an open relationship, I'm just not, Jay. I know that's kind of 'in' right now, what with the new stuff on Netflix and that three-way couple on *Say Yes to the Dress* and all, but I guess I'm just a little more traditional—"

And then he had the nerve to start laughing at me.

I felt my face flush in an instant. "I won't sit here and be made fun of," I said and stood up and grabbed my purse off the back of the chair. "See you around."

"Riley, last night . . . that woman, the one you saw at my apartment—"

But before Jay could finish his sentence I heard the squealing of tires and then a second later something came hurtling through the plate-glass window where I had been sitting just seconds before. I had barely processed what had happened when Jay jumped across the table and threw me to the side, shielding me with his body.

"Stay down," he ordered, now sounding every bit the DEA agent he was. Glass pebbles scattered everywhere while people screamed and ducked for cover.

I felt dizzy with panic as I snuck a glance out from under Jay's arm. There was a hammer lying on the tile floor surrounded by puddles of beaded glass. It had a massive iron head and a long wooden handle, almost more like an axe than a hammer. I immediately pictured what would have happened had I still been sitting when that thing came flying in, and for a second I felt like I might throw up.

"Everybody stay down," Jay announced, and he stood up slowly and drew a gun that I didn't even know he had been carrying. "I'm DEA. I need you all to remain calm and stay put."

Mrs. Swanson and Betsy Norbitt huddled under the overhang of the counter, looking terrified. And Jonathan Gradin clung to the bottom of the cherry-printed café curtains that hung down against the wall, his fleshy face red and sweaty. A calm, grim-faced Rosalee had come out of the kitchen when the commotion began and was now on the phone, presumably to 911. Jay ran outside but the car from which the hammer had been thrown was long gone. I sat crouched under the table, shaking, confused—and wondering if that hammer had been meant for me.

CHAPTER 35

Everyone at Rosalee's was ordered to stay onsite until someone from the sheriff's office took our statements. Jay called in help from his office, and within minutes of the attack there were at least four uniformed law enforcement officers and several other "official" people milling around, snapping photographs, tagging evidence, and taking statements. At one point, Jay checked on me to make sure I was okay, but it was little more than a question-asked/question-answered exchange before he was pulled away.

There are basically two ways one can react to almost being cleaved in half like Newton's apple: frenzied hysteria or complete and utter denial. I opted for the latter. I don't remember making the conscious choice not to panic, but in the aftermath of the attack I found myself surrounded by eyewitnesses who wanted to do nothing more than tell their story. So when I suddenly remembered that I was a reporter, I took out my notebook and got busy doing my job. It not only made good sense, but it made for an excellent distraction from thoughts of *What if?*

I interviewed several people, one of whom was Jonathan Gradin, who gave me an animated account of how he bent backward on his stool—*Matrix*-like—to avoid flying glass and certain death. It didn't exactly square with my memory of him clutching the curtains like a scared cat, but who was I to question his hero's account? I was wrapping up with him when the mayor and Toby walked up to the café.

I extracted myself from Mr. Gradin, who seemed disappointed to be cut short, and ran out to the sidewalk. Upon seeing me, Shaylene Lancett threw her arms around me and pulled me into a tight embrace.

"Oh, Riley! Are you okay, sugar?" She sounded positively distressed at the thought that I might be hurt. "I've just been worried sick about you—about all y'all— in there." She pushed me back to arm's length, still holding me by the shoulders. "Were you hurt?"

"No, not really. Just a little spooked," I said, taking a step backward. "Sorry I missed our meeting."

She waved me away. "Nonsense. You and I can have our little chat any old time. In fact, let me just finish up with Carl here and then we can talk. Can you sit tight a few minutes and wait for me?"

You'd think that given that someone had just thrown a hammer through the window of one of Tuttle's most iconic businesses, the mayor would have bigger fish to fry than being quoted in an obituary, but apparently not.

She turned to Carl, who was standing nearby talking to one of his deputies. "Carl, you don't mind if I steal Riley for a quick few minutes, do you?"

He made sure that I had given my statement and then said I was free to go. "By the way, Lindsey Davis is going to drop the charges against Thad Davenport."

It was the first bit of good news I had heard in a while, and I was deeply relieved.

Toby did not feel the same way. "But that man is guilty as sin!"

Carl ignored Toby and addressed himself to the mayor only. "She said we don't have enough to convict."

That made sense to me. All the evidence that had pointed to Thad was circumstantial, but in light of the attack on David and the threatening note left for me—both of which happened when Thad had an irrefutable alibi—a lawyer could easily make a case for reasonable doubt. It wasn't a resounding declaration of his innocence, but it was good enough to at least kick the can down the road.

Mayor Lancett said nothing, acknowledging Carl's news with a terse nod. She then turned to her nephew, "Would you please take Riley over to the shop? I'll be along in just a few minutes."

Toby turned to me and said a weary, "C'mon."

As we started down the sidewalk I got a view of his always-ironic bib and tucker: a blue long-sleeved T-shirt with the words *Licensed to Thrill*, gray man-joggers, which gave his legs the silhouette of a satyr, and the same white high-tops he had on the other day. However, they no longer looked brand new—the left one had a big blue splotch on the toe.

"Spill something on your new shoes?" I asked as we took the short walk over to Inviting Praise.

He looked down. "Oh, yeah. Shame too, these are brand new. I have a collection, did you know?"

I wanted to ask *Why the hell would I know you collect shoes?* but what I said was, "Really?"

"Thirty-two pairs. All Nikes." He said this proudly, then looked down again and frowned. "Me and Aunt Shaylene were out touring Roy G. Biv's manufacturing facility and some clumsy hayseed spilled dye on me."

Roy G. Biv? That was the elementary school mnemonic for the colors of the spectrum. The thought that somebody named their kid that made me laugh.

"It's not funny, these shoes cost more than you make in a week."

"I wasn't laughing at you," I said, rolling my eyes. "I was laughing because who would name their son Roy G. Biv?"

"It's not a person, Riley, it's a company." Toby's voice dripped with condescension. "A textile dye shop in West Virginia."

We arrived at Inviting Praise and Toby took out his keys, unlocked the door, and let me inside. It was still before shop hours, so Toby locked the door behind us and led me through the darkened store to Mayor Lancett's office in the back. He flicked on the lights and motioned for me to have a seat in one of the two chairs that sat opposite the mayor's desk. He then settled himself in his aunt's chair, which I got the distinct feeling was against the rules.

He sat behind the large white desk and just looked at me. He hadn't offered me any tea or water and we sat in awkward silence, both of us with nothing to say. After a couple of uncomfortable moments I said, "So, what were you guys doing over in West Virginia?"

"Roy G. Biv is looking to move their manufacturing plant, and they're considering Tuttle County. We went to go check it out."

"Really?" I asked, the reporter in me perking up. Presumably the company's move would create jobs, generate tax revenue, boost local businesses, and augment the housing market. This could mean big things for our small town—and would be a huge win for the mayor.

"What do they manufacture?"

"Duh, they're a dye factory. They make dye—you know, for fabrics and such."

I didn't think this information was such common

knowledge that I deserved to be *duh*'d, but I ignored that. Toby had piqued my curiosity.

"So cat's out of the bag, I see." Mayor Lancett appeared in the doorway, scowling at her nephew. Her voice was soft and feathery, even in allegation.

Toby's face went pale. "Oh, hey, I didn't—"

She held up her hand and he immediately stopped talking. "It's fine. I was planning on announcing it soon anyhow."

As if he suddenly realized where he was sitting, Toby stood up in a hurry and knocked his knee on the edge of the desk. "Goddammit!"

"Toby, *language!*"

"I'm sorry, Aunt Shaylene," Toby said, sounding like an eleven-year-old kid.

"Please give Riley and me a minute alone."

CHAPTER 36

Toby scuttled out of the room as Shaylene walked around her desk and took a minute to straighten the Muppets figurines that lined the edge before she sat down. Then she pulled open the top drawer, took out one of those little antibacterial wipes in the small square envelopes, ripped it open, and wiped off the surface of her desk and the armrests of her chair.

"Now then." She looked at me the way one might look at a wounded bird that had landed on their doorstep. "How are you doing, Riley? *Really.*"

"I'm fine," I said, a little uneasily. "Really."

"That must have been terrifying," she said, shaking her head. "I just can't understand what is going on in this town lately."

"I'm sure Sheriff Haight will get to the bottom of things," I said.

"I certainly hope so." And then she straightened herself up and clasped her hands in front of her on the desk. "Now then, you wanted a quote for Arthur Davenport's obituary."

"Well, actually . . ." I wanted to say *It was you who wanted to be quoted,* but I didn't want to start off the conversation in such an adversarial way. So instead I said, "I've heard from a couple of sources that you and Arthur had been close, but then something happened."

Her jaw tightened, but she said nothing.

I prodded. "I was wondering if you could tell me more about that."

"Sometimes this town is just too small." She said this almost under her breath, but I was certain she'd meant for me to hear. And then she said louder, "You'll probably find out sooner or later, so I might as well get it over with."

It turned out that once again, part of what I knew was true. I just didn't have the whole story. Shaylene Lancett and Arthur Davenport had been high school sweethearts. They dated for two years in high school but broke things off when Arthur left for college (he was a year ahead of her). She said the breakup had been both mutual and amicable. While at school in North Carolina, Arthur met and married Maribelle, Thad and David's mother, and brought her back to live in Tuttle once he finished medical school. Shaylene said that after that, they remained friendly, but didn't socialize.

"I married much later in life, as you know, and I don't think Maribelle liked the idea of her husband spending time with an unmarried ex-girlfriend—understandably. But after she passed away, Arthur leaned on me for support."

I wonder what she meant by *leaned*. "So did you and Arthur ever rekindle the old flame, you know, after Maribelle passed away?"

A deep blush colored her cheeks. "Arthur was one of my oldest friends," she said. "He was funny and charming and brilliant and irreverent, and we had a terribly strong bond." She paused, and a sad ghost of a smile crossed her face. "At one point, I think I'd hoped that we'd reconnect, but as the years passed it became clear that he didn't think of me that way."

I wasn't sure what to say to something like that so I said

nothing, and waited for her to continue. Eventually she did.

"Until the night before my wedding," she said, her soft voice taking on a harder edge. "He came to me, told me he loved me, begged me not to marry Theo—said everything I'd always wanted to hear . . ." Her eyes were locked on one of the figurines on her desk. "I'm not sure if it was how he really felt, or if he was just saying that because he didn't want to lose me to another man. But either way, it made me angry. I'm afraid I didn't handle it well."

"What do you mean?"

"I threatened to kill him." She must have read the impact on my face because she followed quickly with, "I wouldn't have hurt him, obviously, but I was so angry at him for what he'd done, what he was trying to do . . . I'd finally found happiness with Theo after all those years. Arthur had his family, his children, and I didn't have any of those things. And there he was trying to ruin my chance for love. It was cruel, and I guess I snapped. I grabbed a knife from the kitchen and told him if he ever set foot in my home again, I'd make sure it was the last step he ever took."

I tried to control my shock. Shaylene Lancett seemed like the least likely person in the world to threaten someone with a knife. "When was that?" I asked.

"About two years ago."

"Does the sheriff know about this?"

"Not exactly," she said carefully. "I was hoping to avoid becoming involved in the investigation. What with the scandal this town has just been through, and this deal on the horizon with Roy G. Biv. And, of course, you have to believe I didn't have anything to do with Arthur's death."

My silence indicated that I didn't necessarily believe any such thing.

"I was having dinner with Theo and Darryl and Betsy

Norbitt at the Shack on Monday night. We were there from six o'clock till after nine-thirty. Call Louis and check if you want."

I made a note of her alibi. I would most definitely check it out. "I'm going to have to tell Carl about this," I said.

"That's fine," she sighed. "But just know that the anger I had toward Arthur burned out a long time ago." She looked at me with a pleading in her eyes. "Please don't judge me too harshly. It's just a very complicated thing. You spend your whole life loving a man who doesn't love you back—at least not the way you need him to—and just when you're ready to move on, he comes back and messes everything up."

Boy, did I understand that. "I'm not judging you, I'm just trying to"—I almost slipped and said *figure out who killed Arthur*—"write an accurate portrayal of who Arthur Davenport was."

At that, she perked up and talked for a while about all the things she had loved about him. His wicked sense of humor, his love of basketball and Christmas music, and how dedicated he was to his work. I took notes and listened as she wound her way through memory lane.

"Thank you for talking with me, Riley," she said after she'd run out of stories. "I've been carrying around all this guilt ever since he died, and it feels good to just talk about the man I knew for over forty years."

"Guilt?"

She nodded. "We hadn't spoken beyond social pleasantries in over two years. After I did what I did," she looked down, "Arthur stayed away like I asked. According to mutual friends, that's also when he started drinking more and took up with some unsavory companions." She said the word like it tasted bad in her mouth. "A small part of me wondered if he actually was sincere when he'd come to me.

What if he really did love me and wanted us to be together? And my violent rejection set him on a path to self-destruction that ultimately ended with him being . . ." She took a deep breath to clear the emotion from her voice. "I just want it all to be over."

"But surely you want to see whoever is responsible for this to be brought to justice?"

"Of course," she said, quickly. "I also know that it's time to close the books on this one for the good of the community."

And there it was. *For the good of the community.* Thanks to Holman and me, Tuttle Corner had just made headlines for drug-dealing taco trucks and homicidal officials; having another high-profile murder case not even three months later didn't exactly reflect well on us as a community. That explained why she was pushing Carl so hard to make an arrest. It all made sense now. The reason Mayor Lancett was trying so hard to close the books on Arthur's murder wasn't because of her guilt—although I believe she did feel badly about what happened between them—but because she was trying to woo Roy G. Biv Industries to the county. A mayor who brought jobs to town was far more likely to get reelected than one who let the town become embroiled in crime and corruption.

I decided to call her out. "Is this about Roy G. Biv?"

"It would be a huge boon to our economy," Mayor Lancett said deftly, avoiding the question. "But nothing is set in stone. They're looking at a couple of possible site locations. But Tuttle County would be a great fit because we have the natural resources they're after."

"And what resources are those?" *Other than an over-eager mayor,* I thought.

"Indigo, mostly."

"Indigo?"

"Why do you look so surprised? Their focus is on all natural dyes and indigo is by far the most common plant used in textile colorants."

A light bulb went on in my head. "And indigo grows in the same soil as tobacco."

"Yes, exactly," Shaylene said. "That's one of the reasons Tuttle County is so attractive to them."

I'd heard more about tobacco farms and indigo plants in the past two days than in all my previous twenty-four years on the planet. "Shaylene," I said, a new thought occurring to me, "this may seem like an odd question, but did Arthur have anything to do with this possible deal with Roy G. Biv?"

She shook her head. "No. Why?"

"No reason, I was just wondering." For a moment I thought perhaps this was all connected somehow to Arthur's death, but that was probably just wishful thinking. That would definitely be too easy. The bottom line was that even after finding out that the mayor did in fact threaten to kill Arthur, and finding out why she was putting pressure on Carl to close the case, we weren't any closer to finding out who killed Arthur Davenport. I felt deflated.

"The only local people involved are some farmers the company contacted to see if they'd be interested in becoming indigo producers, should the company end up relocating here."

I held my breath and asked one last Hail Mary of a question. "And which families are those?"

"One of them is the Luetkemeyers—they own Luke's Farm," she said. "And the other one I've never met. A family by the name of Krisanski."

Touchdown.

Chapter 37

It was past 10 a.m. when I arrived at the *Times* office. So much had happened since the incident at Rosalee's that it took me a minute to figure out what she was talking about when Kay asked if I was okay as soon as I walked in the door.

"Yeah, I'm fine."

"Were you hurt?"

I shook my head. "Just a little scared." I had a few marks on my forehead and left elbow from flying debris, but thankfully the window had been made from tempered glass, so it shattered into small granular pieces instead of sharp fragments. It could have been a lot worse.

Kay eyed me with suspicion, yet spoke in an uncharacteristically gentle voice, "Are you sure?"

"Would I have been able to get interviews from four eyewitnesses and three emergency personnel workers if I wasn't?" I pulled out my notebook and flashed a triumphant smile.

Kay laughed. "I'm glad you're okay. Have the story uploaded as soon as you can. This is front-page material, Riley. Good work." She turned to walk back to her office.

"Kay?"

She gave me a half turn. "Yeah?"

"Um, there's more. Can we talk in your office?"

I told her what I'd learned about Roy G. Biv Industries
and the possible move to Tuttle County and how I believed
it was behind Mayor Lancett's intense interest in the murder case. For the time being, I left out the stuff about her
personal relationship with Arthur. At the moment, the murder investigation was still stupid Spencer's story; let him
chase his own leads.

"Wow," Kay said when I'd finished talking. "This is big.
Think you can have a story on it by tomorrow?"

"I'll do my best."

Just about everyone in the office came by my desk at
some point to ask what had happened at Rosalee's, if I was
okay, and if anyone had any leads on who might have done
it. I shared the little information I'd learned from talking to
the emergency responders on the scene: no serious injuries (thank goodness) and no leads. But I hoped the latter
would change as the police continued their interviews with
witnesses. There'd been at least a handful of people on the
street and in the park when the car drove by and hurled the
hammer into the café. Surely somebody saw something.

I had some more interviews to get before I could finish
the story about the attack at Rosalee's, specifically one with
Sheriff Haight. I texted him and he agreed to let me come
by the station in an hour.

With the mayor's comments fresh in my head, I also
wanted to talk to Lauren McCarty and ask more questions
about her family's farm. I knew it was still in operation
based on what Tabitha found, and now it seems that someone from the family had also been in touch with Roy G.
Biv—the question was, did Lauren know that?

I decided to interview her in person this time, hoping
that the face-to-face conversation might yield more information. So I drove over to Smythe & Breidenbach, the

accounting firm in town where Lauren McCarty worked.

"Can I help you?" a woman asked as I walked in the glass-front office. I checked her nameplate by the reception desk—Lauren.

"Hi Lauren. I'm Riley Ellison, from the *Times*. We spoke on the phone yesterday?"

She reached out to shake my hand, while shooting a quick glance over her left shoulder. "Hey. What can I do for you?"

"I'm working on another story, this one to do with farming, and I came across a plot of land that is registered to your father, Charles Krisanski. I remember you telling me that he passed away a couple of years ago . . ." I purposely left the statement open-ended, hoping Lauren would fill in the blanks for me.

"Yeah, that's our family farm, the one I was telling you about. I guess the deed was never updated after Daddy died."

"Your family still owns the farm then?"

"Yes, it's been in our family for years. There's no bank note on it, so technically we own it, but like I said yesterday, it's pretty much just dormant land now. After Daddy died, Mom didn't have the energy to take it over, and John and I had no interest—so we just let all the crops go to seed. We're just hoping someone comes along and makes us an offer on it."

I knew this wasn't true. What I didn't know was if Lauren knew it wasn't true.

"Have you been by the farm lately?"

"No, why?"

"I have reason to believe that someone is using your family's land, Lauren. My associate drove out there yesterday and saw rows of healthy crops, fresh tire tracks, irrigation systems running. It looked like a fully functioning farm."

"*What?*" She looked gobsmacked.

"So you don't know anything about this?"

She shook her head slowly, her brow deeply furrowed. "No, I mean, I can't imagine . . ."

"Has anyone been in touch with you about buying or leasing the land?"

Again, she shook her head. She was clearly thrown off by this information. "No, no one has even mentioned it to me since Mom died."

She was so obviously surprised by this information that I had no reason to doubt her. Plus, I couldn't think of a reason someone would lie about farming their own land. It's not like that's a crime. "Could I talk to your brother? Maybe he knows something?"

"Sure," she said, just as the phone rang. She scribbled down his phone number on a Post-it note and handed it to me as she answered the phone. "Smythe and Breidenbach, how may I help you?"

I mouthed a silent *thank you* and left the office. I had about thirty minutes till I was due at the sheriff's office, so I ran by Tuttle General to check on Tabitha. On my way over, I left a message for Lauren's brother, John, asking him to call me back. As I pulled into the visitor lot at the hospital, I saw that Jay had texted me.

R u okay? We need to talk. Can I come by later?

I felt a lump in my throat. I wanted nothing more than to talk to Jay, to let him comfort me after the scare this morning, but I knew I had to be strong. It was obvious he didn't feel about me the way I felt about him, plus we clearly wanted different things. I ignored the text, chucked my phone into my purse, and walked inside the hospital.

I headed straight for Tabitha's room. Before I got there, however, I found Thad sitting in the waiting area just outside the third-floor elevators. He was in the same clothes he'd been wearing the night before and looked like he hadn't slept. In front of him was an empty cup of coffee and an untouched muffin.

"Hey," I said as I walked up.

He looked at me through bleary, red-rimmed eyes. Thad looked as worn out and tired as I'd ever seen a person. His father had been murdered, he'd been held in jail for days, and then his brother and his fiancée were both hospitalized. That kind of stress would wear out anybody.

"They've got her in surgery now. Doc said they should be out soon."

I nodded. "How's David?"

"He's being released today. He's still weak, but Dr. Cavell thinks he's past the worst of it." Thad ran a hand through his hair as he leaned back against the blue vinyl seat. "I'm worried about him going home alone though, so he's going to come stay at the house with me."

The last thing I wanted to do was add to his stress, but I felt like he needed to know about the threat I'd received, since he and Tabitha knew almost everything I did about Arthur's death. I told him all about it as gently as I could and made sure he knew Carl had the note and was looking into Brandon Laytner's alibi for the night of his father's murder.

"God, I'm so sorry, Riley." He shook his head. "I wish I knew what to say . . ."

I felt for him. He'd been through so much in the past few days, and despite everyone's best efforts, we were no closer to figuring out who was behind it all.

"I'm just glad the prosecutor dropped the charges."

"Me too—but I won't feel like any of us are safe until we find who killed Dad and tried to kill David. I'm thinking of hiring protection for us out at the estate."

"Not a bad idea," I said, wishing I had the resources to hire some protection of my own.

CHAPTER 38

I walked into the sheriff's office a few minutes later than expected. The place was buzzing with the kind of frenetic energy brought on by stress, fear, and shared purpose. In Tuttle Corner, an attack on one of us was an attack on all of us, and finding out who threw that hammer was now the priority of everyone in the office.

Gail had the phone crooked between her ear and shoulder and was typing something into her archaic desktop computer at the same time. When I walked in, she nodded her head toward Carl's office as a way to let me know I was free to go on back.

I walked to the back of the large rectangular room and saw through the window that Jay was in with Carl. My mouth went dry as I mentally calculated if there was any way I could turn and run out of there without being seen.

"Riley," Carl called to me from his desk. *Damn.* He looked at his watch. "Give me a minute to finish up with Jay."

Jay looked at me but said nothing, his face completely unreadable. He was a consummate professional and I knew he wouldn't try to talk to me about personal issues here. I stepped back out of the office, pulling the door closed behind me.

My heart thumped against my chest wall. Was this

going to happen every time I ran into him? I was going to have to find a way to make peace with the fact that we were over, that he wasn't the man I thought he was.

I pulled out my phone and pretended to be busy while I waited. A couple of short minutes later, Carl's door opened and Jay walked out alone. He paused in front of me.

"We need to talk," he said in a low voice as his eyes looked over my head, scanning the room.

"I don't think there's anything left to say."

"There is, trust me," he said. "Things like—"

"Like how a person could be so cruel?" I said in a shouty-whisper.

"Riley—"

"Riley, come on in," Carl called from behind his desk.

"I have to go," I said, not even looking at Jay as I walked past him into the sheriff's office. I heard him exhale loudly as I did, but I was right about his professionalism preventing him from causing a scene.

I took a deep breath as I sat down in a chair opposite Carl's desk.

"Trouble in paradise?"

I gave him a look that said *Drop it*. Thankfully, he did. We spent the next ten minutes on my questions about the incident at Rosalee's and the status of the investigation. The hammer had been sent to the lab for prints, and they had a few descriptions from witnesses that they were trying to match. After I had enough information for the article, I screwed up my courage and asked him the one question I wanted to know the answer to more than any other: "Do you think this could have anything to do with me?"

"Riley," Carl said, his face softening, "you were sitting in that restaurant next to a man who has angered a number of dangerous criminals over the course of his career.

There's a far greater likelihood that hammer was meant for him than for you."

I let out the breath I'd been holding in, unsure of whether that made me feel better or worse. Either someone was trying to hurt me, or someone was trying to hurt Jay.

"By the way," Carl said, "I sent Butter over to talk to Brandon Laytner." He pulled out a sheet of paper and read from it. "He told Butter that on the night of the murder he'd been home alone. No alibi. Same thing for early this morning. Butter said he got real belligerent when he asked him about that. He said, 'Where the hell do you think I was at 2 a.m.?' "

I could totally see Brandon being rude to Butter. I'm sure he would have treated me the same way had I not been with Ridley. But being a bully didn't give you a free pass on anything.

"Are you going to look into it further? I mean, there were tobacco leaves at the scene and this guy had a clear problem with Arthur *and* he works with tobacco plants . . ."

Carl held up a hand to stop me. "We are looking into it. Rest assured." Evidently Carl hadn't changed his mind about letting me help. "And I sent the note over to the lab in Richmond to see if they can get any prints off it. I'll let you know what we hear."

He stood to walk me out, and his police scanner crackled to life. I heard him mutter under his breath, "Good Lord, what now?"

"Sheriff, this is unit five and we are responding to a ten-one-hundred off Route K."

"What's a ten-one-hundred?"

"Dead body—*shhh*," Carl whispered.

The voice on the radio continued. "Officers were driving

on Route K just past mile marker eight-nine when we were flagged down by two men in hunting gear. The men said they were out turkey hunting and found a deceased male lying in the field."

The scanner cut out and I sucked in a sharp breath. Carl put a hand out to tell me to calm down. A second later the scanner came back on. "We were able to confirm the presence of a body. We have a white male with what looks like a gunshot wound to the head." Another cutout, more static. "We found a hunting license identifying the man as one Bennett Nichols of Tuttle Corner, Virginia."

CHAPTER 39

W e'll have to run some tests to be sure, but looks like it was a hunting accident," Tiffany Peters said to us as we walked up to the spot where Bennett Nichols's lifeless body lay shrouded by tall grass. "My guess would be that his gun accidentally discharged, hitting him once in the neck, shot clean through his carotid." She spoke with equal parts authority and glee, her tiny witch-hat earrings dangling as she talked.

I stayed back a few paces, not wanting to get too close.

"All right," Carl said. "Call Dr. Mendez and get him out here." Then he turned to his deputies and asked, "See any signs of foul play? Any other footprints, anything like that?"

Deputy Wilmore spoke first. "Yeah, but they're probably from the two guys that found him. They were friends of Jim Nichols, this is his land. They said Jim told them his son was going to be hunting from 5:30 till about 8 a.m. They didn't come out here till after 1 p.m."

"Tiffany, how long would you guess the body's been there?" Carl asked.

"Hard to say without testing it, but I think it's safe to say at least six hours, since rigor mortis has started."

"Okay," Carl said, turning to Butter. "Did we check those guys' guns to see if they'd been fired recently?"

Butter nodded. "We'll send 'em to the lab to be sure, but I don't think so. Those guys are real shaken up over this. I don't think they had anything to do with it."

"Has anyone talked to the family yet?"

Both Butter and Wilmore shook their heads. I didn't envy that job. I can't imagine anything worse than having to tell a woman her husband just died, except maybe having to tell parents that their son did. I thought of Libby. How would she take the news? Her relationship with Bennett had been complex and toxic, but longstanding all the same.

Carl rubbed the back of his neck as he looked over toward the body. "Chances are this was just an accident," he said, "but I can't close my eyes to the possibility that it was something more given his involvement with Arthur Davenport. We've now got two dead bodies and one attempted murder on our hands. And the common denominator seems to be Libby Nichols."

I had to agree with him. I'll admit I had trouble thinking of Libby as a stone-cold killer, however years of abuse and stress can do terrible things to a person. I guess I could see her wanting to kill Bennett after everything he'd put her through. Less clear was what would have been her motivation to kill Arthur, or David, for that matter? My mind ticked through the possibilities, coming up blank each time.

"Sheriff?" Deputy Wilmore called out. "Found something interesting over here." He held up a small gold key with a rounded top. I recognized it right away as the key to a post office box.

"Now why would a person have a PO box key while he was out hunting turkey?" Carl muttered.

"Maybe he was planning to stop by the post office later—actually that doesn't make a lot of sense, because this was an early morning hunt and would be over before the post office even opened," I said. "Or maybe he didn't want to leave that key lying around for some reason."

Carl picked up on my train of thought. "Ted, can you go down to the post office and find out what's in that box. If Leon gives you any trouble, call Judge DeFreitas and ask her for a warrant." Then he turned to me. "I need you to go back to the *Times* office and wait for me to call. I'm going to go see Libby"—I started to argue and he put up a hand to stop me. "You'll get the story, don't worry. But I've got to go tell a woman she's lost her husband, and trust me when I tell you that is no place for the press."

CHAPTER 40

I spent the next couple of hours walking around the newsroom trying to act busy. I fed Aunt Beast, bounced on Holman's chair, looked over the obit draft, called a few sources to interview about the Roy G. Biv story—but I spent most of the time checking my phone. When Carl finally called and asked if I could come down to the station, I was out the door in three seconds flat.

First, Carl told me that Dr. Mendez had called and said it would be a while till he could say for certain, but he believed Bennett's injuries were consistent with a self-inflicted gunshot wound. This meant that in the absence of any evidence to the contrary, medically speaking, it appeared to be an accident. When I asked if there was any evidence to the contrary as of yet, Carl said, "Just wait. There's more."

He told me about his difficult conversation with Libby Nichols, and that while she was stoic upon hearing the news that Bennett had died, during the course of the conversation she broke down several times. "She said she told Bennett he wasn't strong enough to go hunting and he just blew her off. Told her it was his form of relaxation. That woman's emotions were all over the place. If she was acting, someone ought to give her an Oscar."

When I asked whether Carl thought Libby could have

been involved in Bennett's death, he said, "Just wait. There's more."

Deputy Wilmore was able to get access to Bennett's post office box and inside found a picture of Libby and Arthur Davenport locked in a passionate embrace. The photo, which Carl showed me, looked like it'd been taken from a distance through a window. It had been printed out on computer paper and the resolution wasn't great—but even still, the two were clearly visible. It had a date stamp on it: the day before Arthur was killed.

When I asked if Carl thought this made it look like Bennett might have been the one who killed Arthur, I answered my own question before he had a chance: "Don't tell me: *just wait. There's more.*"

Carl nodded. "The box also contained several empty sample bottles of Digoxicon, the drug that was used to poison Arthur and David Davenport. The way it looks right now is that Bennett found out that Libby and Arthur were still seeing each other, and he killed Arthur because of it. Libby confirmed Bennett was taking this for his heart condition and the pill bottles are being tested for prints."

"What about Bennett's alibi?"

"All we know for sure is that the time of death was 11:13 p.m. Dr. Mendez confirmed that the lethality of this drug really depends on the quantity used and how quickly it's ingested. It's possible that Arthur had been sipping on the poisoned whiskey for hours before he actually died. Libby said Bennett came home Monday evening about 7:30, and before that had been at his office alone—"

I finished his thought: "—which means if Bennett was the killer, he could have given Arthur the poisoned whiskey earlier in the night and then come home to arrange for the world's most perfect alibi: the sheriff himself."

"Exactly." Carl clenched his jaw. I could see that he was discomfited by the idea that Bennett had played him for a fool.

Another thought leapt to my mind. "That could also explain why Bennett stabbed Arthur after he was already dead."

"How so?"

"Think about it from Bennett's perspective: he gives Arthur the whiskey at some point, maybe he stops by his house on his way home from work, let's say around 6:30. That would have been before Thad got there. Maybe he says it's a thank-you for saving his life, or gives it to him as a peace offering or something . . ." I was making this up as I went along, my imagination dreaming up the scenario like it was a movie. "Bennett wanted Arthur dead, he told me as much when I interviewed him. Of course, he wouldn't have wanted a violent confrontation because he wasn't strong enough after the recent episode with his heart. So he crushes up his pills, gives the tainted bottle to Arthur, and then goes home to work on his alibi.

"Bennett was smart enough to know that if you found Digoxigon in his bloodstream, you could easily find out he had a prescription for it, so in order to make it look like Arthur died from a knife wound rather than digitalis poisoning, he goes back into the house after Arthur is already dead and plunges a knife into his chest. He was betting on the fact that you'd probably just take the scene at face value and call it a stabbing death."

Carl dropped his head into his hands and I heard him mutter something under his breath.

"What?" I asked.

"We left the Nichols house just after midnight. And it never occurred to me to check Bennett's alibi for the rest of the evening. *Dammit.*" He smacked his hand on his desk. "If what you're saying is true, I bungled this entire investigation."

I felt for Carl in that moment. No one could relate more to that feeling than me—after all, hadn't I just made an equally stupid rookie mistake at my job?

"It's just a theory," I said to try to make him feel better. "And honestly, it doesn't explain why he'd poison David."

"Yeah, still no leads on that," he said, drumming his fingers on his desk, now noticeably more agitated. "But his threatening you fits."

I nodded. "If Bennett left his house before dawn to go hunting it's possible he came by my house on his way to his parents' land."

I didn't know for sure that I was right, but just the thought chilled me to my core. Any other day, I would have been at home. Had Thad not called me to come to the hospital, Bennett would have broken into my house and found me there very much asleep. What would he have done? Would he have stopped at a warning, or would I have become his next victim?

"Okay. This is good guesswork, but we'll need confirmation before we can make any kind of official determination. Let me put Wilmore and Butter on some of this and talk to Lindsey Davis. Until then, let's keep the details of the PO box out of the paper."

I agreed and stood up to leave. "Let me know what you find out."

"Thanks for your help, Riley," Carl said as he walked me out. "It looks like we may have finally found our killer."

Chapter 41

As soon as I got back to the office, I decided to come clean to Kay and let her know exactly what I'd been up to over the past few days. She listened without comment as I detailed all the ways that I'd ignored her directive to stay off the story. I held nothing back, starting from my meeting Carl at the hospital, my visits to the Nicholses and Brandon Laytner, and even the threatening note.

Her eyes narrowed and widened at a few points in my story, but she said nothing until I caught up to the present moment. I thought there was a good chance she was going to fire me when I finished talking, so I decided to make my last comment count. "But now that it seems to be over, I think you should let me write up the story."

Kay crossed her arms in front of her and lifted an eyebrow at me. "You want to be rewarded by getting the byline after you directly disobeyed me and went behind my back to do your own reporting?"

"Yes."

Kay gave me an eagle-eyed stare that I returned without flinching. After a few long seconds, the corner of her lip tugged upward. "Holman would be so proud of you right now."

It ended up being a long night at the *Times,* and by the time I had gotten all the stories written it was past 11 p.m. Kay decided the attack on Rosalee's would go on page one and the update on the Davenport murder would be on page two. I was getting my first front-page byline, and although I was physically exhausted, I was fizzing with adrenaline.

While I was waiting for Kay to tell me I could go home, I called my parents, who would be back in town just in time for Sunday's paper. My mother said she'd never been so excited to read a newspaper in her life, and my dad, predictably, cried. Mom asked how Jay was and I told her he was fine, which was sort of true because I had no reason to believe he wasn't. There'd be time to tell them what happened once they got home; no need to worry them while they were away.

I texted Ryan and asked if he could keep Coltrane until I got home, and he said he would. So once I got the word from Kay that I could leave, I told him that I'd be home in ten minutes. As I walked toward the newsroom door, I saw Gerlach Spencer sitting at his desk. I didn't know why he was still at the office; as far as I could tell, he was just sitting there playing *Candy Crush* on his phone.

"Hey Spencer," I said. "No hard feelings about the Davenport story, right?"

"Wrong." He shot me a death stare. "You poached that right out from under me."

"Aw, c'mon," I said. "Your loss was my gain, *amiright?*" I put my hand up to give him a high-five—and I swear for the briefest of moments he considered doing it out of some sort of Pavlovian response. Ultimately he left me hanging, which was what I hoped he'd do because it gave me the perfect opening to say, "Geez, someone needs to *relax!*"

CHAPTER 42

I walked out of the office and noticed the temperature had fallen quite sharply since the last time I'd been outside. I was glad I'd taken my car to work that morning because after the day I'd had, a two-minute drive sounded better than a ten-minute walk. Thad's phone call about Tabitha seemed like it happened a lifetime ago, but it had only been just under twenty-four hours. I did a quick mental calculation and realized I'd been up for almost twenty-two hours. I could feel the stress of the day catching up with me in the form of a stiff neck and the beginnings of a headache. I couldn't remember a time when I'd been more excited to get home and climb into bed.

Until I got there.

Parked in my driveway was Ryan's massive truck and Jay's sporty BMW convertible. As I turned the corner and saw them both there waiting for me, I considered driving right on by. If it hadn't been for Coltrane I probably would have.

I parked on the street and got out of my car. "Hey guys."

Both were standing outside of their respective vehicles, leaning against them, Jay with his hands in his pockets and Ryan with his arms crossed in front of his chest. It was like they'd both taken a class on How to Stand Like a Dude. Coltrane, sweet boy that he was, didn't try to play it cool.

He bounded over to me with unabashed excitement and gave me a proper hello.

"Thanks for taking him today," I said to Ryan.

"Happy to," Ryan said. "I love this guy."

"Riley, can we talk?" Jay cut in, impatient for my attention.

My hand automatically went to my forehead as the pounding began to strengthen behind my eyeballs. "Listen, it's late and I've had a hell of a day . . ."

"It won't take long, I promise."

I sighed and looked down the street.

Ryan immediately picked up on the tension. "If she says she's tired, then maybe you ought to lay off?"

Jay stiffened. He didn't seem to appreciate being told what to do by my ex-boyfriend. Ironically, that title now applied to him as well.

"Ryan, it's okay."

"Yeah, Ryan, we don't need your input here," Jay said with more vitriol than I'd ever heard him use before.

"Hey," I spun around and pointed at Jay. "You don't get to talk to him like that—"

"Yeah, you—"

"Shush." I swiveled my finger toward Ryan. "You're just here to drop off Coltrane, *thankyouverymuch*." And then I felt bad about being snippy so I added, "I really do appreciate the help."

"Fine," he huffed. "But I hope you'd tell me if you needed something . . ."

"Goodnight, Ryan."

Ryan gave Coltrane one last pat on the head and got into his massive truck. As the engine roared to life, Jay and I stood framed in its headlights.

"Five minutes? Please?"

The last thing in the world I wanted to do at that moment was to have a difficult conversation, but I could see he wasn't going to leave me alone until he "unburdened himself." I nodded my weary consent and unlocked the door and the three of us went inside.

"How are you after what happened this morning?" Jay sat on the couch and I purposely sat across the room in the armchair. Of course, Coltrane sat at *his* feet. I needed to have a talk with that dog about where exactly he thought his bread was buttered—and by whom.

"It has been a long day," I said, which didn't really answer the question. The truth was I didn't know how I was feeling. I had been so busy all day that the last thing I had time for was to reflect on my feelings. Besides, my feelings were no longer Jay's concern.

He took a deep breath and exhaled audibly, like he was in yoga class. That made me nervous. What was he about to say that he needed yoga breathing for?

"I'll get right to it. The woman you saw at my apartment, her name is Ginny, and she's my partner."

"Okay, great," I said, standing up. "Thanks for telling me. I hope you two are very happy together."

"No," he said, and he stood up too, so we were standing face to face. "You don't understand—"

"Jay," I said, aware of how close we were standing to each other and how much harder that made this conversation. "You don't have to say anything else. It's fine. We want different things, apparently. Just go home to your girlfriend—oh sorry, partner," I said. "Excuse me for not being up on the current terminology."

"What?" A deep crease appeared over the bridge of his nose. "No, from the DEA. Ginny was my partner at the agency up in Camden for five years."

Oh. That kind of partner. I should have been more embarrassed for myself, but I honestly didn't have the energy. I didn't even try to hide the hope from my voice when I asked, "So she's not your girlfriend?"

"No. *You* are my girlfriend."

"I am?" The stress of the day caught up to me and I could feel tears building at the base of my eyes. I looked down. "The only one?"

Jay's finger swept down my cheekbone and rested under my chin. He tilted it up so that we were once again eye to eye. "The only one."

I threw my arms around his head and kissed him with enough enthusiasm to hopefully make up for being so crazy the past couple of days.

He kissed me back and then, just when it seemed like things were going to get more interesting, pulled away. "There's something else I need to tell you though."

"Anything," I said, my arms still around his neck.

"Ginny came to town yesterday to give me some big news . . ." He paused, staring at me for an unreasonably long interval.

She won the lottery? She's getting married? She got pulled onstage at a Maroon 5 concert? "Well—what is it?"

He sighed, looked down, and then straight up into my eyes. "She's been made the special agent in charge of the DC office . . . and she's asked me to come work for her." He hesitated, and it was as if I could see the guilt settle on his shoulders like a cloak. "And I said yes. I leave in two weeks."

I unclasped my hands from around his neck. "Oh." It was all I could think to say. I had gone from crushed to blissfully happy to crushed again in an instant. Jay was moving away.

"I've been struggling with how to tell you," he said.

"Mobility is a condition of the job, and I think I always knew I'd be transferred away from here, but I've just been having so much fun hanging out with you, I didn't want to think about it." He took a step closer to me and reached for my hands, which now hung limp by my sides. He then lifted them to his mouth and kissed them one by one.

"DC is only a couple of hours away . . . we can still see each other on weekends?"

It was the kind of thing you say because you want it to be true, but I think we both knew we weren't going to take our relationship long distance. We'd only been together for a few months, and as busy as we both were with our jobs, it'd never work. Plus, what was the endgame? I wasn't planning on moving to DC and he wasn't likely to move back here.

I looked up at him, my bleary eyes saying what neither of us wanted to admit. This meant it was over. It had to be.

Jay lowered his head and said in a near-whisper, "I'm so sorry."

I think I was almost too tired to feel anything at that point. I nodded silently and took a step closer to him and let him wrap his arms around me. It was my way of saying "I understand," even though I didn't want to. I let him hug me tight and kiss my neck and then eventually take me into my room where he tucked me into bed. I lay on his chest while he ran his hands through my hair and we talked until I fell asleep.

When I woke up the next morning, he was gone.

Dear Jenna,

Turns out, my guy wasn't dating other people after all. But he just
told me he's moving away. I'm heartbroken and I could really use a
little advice, or maybe just a (virtual) shoulder to cry on.

All best,
Riley

Dear Jenna,

Haven't heard back from you yet. Usually you respond so quickly.
Anyway, still feeling bummed about things and could really use
some words of wisdom. I can't believe I'm saying this, but I've
actually really grown to rely on our little "talks." I think I may even
spring for the $89.99/month after the free trial runs out!

All best,
Riley

Dear Jenna,

I was looking for some wisdom, but I'll take anything at this point.
Do you have any "wise words" from celebrities for me, or can you
tell me WWBD (What Would Beyoncé Do)? I'd even consider
downloading one of your apps—haha, lol. I'm only kidding—
kind of.

But seriously, I'm starting to get worried about you. Are you okay?

All best,
Riley

Dear Riley,

My name is Dylanne M and I am a supervisor at
Bestmillenniallife.com. I'm sorry to report that Jenna B is
no longer with the company. She left very suddenly when
she was offered the role of "Woman Eating Bagel" in the
next Eddie Redmayne film. One of the perks of working at
Bestmillenniallife.com is that we encourage our Personal
Success Concierges™ to FOLLOW THEIR BLISS, just as we
encourage our clients to do the same. We like to think this
breeds CONSISTENCY OF MESSAGE, though I don't mind
telling you it can create some staffing challenges!

As a gesture of goodwill for your understanding of this
unforeseen circumstance, we would like to offer you 50% off
your first full month of Bestmillenniallife.com. And we will
immediately get you set up with Kenny R, one of our highest-
rated Personal Success Concierges.™

We apologize for this speedbump on your road toward
PERSONAL FULFILLMENT. We hope you'll decide to continue
on this journey with us (at half off!).

Warmest regards,
Dylanne M
Supervisor, Level II
Bestmillenniallife.com

Dear Dylanne,

Is there any chance that you can apply the 50% off to
Click.com? I think I'm in need of Regina H's services again.

➤

PS: If you can get a message to Jenna B, please tell her I said, "In the wise words of Adele, 'I wish nothing but the best for you.' Haha lol."

All best,
Riley

Chapter 43

My parents insisted on taking me out to dinner Sunday night to celebrate my big professional success. They came over to pick me up wearing matching T-shirts they'd made that read *We Read Riley* in huge block letters on the front and *Proud Parents of a Newspaper Reporter* on the back. I was at once mortified and touched, and as soon as I saw them I started bawling like a three-year-old who just lost her binky.

My dad, who suffers from sympathetic crying syndrome, immediately started crying too. "I told you it was too much, Jeannie."

"Hey, hey," my mom said, pulling me into a tight hug. "What's all this about?"

So unfortunately, instead of celebrating my success, we ended up spending most of the evening talking about my broken heart. I explained to my parents about Jay's job offer and how he'd already accepted it and would be moving soon. I told them how we'd decided to end things before it got weird or ugly with the distance, and how it felt like the emotional equivalent of dancing to a song you love and then having some jackass DJ stop it suddenly partway through.

"You never know, honey," my dad said. "Maybe another big drug lord will move down to Tuttle and Jay can come back?"

"Cheers to that!" My mom laughed and lifted her drink.

"Yes, cheers to an increase in the Tuttle Corner drug trade—" My dad fell silent mid-toast. We followed his eyes to see Hal Flick walking up to our table. My mom set her glass down without taking a sip.

I had yet to fill my parents in on how well Flick and I worked together on the Davenport obit, so I couldn't blame them for their chilly reception.

"Hi, Flick!" I said, hoping my tone would signal my parents that there'd been a shift in our relationship.

"Hello," Flick said, his eyes triangulating the table. "Sorry to interrupt. I saw your car out front and . . . " He broke off.

As close as I had been to Flick as a young girl, my parents had been even closer—my dad, in particular. He'd gone on many a weekend fishing trip with his father and Flick, and Flick was a regular at our holiday table because his own family was scattered throughout the country. But in large part because of me and how betrayed I'd felt when Flick refused to see granddad's death for what I thought it was, my parents had stopped talking to him. If there was one thing you could say about my parents, it's that they were firmly on my team, for better or worse. (One needed look no further than their shirts as evidence of that.)

"Riley did a hell of a job this week at the *Times*," Flick said, shoving his hands into the pockets of his cotton Dockers.

My mom smiled automatically. My dad looked at Flick, then looked to me.

I wanted to show them that it was okay, that my position on Flick was changing. "Thanks." I smiled at him. "You helped me a ton."

He shrugged. "Eh, you didn't need much help."

An awkward silence settled around us, made more awkward because there was one empty chair at our table. I saw Flick's eyes dart to the chair. Dad saw it too. He looked at me again and I gave him a small nod.

"Would you like to join us?" My dad's voice sounded tight but sincere.

I thought I saw some color creep into Flick's cheeks, but he shook his head. "I was just hoping I could talk to Riley for a minute?"

Surprised, I got up and followed Flick toward the front of the restaurant, where he pushed open the door and walked to a spot far enough away from anyone who might be listening in on our conversation.

"What's up?"

"Listen," he said. The tentative, shifty-eyed manner was gone now. He looked directly into my eyes. "Something has come up. Something about Albert's case ..."

Albert's case. My stomach got that swoopy feeling. "What is it?"

"I'm going to be up in DC for a few days looking into some things that Albert was working on when he died."

"What things?"

He shook his head. "I can't say. But I wanted you to know that if I—if I'm not able to get back here, there's a file at the *Times*. Kay knows where it is. I've given her instructions to give it to you and Holman if anything should happen to me."

"What're you talking about? What do you mean if anything should happen to you?" This conversation was scaring me.

"It's just a precaution, I'm sure everything will be fine. But I just wanted you to know ... it's just important to me that you know I've been working all this time to find out what really happened to Albert. I didn't tell you before because . . . well, because it felt like I was betraying him. He wanted me to keep you safe, and I thought if you knew what I'm looking into you might—might—"

"Might what?"

"Not be." His mouth flattened into a thin line.

"I don't understand, Flick, you have to give me more. You can't just come here and—"

"As soon as I have something concrete, I will, okay?"

It was not okay. I wanted to know more. I wanted to know exactly what "things" he was looking into, and I wanted to know for sure if he thought my granddad killed himself or was killed by someone else, and I wanted to know that if it was the latter, who did he think was responsible? I wanted to know why he wasn't working with the police on this, and what was so important up in DC, and why he had a secret file hidden at the *Times,* and why I couldn't see it right away.

But I could tell by the steely look in his eyes that he wasn't going to answer any of those questions.

"Okay," I agreed.

He looked at me a moment longer. "Thank your parents for the invitation to sit down," he said. He spoke with more than a twinge of softness in his voice. "And tell them those T-shirts are ridiculous."

I laughed and then, out of pure instinct, I put my arms around him and gave him a hug. "Be careful."

It took a moment, but eventually he hugged me back. And then a moment later, without a word Flick turned and walked back toward the parking lot, leaving me as he so often had, with more questions than answers.

CHAPTER 44

T he last place you want to be when you've just realized your relationship has no future is at a friend's
wedding, but that's exactly where I found myself a
little less than a week later.

When the back patio doors opened and Tabitha St.
Simon appeared under the dramatic antler arch, she looked
positively radiant. She wore a long ivory dress made from
hand-stitched lace with a long train that took two bridesmaids to lift down the stone steps. She looked like a por-
celain doll with her big brown eyes and impossibly long
lashes, light pink cheeks, and dark hair swept up in a loose
chignon. True, she had a rather bulky cast on her left ankle
and she had to walk down the aisle using crutches, but she
made it work. And by the time the reception came around
she had changed into a shorter dress and broken out her
wheeled knee-walker, and she was cutting it up on the
dance floor without a care in the world.

While it was great to see Thad and Tabitha so happy—
especially after everything they'd been through—it had
been a tough week for me personally. The bright spot was
that Holman had come back from his undercover assignment; a nice comfort. Until he started driving me crazy.

The day after Arthur's obituary ran in the paper, Holman returned to Tuttle with the proof he needed to expose

TransVirginia Shipping Company's illegal dumping prac-
tices. In fact, he said that by his second day at sea he'd wit-
nessed enough to prove the allegations, but was stuck on
the ship for the rest of the weeklong voyage.

On his first day back in the office, I filled him in on
everything that had happened since he left town. He was
proud of my work on the Davenport story, which he showed
by saying simply, "I told you so." Then without further comment he said, "Aunt Beast looks thin." He pursed his lips as
he watched her swim around the bowl. "Are you sure you
followed my instructions?"

"Yes, Holman."

"Hmm." He put his bug eye right up to the side of the
glass. "Her scales aren't as vibrant as usual either. I'm giving you a C- on fish feeding."

I rolled my eyes. "But what do I get on reporting?"

He blinked. "What do you mean?"

"I mean, if I get a C- as a fish feeder, what grade do I get
as a reporter?"

"Reporters don't get grades, Riley." He looked confused.
"We aren't in school."

"Yeah, but if fish feeders—" I stopped myself. It was
good to have Holman back, and I didn't want to argue
with him.

Jay and I had mutually agreed that it would be a bad
idea for him to come to the wedding as my date—why make
a difficult situation even worse—so Holman had been kind
enough to be my plus one. And even though he'd been re-
galing everyone we talked to with stories of his maritime
adventures (which mostly included the irony of how many
frozen fish sticks the crew ate), I was grateful not to be there
alone. Romance was in the air and Holman, bless his heart,
provided the perfect antidote.

The wedding ceremony took place on the Davenport estate's massive stone patio, and the reception extended down the steps to the back lawn. Tables with white cloths and lavish flower arrangements surrounded a parquet dance floor covered by crisscrossing strings of twinkle lights. It felt like dancing under the stars. It was a beautiful event, down to the last detail, and I was in awe of Tabitha's ability to pull it off given the events of the past two weeks.

The toasts were in full swing, and we'd just suffered through a multi-stanza poem by all nine bridesmaids, who each recited one verse and passed the mic down the line. (I never knew you could rhyme so many words with *amazing*.)

When it was the Best Man's turn, David Davenport, looking back to health and extraordinarily handsome in his jet-black tuxedo, told a charming story about how Thad had come home from his first date with Tabitha three years ago and said, "Tonight I think I met the girl I'm going to marry." When David asked how he knew, Thad said, "She told me so." Everyone laughed, and Tabitha's cheeks turned a deep pink, which made her look even more beautiful.

Then David paused, his tone turning serious. "We all know that these past couple of weeks have been hard for our family. We lost our father, many of you lost your doctor, and many more still, your friend. Arthur wasn't perfect by any stretch of the imagination—he probably worked too much, drank too much, expected too much from the people closest to him—but he was a good doctor, a good friend, and a good father. He loved Thad and me, and our mom, God rest her soul." He paused, looking out over the crowd, whose faces had all turned serious too. I saw him share a look with Thad from across the lawn, a shared understanding of a common loss.

David went on. "And he didn't deserve what happened to him. But if there's one thing Dad believed down to his very soul, it's that this life doesn't owe you anything, so we will try to focus on the good he did while he was in this world rather than the injustice of how he left it." The crowd was so quiet you could have heard a pin drop. None of us were sure where exactly David was going with this toast.

"So, in that spirit, I'd like to share something from Dad's obituary that I think lends itself particularly well to this moment. Tuttle's newest intrepid obituary writer, Riley Ellison, who is here tonight, uncovered this quote that Dad said at a 2014 awards banquet." David's eyes found mine and he gave me a little wink. "He was being honored with an award for excellence in healthcare, as voted on by his patients. Those of you who knew him know my dad didn't miss an opportunity to grab the spotlight, so as he looked out into the crowd of his former patients who'd turned up for the reception, he said, 'All you ladies out there remember that I was the only man who ever truly found his way into your heart.' "

That broke the tension and everyone laughed, including David, who wiped at the corner of his eye before continuing.

"I wanted to share that story not only because Dad found his way into the hearts of so many, both literally and figuratively, but I know if he were here right now, he'd be so gratified to see that my big brother Thad was lucky enough to have found his way into Tabitha's heart, and her into his. He'd be so proud of you both, and I am too." Then he raised his glass and said, "To the happy couple!"

We all clinked glasses and drank to Thad and Tabitha, the music came back up, and the party continued. A few minutes later, a breathless Ridley walked over and plonked herself down at the table where Holman and I sat eating cake.

"I am too big to dance."

David followed in her wake, a wide grin on his face. "You were the most beautiful woman out there." He kissed her cheek and sat down next to her. "And you're equally as lovely right here."

At almost the exact same moment, Holman looked at me and said, "You have some frosting on the side of your nose—either that or a booger."

"So Ridley," I said, wiping my face with a napkin. "How are you feeling? You're getting close, right?"

She leaned back in her chair, a contented and drowsy expression on her face. "Thirty-seven weeks. Dr. Wilson says I could go at any time." She rested a hand atop her belly, which was now quite a bit more pronounced than it had been the last time I saw her. She was wearing a yellow chiffon Grecian dress with a plunging neckline to show off her ample chest, and of course, she looked amazing. But for the first time I noticed that her face was beginning to look just a tad bit swollen. *Finally.*

"Did Sheriff Haight ever figure out who poisoned you?" Holman dropped the question on David like a lead balloon. Small talk wasn't Holman's strong suit.

"Not conclusively," he said, tearing his gaze from Ridley. "But we think it must have been Bennett. Wouldn't you agree?" He looked at me.

It was a good question. I was bothered by the fact that there hadn't been any physical evidence linking Bennett to David's poisoning.

"Maybe Bennett just had a grudge against our whole family—who knows?" David said.

"If it were me, I'd want to know for sure," Holman said.

"I do want to know," David said. "But not tonight. Tonight I want to enjoy seeing my brother happier than I have in a long time, and the company of this gorgeous lady."

Ridley gave David a blinding smile, I fought the urge to barf, and Holman furrowed his brow. "Well, that certainly seems shortsighted. You're like Scarlett O'Hara—*I'll think about it tomorrow . . .*" he said in a laughable impersonation of a Southern belle.

David, like his father, was not one to miss an opportunity. He stood up with glass in hand and said, "Frankly, my dear, I don't give a damn what you think." Then he walked off toward the bar to freshen their drinks.

<hr>

A few minutes later, Holman and I were debating whether or not the lead singer of the band was lip-synching Norah Jones's "Come Away with Me" (she so wasn't) when Dr. H walked over to our table. "Ah, Mr. Holman and the lovely Riley!"

His warmth brought a smile to my face as it always did. I stood up to give him a hug.

"I dare say Tabitha planned everything perfectly. Not that we had any doubts about her planning capabilities," he said with a chuckle. But after a moment, his face grew more serious. "How are you, my dear? You don't seem quite yourself."

"I'm okay," I said, forcing a smile. "Or at least I will be."

"She's upset because she and her boyfriend Jay broke things off. He's moving to Washington, DC, to take a higher position within the DEA. Riley understands this intellectually, but is having a hard time processing it emotionally." Holman rattled off all of this like he was an anchorman on the six o'clock news. Then he added, "Particularly in this romantic setting."

"*Holman!*" I hit his arm.

"What? Was that not an accurate description of why you're in a funk?"

Dr. H looked from Holman to me. "Well, I wouldn't lose hope. These things have a way of working out!"

I don't know if it was Holman embarrassing me, or Dr. H's kindness, but I felt tears sting the back of my eyes.

Dr. H again deftly swooped in. "Did I ever tell you about the time Louisa almost threw me out of the house?"

I shook my head, the abrupt change in subject stopping my tears.

"It's true. We were talking about how we would each want to spend hypothetical lottery winnings, and she just couldn't understand why a man my age would want to open a riverboat casino!" He laughed and got the fond faraway look that always accompanied a story of his dearly departed Louisa. "I told her, 'The house always wins! We could be the house!' And she screeched that she wasn't going to end up married to a house, and threatened to throw me out if I was the sort of man who wanted to own a casino. Eventually we settled on the hypothetical decision to open a bird-feed store instead. Her compromise was that we could call it the Flamingo."

Dr. H's stories, particularly about Louisa, often left me both scratching my head and charmed, and I knew he had told this one to stop me from getting upset. I stood up and gave him another tight squeeze. "Thank you," I whispered.

"All right, all right," Dr. H said, as he released me. "I'm going to leave you young folks to carry on. It's past my bedtime."

The reception was beginning its third hour and I wondered how much longer I had to stay. Being surrounded by all of this happiness was getting tougher by the minute. So far I hadn't humiliated myself by texting or calling Jay, but one more glass of champagne and who knows what I might do. Holman was deep in conversation with poor Ridley on what she planned to do with her placenta after she gave birth and since I wanted no part of that conversation, I pulled my phone from my tiny sparkly purse to check the time, and saw that I'd missed a call.

> *Hey Riley, it's Lauren McCarty. Just wanted to let you know that I talked to my brother and he said he had given permission for someone to use our land as a part of some kind of investment or something. He said he'd done it months ago, back when Mom was still alive. I guess no one thought to tell me. But I'm glad you came around asking questions because my brother and I are co-owners of that land and we both stand to make a pretty penny if the pharmaceutical company who is leasing it hits it big with this tobacco-based drug. Anyway. I didn't know if John ever got back to you. He's been super down lately— his best friend from high school just died in a hunting accident and he's taking it real hard. Okay, well, that's all. Thanks. Bye.*

CHAPTER 45

"I have to go," I announced as I pushed back from the table and stood up.

Holman and Ridley looked surprised, the same question on both of their faces. "Uh, something has come up," I said, vaguely. "Holman, you'll be okay getting home, right?"

Holman had insisted on driving himself here on his bright yellow 1972 Honda Hobbit, which was a cross between a bicycle and a scooter. It looked like the love child of a giant praying mantis and a banana and was the most ridiculous contraption I'd ever seen. But he loved it and liked to take it out on special occasions.

"Yes," he said, eyeing me with suspicion. "But what has come up?"

I didn't want to tell him about the call from Lauren and all the questions it raised—basically connecting her brother John to Brandon Laytner and Bennett Nichols—because the investigation was essentially over. I didn't want to look like a schmuck reopening the story if it was all smoke and no fire. I'd look into it myself first and then I could tell Holman or Carl if anything interesting turned up.

"It's...uh...Jay," I said, his name popping into my head at the last second. "He called and wants to talk."

"Would you mind giving me a ride home?" Ridley stood up too. "I'm so tired and I don't want to make David leave now. He's having so much fun."

Damn. There was no way I could get out of that without looking like a huge bitch *(No, I won't take you home, super pregnant lady)*, and there was no way Holman could fit her on his Hobbit. I reluctantly agreed, and she went in search of David to say goodbye. I told Holman I had to run to the ladies room and ducked into the house, where I tried to call Lauren back, but there was no answer. I then scrolled through my phone and found John Krisanski's number from last week and called him. He didn't pick up either, so I left him another message saying I had a few questions about his connection to Invigor8, Bennett Nichols, and Arthur Davenport. That ought to get his attention. Maybe now he'd actually call me back.

Holman and I found Thad and Tabitha on the dance floor and I interrupted their Electric Slide for a quick minute. I pulled her into a tight hug, being careful not to mess up her perfect hair. "Congratulations, Mrs. Davenport."

She wrenched away like I'd slapped her. "Oh, I am *not* Mrs. Davenport." She wagged a finger at me. "I will be keeping my name, thankyouverymuch. I take a lot of pride in being a St. Simon girl. Plus, it's my professional name and I wouldn't want to lose any of the clout I've built up under this name."

I was pretty sure Tabitha's professional name according to Tuttle library patrons was "Excuse Me, Miss," but I didn't say anything. This was her big day after all, and my gift to her (in addition to the monogrammed hand towels) was to let it slide.

"Sorry," I said, winking at Thad. "Thanks for everything, guys. It was a perfect evening."

"Thank *you* for everything," Thad said, and I could tell

he meant it. He might not have been the most interesting man in the world, or as charming as his brother, and he might have been at least thirty-seven percent Sasquatch, but Thad was a good guy—and the perfect opposing force for Tabitha. It was nice to see them heading off into their happily ever after.

Ridley was at the front waiting for Holman and me. We all walked out together, holding our favor boxes containing two bear claws from Tuttle Donuts, a beloved local institution, and two small bottles of milk.

"The Hobbit doesn't have storage, will you take mine?" Holman asked, a slight edge coming through in his voice. I recognized this edge as food stress. Holman loved doughnuts like Winnie the Pooh loves honey. "Don't eat them though, okay?"

"I won't."

"Because it would be incredibly disappointing if I were to come over to your house in the morning to retrieve them only to find them gone."

"I won't eat your bear claws, I promise."

Moments later, after a few more assurances that I wouldn't snarf his doughnuts, he sputtered and tutted his way out of the long brick driveway on his preposterous vehicle.

Ridley and I got into my car and headed toward Ryan's parents' house. As we turned left out of the driveway, I could feel her eyes on me.

"What?"

"So Jay called, huh?"

I had told Ridley the whole story about Jay breaking up with me in a moment of weakness at the wedding reception. She'd asked why I brought Holman and it just sort of spilled out. Not that she and I were becoming friends or anything.

"Um, yeah. He says he wants to talk."

"You lie."

"I'm sorry—what?"

"You're lying."

I sat there stung speechless for a moment—how dare she accuse me of lying! I mean, I was, but still.

"Riley," she said calmly, "one of my gifts is I can always tell when people are lying. I've had this ability since I was a girl. It is how I know Ryan still loves you, despite his denials, and how I know this still pleases you. So this lie about Jay calling you was very easy for me to spot."

"What're you"—I started to argue, but stopped myself. The truth was I was a terrible liar and it didn't take someone with a "gift" to sense it.

"Fine. I just wanted to leave. It was a little too much 'love' for me, given my personal situation right now."

Ridley was quiet, but I felt her eyes on me from the passenger seat, like she was running what I said through her internal polygraph. After a beat she said, "Nope. You're still lying."

"Ridley!"

"Who called you? I saw your face when you listened to the message—you went pale. Who was it?"

Damn. She was good. I thought it over quickly and decided, *What did it matter if I told Ridley who called?*

"It was Lauren McCarty. Her mother was a patient of Dr. Davenport's and her family owns a tobacco farm in the area. She said something that made me wonder about the relationship between Bennett Nichols, that creepy Brandon Laytner, and her brother, this John Krisanski who I don't know anything about, but whose name keeps coming up. Something about this seems odd to me and I just want to do a little research, that's all. Plus, a wedding really isn't the best place to be when you've just been broken up with."

Ridley was quiet as she typed something into her phone, apparently already disinterested in what I was talking about. But the more I thought about it, the more interested I became. All three of those men had ties to Dr. Davenport, and more significantly they all had reasons to dislike him. Why hadn't their connections come up earlier? Was someone trying to hide something? My mind was busy tossing around theories when Ridley held up her phone. "Look."

I snuck a sideways glance at the screen. "Why are you showing me a picture of the custodian from Tuttle General?"

"According to Google, this is John Krisanski."

Shocked, I pulled the car over to the side of the road to process this. John Krisanski was Jack the custodian? How was that possible? I ticked back through the few conversations I'd had with Jack over the past few days. We'd talked about Arthur's obituary—but he hadn't mentioned that Arthur had taken care of his mother. And now I learn that this guy was Bennett Nichols's best friend from high school, *and* he was leasing his family's farmland to Brandon Laytner's Invigor8? There were a lot of coincidences starting to rack up here. I stared out of the windshield into the dark night, my eyes unfocused as I thought through what all this could all mean.

"Riley?" Ridley's voice brought me back to the moment.

"I'm sorry," I said, shaking it off. "I'm just shocked, that's all—" I put my turn signal on and started to pull back onto the road. "I know you're exhausted, I'll get you home."

"It's not that—" Ridley said as she looked from the floorboard to me and back again. "I think my water just broke."

CHAPTER 46

I had never driven so fast in all my life. All of a sudden
every bump in the road seemed like a threat, every stop-
light an obstacle. As I flew down back county roads toward Tuttle Gen, I had visions of being forced to deliver
Ridley's baby on the side of the road. I was in a near panic.
I wasn't proud of it, but at one point Ridley looked over and
said between contractions, "It's going to be fine, Riley. Just
breathe."

I flew into the circle drive of the hospital, put on my
hazards, and led (an infuriatingly calm) Ridley inside.
She had called Ryan on the way over but we'd made it
there first. The woman at the reception desk called for a
wheelchair and told me they'd be taking Ridley straight to
Labor & Delivery.

I ran back outside, legally parked my car, and went
back to wait with her until Ryan got there.

When I got to her room, she was already hooked up to
what they called a fetal heart-rate monitor. The nurse in
the room explained that Ridley was in "active labor," which
meant the baby was ready to be born.

"You look scared silly, hon," the nurse said. "Are you
Ridley's partner?"

I'll admit my first reaction was to be flattered—I mean,
the thought that I could be with someone like Ridley . . .

and then I mentally slapped myself for falling under the Ridley-spell like everyone else. "No," I said quickly. "I used to date her partner. I mean, her baby daddy. I mean, the baby's father."

The nurse looked at me like I was insane, since I was now clearly irrelevant, not to mention full of TMI. Then she turned back to Ridley. "Hon, do you have a partner who's going to be involved in this birth? I don't think it's gonna be too long now."

"Yes," Ridley said between deep breaths. "He's on his . . . *warggggh!*" She let out an anguished cry. I have to say: watching Ridley in active labor put off any ideas I had about having kids for a good long while. Not that I felt it had been in my immediate future or anything. But still. It did not look fun.

"I'm going to get the doctor and then we'll get some more information on where you are. Okay, sugar?"

Ridley was sitting propped up by two pillows behind her, a death grip on the railing of her bed with each hand. Incredibly, she didn't seem scared or nervous, just hyper-focused. It was almost like she was in a trance; she was star-ing at a point directly across the room, puffing out short, forceful breaths every couple of seconds. I felt like I should be doing something, so I took a few delicate steps toward her bedside. Should I breathe with her? Should I help her count—was that a thing? I had no idea.

"Can I get you anything?" I asked tentatively.

"No," she said, and her voice had a definitive edge I hadn't heard before. Not exactly harsh; more like firm.

"Ice chips? Another blanket?"

"No."

"Do you want a magazine?"

"Riley," she sighed, finally breaking her gaze at the

point across the room. "I'm trying to meditate. It's supposed to help the baby and me relax."

"Ohhhhh," I said. "Okay. I'm sorry. I'll just be quiet."

She went back to breathing/staring and I stood there
silently like an idiot. This went on for some time. And then
Dr. Wilson walked in the room, her eyes down on the chart
she was holding. "I hear there's a baby ready to be born in
here—oh, hi, Riley!"

Dr. Wilson was an old friend of the family and had been
my gynecologist since my mother first took me to see her
at the age of seventeen. She was a lovely woman, but I always felt a little weird when I saw her in social situations.
Probably because most of our conversations took place
with my feet in stirrups.

A second later Ryan flew into the room. "How is she?"
He seemed to be addressing Dr. Wilson, but before waiting
for an answer, he looked at Ridley. "How are you?" Then his
face swiveled back to Dr. Wilson. "Is the baby okay?" Then
back to Ridley. "What do you need? What I can do?" He
was panting and his cheeks had taken on the muddy red
color they used to get in summertime when we'd go roller-
blading through the park.

Dr. Wilson put a hand on Ryan's shoulder. "Just relax,
she's fine. Everything is fine. Baby looks good, a little early,
but that's not abnormal. We're going to continue to monitor his or her heart rate as Mom progresses, but there's no
reason for concern."

Ryan ran a hand though his hair and exhaled loudly,
and only then did he look my direction. "Thanks for getting
her here so fast, Riles."

Ridley, still meditating or whatever, barely acknowl-
edged Ryan when he came in. She was deep in the throws
of concentration, like a warrior. It was actually super

impressive and made me think that maybe I should learn to meditate.

Dr. Wilson turned to Ryan and me and said, "I'm going to need to check her, so if you guys could give us some privacy . . ."

We stepped into the hallway. Ryan was still breathless from his run to the room, and I could see he was sweating a little, though I suspected that was more from nerves than anything else. He leaned against the wall and looked like he might collapse under the stress of the moment.

"They're going to be fine," I said. "Dr. Wilson says everything is okay."

He turned to me and I knew in that moment that his fears had nothing to do with Ridley or the baby. It wasn't that he didn't care about them, but I could see the worry on his face was of a more personal sort. He was afraid he wasn't up to this challenge. Ryan was rarely a victim of self-doubt; it was one of the things that had drawn me to him all those years ago. But standing in that hallway on the precipice of becoming someone's father, I could see that insecurity consumed him.

Without any words of wisdom to offer, I did the only thing I could think to do: I pulled him into a hug. The ferocity with which he hugged me back surprised me, and I held him tight in return. He buried his face in my hair and clung to me like a baby koala.

"Hey, it's gonna be okay," I said, allowing him his moment of self-absorbed fear.

"What if it's not?" he said, pulling back. "What if I can't do this?"

"Ryan," I said. Moment over. "Stop it. You are about to become a father, but that woman in there," I pointed toward the room, "is about to *give birth*. I'm sorry—but who cares about you right now? Take a deep breath, splash some water on your face, and get it together. You need to be there for her right now. Got it? This isn't about just you anymore."

He looked surprised at first, and then a second later, he nodded. "You're right. How do you always know exactly the right thing to say to me?"

"Because it's almost always 'Get over yourself.' " I smiled at him.

When we were together, that had been our dynamic. He was the crazy one always flying off into the stratosphere and I was the levelheaded one who brought him back to earth. It had been nearly a year since we'd been together, but we fell back into the old pattern instantly. It worried me how comfortable it felt.

"Ryan," Dr. Wilson popped her head into the hallway. "She's asking for you."

He looked back at me. "Wish me luck . . ." And then he walked into the room and closed the door behind him. This was a big moment for him—for them—and I was proud of him for showing up despite his fears. Not that I had any doubt that he would.

My feelings for Ryan spanned every color in the rainbow, and odd as it was, my feelings for Ridley were fairly complicated as well. But in that moment, I was genuinely excited for them both. They were about to bring another life into this world. The enormity of that swept over me and it seemed impossible that this sort of thing had happened every minute of every day since the beginning of time. It was one of those moments, like standing under the stars on a clear night, when the weight of your insignificance folds around you, in equal parts comforting and depressing.

I walked toward the elevators and saw Mr. and Mrs. Sanford checking in at the nurses station. I didn't want them to see me. I didn't belong here, and seeing me would be awkward for us all, so I found the nearest exit marked STAIRS and pushed it open.

The maternity ward was on the third floor, and it didn't take long for me to get down to the main level. It was close to midnight and the hospital lobby was nearly empty. All the shops and offices were closed and locked. I walked quickly out of the building, thinking it was a wonder more horror movies weren't set in hospitals after hours.

It was a dark night, and as I walked toward the parking lot the corner of my eye caught an orange dot glowing out of the blackness. A cigarette.

"Riley?" It was Jack, or John, or whatever the hell his name was. He was standing half in shadows but I recognized his voice and his large, hulking silhouette.

A ripple of nerves went through me. There was no point in pretending he was just a kindly custodian anymore. "Hey," I said, purposely not using his name (after all, which one would I use?).

"Listen," he said and let the cigarette fall to the ground. He stomped it out while releasing a cloud of gray smoke into the night air. "I think you and I need to talk."

"I agree," I said, now hyperaware that I was alone in a dark parking lot with a man I didn't know. "But it's late. Maybe we could talk tomorrow?"

Jack took a half step forward, and something in his hand glinted in the dim light of the moon. It was a gun. "I think we better talk now."

Instinct took over and I turned to run back toward the hospital. Jack didn't move to follow me, but I heard the click of the safety being released. And then in a voice as sweet as cherry pie, he said, "I don't want to shoot you in the back, honey, but I will."

CHAPTER 47

J ack forced me at gunpoint to drive to my house, un-
lock the door, and put Coltrane outside in the fenced
yard. He took one of my kitchen table chairs and set it
in the middle of my living room and told me to sit. He then
tied my hands and ankles to the chair with zip ties he had
in his jacket pocket. He had come prepared.

He sat down on the couch opposite and let out an exasperated sigh. "Riley, Riley, Riley . . . what am I going to
do with you?"

"If you're taking suggestions, 'let me go' gets my vote."

Jack laughed. "You're gutsy, I'll give you that."

He was a big man, maybe six-foot-three or -four, and
had a beer gut that hung over the top of the waistband
of his jeans. Our conversations had always been short in
the hospital, and I don't think I'd ever really looked at him
until that moment. He had a long face that looked weath-
ered from years spent in the sun. His eyes were small and
light blue, so light that they seemed almost colorless, like
a goat's. I knew now that he was the same age as Bennett
Nichols, but Jack definitely looked older.

And then it hit me like a flash of lightning: Jack was
the third man I'd seen in the picture with Bennett and
Brandon, the one where they were fishing. They were all
friends—good enough friends that they'd been on a fishing

trip together at some point. This raised so many questions, chief among them, *Had the others been involved in killing Arthur, or had that been Jack alone?*

"You're friends with Brandon Laytner and Bennett Nichols," I stated more than asked.

"Yeah. Been friends almost all our lives." His eyes snapped up to mine, a challenge set there that I couldn't identify.

"Did they help you kill Arthur, or did you do that all on your own?" It was a risk to be so combative, but I wanted to get him talking. The more time he spent talking, the less time he spent shooting me.

Jack laughed again; this time the laugh turned into a wheezy cough after a few seconds. "What—you think we're going to have one of those chats like in Scooby-Doo where I tell you the whole story of what I did and why?" He leaned forward and narrowed those goat eyes at me. There was not one ounce of pity in them, and that was the first moment I felt actual fear. "Nun-uh. What's gonna happen is I'm going to sit here and think about what to do with you, then I'm going to do it. I've come too far to get busted now."

Terror stole my voice. I stared back at him silently.

He shook his head. "I tried to warn you. You shoulda left it alone. Bennett was the same way. He kept asking questions—I don't know why he cared so much, he hated Arthur almost as much as I did. If he had kept his mouth shut, he might still be here, the dumb bastard."

"You killed Bennett?" I gasped, honestly surprised.

"It wasn't like I wanted to or anything." He rolled his eyes. "Benny acted so high and mighty when I told him what I'd done—even though I think he knew all along. Laytner, too. They knew I had no choice—hell, I did it as much for them as for me. But that's how they are, they act

like they're above all the dirty work yet they're always glad
I'm there to do it."

I sensed discord. "But not this time?"

He let out a snort. "Bennett acted all shocked and like
I'd done something wrong even after all that man had done
to him. Pathetic. Laytner wasn't as bad, but he got nervous
when you found out about the farm."

"So you're an investor in Invigor8?"

"Investor, yeah, I like that." He puffed up like a rooster.
"I let Brandon use my land in exchange for a share in the
company. See, I've encountered some challenges in the
professional realm of employment, which is why I'm working as a lackey down at Tuttle Gen. All that's gonna change
when Invigor8 hits it big with this new drug. Then we're *all*
going to be rich."

"So when Arthur withdrew his support from the drug
trials, he threatened that," I said as another piece of the
puzzle locked into place. "It was you arguing with Arthur
Davenport on the street that day, wasn't it?"

It hadn't even occurred to me before, but Jack Krisanski fit the description of the person Susan Pettis said she
saw. He was definitely big and although he was not entirely
bald—a thin halo of fine hair still stretched around the back
of his head—from a distance he would have looked bald.
I checked his forearm and sure enough, there was a large
tattoo of a wolf baying at the moon.

Jack stood up suddenly and I flinched.

"Don't worry, I haven't decided what to do with you yet."
He looked amused by my fear. "You hang tight, I'm going
to use the facilities and have a think on what to do here."

He walked out of the living room and into my bedroom.
I heard him close the door to the master bathroom and pictured him in there among my toiletries and hair products

and it made me shiver. I wanted this man out of my house. Or *I* wanted to be out of this house. I wasn't picky at that moment, and would have taken either.

I struggled against the restraints, but only managed to cut the skin around my wrists. Jack had tied an ankle to each of the front legs of the chair so there was no way I could get up enough momentum to hop the chair toward the door. He had taken my cell phone and I no longer had a landline, so even if I could somehow manage to get this chair to move I wouldn't be able to call 911.

From the bathroom, I could hear Jack whistling. A slow rage started to burn inside me. I don't know why that was the tipping point—because arguably kidnapping me at gunpoint and zip-tying me to a chair was way worse—but to hear this man whistling like he was just out for a summer stroll sent me over the edge. Since the only weapon I had at my disposal was my voice, I started screaming. And I mean *really* screaming.

"JOHN KRISANSKI IS GOING TO KILL ME!"

"CAN ANYONE HEAR ME?"

"HELP MEEEEEE!"

And then I let loose a chorus of shrieks and wails that would definitely be heard if anyone were outside. Given that it was the middle of the night and most of my neighbors were the early-to-bed/early-to-rise sorts, I wasn't holding out much hope, but it was better than sitting there doing nothing. At least Coltrane heard me, and he started barking like crazy from the backyard.

A few seconds later, Jack came running out of the bathroom, pants around his ankles. "Shut up!" He pointed the gun directly at me.

"HE KILLED ARTHUR DAVENPORT!"

"Shut. *UP.*" He stepped closer to me, gun extended, the

distance between me and the barrel less than ten feet.

I didn't care. If he was going to kill me, he might as well get it over with. I wasn't about to sit around and wait for him to do it on his terms where he could cover his tracks. If he shot me right here in my living room, there was a good chance he'd leave some DNA evidence behind. I figured at least if I was going to get murdered, the sonofabitch who did it was sure as hell going to get caught.

"SOMEBODY, PLEASE!!!"

"I won't warn you again—"

"HELLLLLLLLPPPP!"

And then three things happened at almost exactly the same moment: I saw a flash of red light, I heard a deafening blast, and I felt a searing pain rip through me.

CHAPTER 48

When I came to, I was lying on the floor of my house. A savage pain burned in my leg and I didn't have to look down to know I'd been shot. My eyes felt heavy and I had to fight to open them. I saw feet, big feet, attached to legs wearing khaki pants. Had Jack been wearing khakis? I couldn't remember. All I could remember was the burst of light and the crack of the gun. Everything faded to black again.

Moments later (or was it hours?) I heard voices, more than one person, all men. I tried to listen to what they were saying, but my mind was having rolling blackouts. The power would come on for moments at a time and then switch off without warning. I don't know how long I lay on the floor. When I opened my eyes the next time, there were more feet. Four of them, all furry. *Coltrane.* Seconds later I felt his wet tongue licking the side of my face and heard his soft whines.

"Will someone get rid of that dog?"

I tried to say, "No," but what came out was more like, "Nuuuurb."

"She's waking up." Another voice. Who were all these people?

"C'mon," the same disembodied voice said. "Let's get him out of here."

The pain in my leg was making it hard for me to keep a focused thought. My eyesight was blurry and I thought I smelled smoke. Was there a fire? I marshaled all the energy I could and tried to turn my head to see who was in my house. I used what little strength I had in my upper back to turn around to get a better view. From my limited vantage point, I could make out three people. They must have noticed my movement, because soon after they all three spoke at once.

"I think she's coming to."

"Is the ambulance here yet?"

"Did anyone happen to see a small box of bear claws?"

CHAPTER 49

The next conscious moment I had was in the hospital. I woke up to the intermittent beeps and buzzes and anonymous sounds of medical machinery. I rolled my head to the side and saw a person-shaped blob sitting in a chair next to my bed. I blinked a few times to clear the fluid from my eyes. The blob was Holman. And he was watching me like a person watches a setting sun, afraid to look away in case of missing something.

"Are you really awake this time?"

"Mmm?"

"You've had a few false starts. You open your eyes for a second or two and then you fall back asleep."

"I think I'm awake now," I said. My throat felt dry, thick.

"You got shot."

I knew that much, but hearing Holman say it out loud was surreal. I looked at him, my eyes asking the questions my brain couldn't quite formulate.

"In the leg. The bullet grazed the inner part of your calf, sparing the bone, but it still caused a significant amount of blood loss. That's why you feel so weak. But the doctor says you should make a full recovery."

I nodded like this was everyday information. *Shot in the leg. Lost a lot of blood. Full recovery.* I thought of my parents. Had anyone told them what happened? They'd be worried sick. "Mom and Dad . . ."

"They just stepped out for coffee," Holman said. "They'll be back soon."

I closed my eyes and an image of Jack's face swam beneath my eyelids. Had he been aiming for my leg? Or had he missed? Where was he now? How had I gotten here? I had a million questions, but the energy to ask only one. "What happened?"

"I pretty much saved your life."

My blank stare told him I was going to need more to go on.

"Well, technically, you saved your own life by screaming. But I helped."

My brain was processing things so slowly. I struggled to reconcile what he was saying with my last memories before waking up in the hospital. I didn't remember Holman being at my house . . .

"Actually," he continued, oblivious to my confusion, "if we are going to give credit to someone or something, we should really give it to the bear claws. As soon as I got home, I couldn't stop thinking about them. I immediately regretted my decision to give them to you. I know you promised not to eat them, but I kept worrying that Coltrane would jump up onto the counter and get them. Even though they were in a box tied with ribbon, I thought it was a possibility. I've seen videos on YouTube of dogs unwrapping Hershey's bars—"

"*Holman.*"

"What?"

I lifted my arm, which felt like it weighed about seventy-five pounds, and rolled my wrist a couple of times.

"Oh, right. So anyway, I decided to ride my hog over to your place to pick them up, and when I got to your driveway,

I heard Coltrane barking his head off and your voice yelling something from inside the house. I looked in through your sidelight window and saw you tied to a chair, screaming bloody murder. I called 911, then I ran back to the Hobbit to get a weapon, but all I had was a flare. As I told you the Hobbit does not have a lot of storage, of course I always make room for a flare because you never know when your hog is going to break down when you're out riding, you know?"

I really wished he would stop using the word *hog*, but I didn't have the energy to ask, so I just nodded.

"The door was unlocked and I crept in while you were screaming; a second later I saw this big guy come running down the hall with a gun in his hand. He was agitated—and for some reason, without pants—and when he raised his gun to shoot at you, I lit the flare and threw it at him a split second before he pulled the trigger. That's why he missed and shot your leg. He was aiming for your chest."

A chill spread through me. Jack had tried to kill me and but for the grace of God and Holman's obsession with doughnuts, I somehow lived through it. "Where is he now?"

"Burn unit. His shoes had some chemicals on them—probably cleaning supplies from work—and when I threw the flare at him they caught fire immediately. It was bad. He was screaming and ran past me out the front door. He only got as far as the stop sign at the end of Salem Street, though. Butter caught him. He wasn't exactly hard to spot running through the dark streets with two flaming shoes."

"He killed Arthur—and Bennett," I started to say.

Holman was already nodding. "I know. A lot has happened since you got shot," he said. He leaned closer to my bed and his eyes went full bug-out. "I have to tell you something."

"Okay . . ." I said, suddenly nervous.

"Riley," he started to say, and then paused. "The thing is, you lost a lot of blood."

"Okay . . ."

"And even though the bullet went straight through your calf, it hit an artery—not the femoral artery or anything, another one, the popliteal, I think. And you lost a lot of blood."

"Yeah, you said that."

"I don't know how to tell you this but," he paused. "You've been in a coma for six months."

It felt like someone had injected ice water through my IV. I stared at him for at least ten seconds, my brain unable to process what he was telling me. Could it really have been six months? Was it April instead of October? Had I missed Christmas?

And then Holman started laughing. "I'm just kidding. You've only been in here a few hours."

I was dumbstruck for a moment. But eventually I found my voice. "Why would you make a joke like that?" I gasped.

Holman blanched. "Are you upset?"

"Of course I'm upset!"

"Why?"

"Because you just told me I'd lost six months of my life!"

"But it was only a joke. And everyone says laughter is the best medicine."

"Do I look like I'm laughing?"

Holman seemed confused by my question. "You're yelling at me, so no . . ."

"So it wasn't funny!"

"Well," he said, lifting one long, bony finger, "humor is a highly subjective construct, so I don't think it's fair to say definitively that something is or is not—" He must have seen the outrage on my face and decided to reverse course.

"Okay. Sorry. Geez."

I sighed, already exhausted from our short conversation. "Tell me what happened after I got shot."

I could tell Holman wanted to continue talking about
why his joke had failed. Fortunately he fought his instincts.
"Jack was in terrible pain when they brought him to the
hospital. He kept screaming that he was going to die. The
doctor gave him some pain medication that calmed him
down, which also made him a little loopy. He was pretty out
of it and started making grand declarations that he avenged
his mother's death and his friend's honor by ridding the
world of Arthur Davenport, blah, blah, blah. We'll see if any
of it will hold up in court, but Carl says they have enough
for several search warrants that may end up proving his
involvement, even if he decides to retract his confession."

"Gosh, this is complicated."

"It certainly is. I guess Brandon, Bennett, and John Krisanski, who goes by the nickname Jack, all went to high
school together. According to his sister, Lauren—who is co-
operating fully with the sheriff by the way—they were close
friends, but Jack was always the odd man out. Bennett and
Brandon were both popular and wealthy, while Jack was
neither. Jack was the guy they'd dare to eat a hot pepper,
or go make a fool of himself in front of a girl, that kind of
thing. Things changed in tenth grade when Jack took the
blame for Bennett and Brandon after they'd gotten caught
with weed on school grounds. It created a strong bond between them and they remained friends all these years even
though their lives had gone in very different directions.

"Lauren told Carl that Jack was diagnosed with Bor-
derline Personality Disorder at the age of seventeen, which
explained his trouble making friends, dealing with authority, holding down a job, etcetera. He didn't go to college

and floated from job to job, even did a stint in Augusta Correctional for assault; he beat up a former boss of his pretty badly. Fast-forward to about a year ago when Brandon got the idea to re-launch Invigor8 around this new tobacco-based biologic. He talked Bennett into investing millions into the company and Jack into trading his land for shares of stock, effectively making the three of them business partners."

I tried to scoot myself up against my headboard with my good leg, the one that didn't feel like it was coated in hot oil, but had trouble lifting my body weight.

"Here, let me," Holman said, offering me his arm to use as leverage. "You okay?"

I nodded, ignoring the painful pulsating sensation coming from my lower leg.

"Then Jack's mom got sick and he took her to see Dr. Davenport, not only because Arthur had the best reputation in the hospital, but on the recommendation of Brandon and Bennett—this was before he found out about the affair. Anyway, when things went south during Helen's procedure—a truly tragic outcome that no one could have foreseen—Jack went out of his mind with a mixture of guilt, grief, and apparently homicidal rage."

"Wow," was all I could think to say. This was all pretty unbelievable.

"According to Lauren, Helen had always been Jack's biggest supporter, the one person in his life who remained constant despite his struggles. Jack blamed Dr. Davenport for his mom's death. And as if that wasn't enough, Dr. Davenport quit the Invigor8 study a few weeks later, which Jack believed would tank the whole project. So then when he found out about the affair between Arthur and Libby, Jack not only blamed Arthur for his mother's death and for ruining his chance to hit it big with the Invigor8 drug, but also for his friend's heart attack. He convinced himself that Arthur Davenport was the devil himself."

"Jack confessed to all of this?"

"Not exactly." He shook his head. "This is all patched together from Lauren, Brandon, and Sheriff Haight."

And then suddenly I remembered the newsroom. Why wasn't Holman there reporting all of this? As if he read my mind, he pointed to his briefcase sitting on the window ledge. "Don't worry. I've been logging updates from here. Kay knows where I am and is fine with it."

"Thanks, Will."

I can't be sure, but I thought I saw him suppress a smile. "Anyway, this is a long story and I want to get through it before you pass out again."

"I'm sorry," I said. "Go ahead."

"Jack told Carl that he laced the bottle of scotch with crushed Digoxigon, which he knew Thad sold because he'd seen him with it around the hospital. He dropped by Arthur's house the night of the murder, rang the bell, and offered him the bottle as a gift to show there were no hard feelings about what happened to his mother. Jack told Carl that Arthur had been so moved he suggested they have a toast right then. Jack made up some story about being a recovering addict but watched as Arthur had himself a healthy pour."

So I had been partially right about what had happened; I had the how down, I'd just been wrong about the who.

"Jack left and then hid out back to wait for Arthur to pass out. He even heard the whole argument between Thad and his father—which of course played right into his plan to set up Thad. When Arthur finally collapsed about an hour later, Jack went back inside to make sure he was dead.

That's when he saw the knife with Thad's initials sitting on Arthur's desk. He said it was a last-minute improvisation to stab Dr. Davenport, to make 'damn sure' Thad took the blame."

"And what about David? Why did Jack go after him?"

Just then there was a gentle knocking sound on the open door. I thought it was going to be my parents, but it was Carl. He peeked his head in the room. "Ah, so you're awake."

"Whatever you do," Holman said, "do not attempt to use humor as medicine."

Carl furrowed his brow; thankfully he knew better than to ask. "How you doing, Riley?"

The pain in my leg was getting louder but I didn't want to tell anyone because I was afraid they'd leave, and I really wanted to hear the rest of the story.

"I'm hanging in there," I said. "Holman was just filling me in."

"Oh yeah? Where was he?"

"She was asking about David," Holman said.

Carl nodded and took up the story from there. "Jack Krisanski used to go by John Krisanski years ago, then somewhere around his middle twenties, he started calling himself Jack. Said it made him feel like a Kennedy." Carl rolled his eyes. "But his legal name is Jonathan Krisanski and that's what he was listed as on all the paperwork for Invigor8. Remember when David told us he wanted to go through the Invigor8 files from his dad's office?"

I nodded.

"Well when he called maintenance to see if they could wheel up the boxes, guess who answered the call?"

"Jack."

"Exactly," Carl said. "Jack got nervous that if David saw

the name Krisanski on the investor declaration notice, he would put two and two and two together. David was one of the only people in a position to make the connection between Helen Krisanski's death, John Krisanski listed as a principal investor in Invigor8, and Jack Krisanski working at the hospital."

"And Bennett?" I asked.

Carl frowned. "Jack won't say much about Bennett except that 'it was a real shame.' I suspect that once we take a look at all the evidence, what we'll discover is that Bennett must have either found out or been suspicious about Jack's involvement in Arthur's murder. Maybe he even threatened to turn him in. In any event, I think it's safe to assume that Jack killed his old friend and made it look like a hunting accident, and then planted all that stuff in his PO box to make it look like Bennett was the one who killed Arthur."

I let this all sink in. Jack was an absolute sociopath. He killed two people, and he'd tried to kill two more. With each passing moment it was getting harder and harder to believe I'd walked away from my encounter with him.

A nurse walked in to check my vitals and Carl and Holman stepped outside into the hall. I knew my parents would be back soon and there was a part of me that ached to see them, to let them reassure me that I was going to be okay. But a bigger part of me felt so sorry for putting them through the worry of seeing their only daughter in the hospital with a gunshot wound. As the nurse checked the fluid levels in the bag hanging next to me, I laid my head back on the pillow and an intense exhaustion washed over me. I closed my eyes and all thoughts of Jack and Arthur and Bennett evaporated into a deep, dreamless sleep.

CHAPTER 50

By the time I woke up the next morning, I was feeling strong enough to try getting out of bed. Addie, the nurse taking care of me, helped me into a wheelchair and asked if I had anywhere special I'd like to go. A few short minutes later, I found myself face to face with my goddaughter, Rosie Elizabeth Sanford.

"She's beautiful," I said, unable to wipe the smile from my face.

Ryan perched on the side of Ridley's hospital bed. They looked tired but happy. "So you'll do it?" Ryan asked.

I had been a little shocked when they asked me to be Rosie's godmother. And even more shocked when Ridley explained why. "You are my best friend in Tuttle Corner. Admittedly you are also my only friend, but I trust you and think you'll make a wonderful role model for our daughter."

I felt a bit startled, but also moved. As much as I hated to admit it, Ridley was growing on me. She was confident and open, kind and self-assured, and for some reason, she really wanted to be my friend. And I wasn't exactly in a position to be turning friends away. The truth was, I really didn't have any girlfriends left because, like an idiot, I had let all my female friendships wither during the years I was with Ryan. Maybe it wouldn't be the worst thing in the world to get to know Ridley a little bit better.

"How could I refuse this little girl anything," I said, looking down at Rosie's half-moon eyelashes pressed against her cheeks in sleep. She had impossibly tiny pink lips that parted slightly as she breathed in and out and in and out. It was mesmerizing. I leaned in to kiss her forehead. "She's just perfect."

"She is, isn't she?" Ryan said, looking at his daughter with so much love I thought his heart might burst right out of his chest.

The three of us talked for a while about all that had happened since Saturday night. I filled them in on Jack, most of which they already knew. Word travels fast in Tuttle Corner. Addie came back to get me and I carefully handed Rosie back to her daddy.

When Ryan leaned over to take her, he kissed my cheek and lingered there for a moment longer than he should have. "Thanks, Riles," he whispered.

It felt good to have him so close, a complicated mix of longing and sadness—and in light of Rosie, hope and joy. And, if I allowed myself to examine my feelings too closely, maybe even a soupçon of envy. "It's an honor." And then I pressed my cheek against his a moment longer than I should have.

CHAPTER 51

W hat else can I get you?" My mom hovered nearby, clutching a vegan banana muffin in one hand and a bottle of painkillers in the other. This had been her constant refrain over the past five days since I was discharged from the hospital and sent home in my parents' care. I had another couple of weeks before I could put any weight on my leg, so we decided that until then it'd be best if I moved back into my old room. And by "we" I mean "they." I didn't argue too much because the fact of the matter was, it was nice to be taken care of. I was feeling a little fragile in the wake of what had happened, and being fussed over by my mom and dad wasn't the worst thing in the world. They even let Coltrane move in, despite his bitter rivalry with Tofu, their evil cat.

"I'm fine, Mom, really. Go to bridge. I'm just going to sit here and continue with this research."

Holman, either out of endearing solidarity or bewildering insensitivity, had been emailing me research assignments to do while I was laid up. He called or came by every day to check on me under the guise of seeing how the projects were coming along, but really I think he just wanted to know I was getting better. I also like to think he missed me. Either way it had been nice because he'd become my main source of information on how the case against Jack

Krisanski was proceeding.

The latest was that Lindsey Davis had filed two counts of murder in the first degree and two counts of attempted murder against Jack. He was still recovering in the burn unit and apparently would be there for some time. Holman said he had lawyered up and was now not talking much to Carl or any of the other authorities. Still, Carl had a mountain of evidence against him and expected Jack would spend the rest of his days in prison.

It appeared as though Brandon Laytner didn't have anything to do directly with Bennett's or Arthur's death, but would probably still face charges for failure to report a crime, depending on what he knew and when he knew it. The prosecutor was planning to offer Jack a deal of some kind to get him to spill about Brandon's involvement. Holman also told me that on a tip from David Davenport, the FDA opened an investigation into Invigor8's patent development research. I had a sneaking suspicion that whatever they turned up would put an end to Brandon Laytner's bid for pharmaceutical fame.

Libby Nichols had also dropped by my parents' house the day after I got out of the hospital. She said she wanted to see how I was doing and thank me for "getting to the bottom of what happened." Jack Krisanski had killed both her husband and her lover—but more significantly, the father of her unborn child. "Yup. I'm pregnant," she told me, "I found out for sure three days ago." She also said she'd decided not to have the baby's paternity tested because "It doesn't really matter, now does it?" Bennett's life insurance policy would go a long way toward helping her on the road to rebuilding her life and her independence. "Ironically, I have more to live for now than I ever had before."

It was four o'clock and my mom had finally agreed to leave the house to go play bridge with her regular group, and Dad had run to the store to get more apple cider, so when the doorbell rang, I was surprised. Holman didn't usually stop by till after work. I hobbled to the door and almost fell over (quite literally) when I saw Jay standing on my parents' doorstep.

We hadn't seen each other since the night he told me he was moving to DC. While I was in the hospital he'd called to see if he could come by, but I told him I didn't think that was a good idea. Him leaving was as inevitable as it was painful, so I didn't see any point in getting even closer. It would just make it even worse. Holman told me he'd been texting every day to get an update on how I was doing.

I opened the door standing on one leg, holding onto the frame to steady myself. "Hi."

"Hi." His eyes held mine for a few seconds until they flicked down to my leg and the huge brace around it. "Oh my gosh, you should be sitting—I'm sorry, let me help." He moved to put his shoulder under my arm and help me back to my couch.

"I'm fine," I said, pulling away. I hopped, looking ridiculous I'm sure, back to the sofa and sat down.

He sat on the ottoman directly in front of me. "I hope it's okay that I came by," he said.

It wasn't, but what was I going to say? *Seeing you is painful. I totally understand why you chose your career over our relationship but it still hurts. I'm scared I'm not strong enough to say goodbye twice.* I went with, "Yeah, it's fine."

"I'm leaving today."

I nodded. "Oh."

"And I just wanted to see you before I go."

I looked down.

"Riley," he started to say, then reached over to grab one of my hands. "You know I wish things didn't have to be like this."

"I know."

"And you know that DC is only a couple of hours away, you could go there, I could come here . . ."

I let my eyes float up to his and cocked my head to the side. We'd been over this. A long-distance relationship didn't make any sense, because I was never going to move to DC and he was never going to move here. "Jay—" I began.

"I know," he said before I could reiterate what we'd already been through. He leaned back and exhaled loudly. "It just sucks, that's all."

"It sure does."

We sat in silence for a few moments, neither of us knowing what to say or what to do next. His phone vibrated and he took it out of his back pocket, glanced at it, and looked back up at me, his eyes wide. "Well, this is unexpected."

"What?"

"They've just made an arrest in the vandalism incident at Rosalee's."

It had been nearly two weeks since someone had thrown a hammer through the front window at the café, and Carl and his deputies hadn't had any leads on who had done it or why, as far as I'd heard. "And?" I asked.

"A local thug by the name of Justin Balzichek, but that's not the interesting part. The interesting part is that he says he was hired to do it by Anna Greer Mountbatten, the wife of Dale Mountbatten, a powerful lobbyist up in Fairfax."

Something about that rang a bell for me. "Why do I know the name Mountbatten?"

He read off his phone, "According to Carl, that was the

family Rosalee worked for as an au pair years ago, before moving to Tuttle Corner."

"That's right!" I remember that had been quite the topic of conversation around town when a young woman from France suddenly moved here and opened up her own restaurant. A fact made even more curious when we learned she had only been in this country for a little more than a year. I was pretty young back then so I only heard rumblings, but the prevailing theory was that Rosalee had had an affair with the father of the kids she was taking care of and instead of breaking things off, he set her up down in Tuttle with some money and a business to keep her nearby.

"Wow," I said, "do they know if that's true?"

"Well," Jay said, "kind of hard to say. They just found Anna Greer's car halfway between Tuttle and DC, the inside covered in blood."

"*What?*" I gasped.

"According to this, no one has seen her for a few days. But the condition of the car raises serious questions about her whereabouts. And I'll give you one guess who the police want to talk to about that?"

I got a sinking feeling. "Rosalee?"

"Yup."

We both sat in shocked silence for a few moments until his phone vibrated again. He checked it, sighed, and slipped it back into his pocket.

"That's the movers. I have to go."

I started to try to stand up at the same time he did, but I lost my balance and he reached out to grab me before I fell. His arm was around my waist and his face just inches from mine. I could smell the soap on his skin and it caused a stirring deep within me. I was really going to miss this man; I already did.

Our eyes locked, and a half second later he kissed me. And then in a move right off the big screen, he swept me up into his arms and held me like a groom carries his bride across the threshold, kissing me with urgency and passion and regret and heartbreak. We stayed like that for a long time. Long enough that I thought his arms might be getting tired.

Finally, he pulled away and buried his face into my neck.

"You'll always be my one who got away," he whispered, and then he set me back down on the couch the way one might set a glass Christmas ornament, fragile and breakable, back into its box.

And even as I watched him walk out the door, my heart twisting with sadness, even in that moment—or maybe especially in that moment—I knew I was going to be okay. I knew it because if I'd learned anything about myself over the past few weeks, it was that despite what anyone else seemed to think, of all the things I was, breakable wasn't one of them.

Dear Ms. Ellison:

Thank you so much for choosing to reconnect with us at Click. com. I appreciate you asking for me by name and for telling my supervisor that I am "as likely as anyone else" to help you find love. To answer your question, I am indeed "up for the challenge" and feel it is important to note that I do not believe you are "cursed" or "destined to die alone" as you suggest. #thinkpositive #nobodylikesadebbiedowner

Now that you have chosen to throw your metaphorical hat back in the ring (please note that we at Click.com discourage the wearing of actual hats on dates unless you're going to the Derby), I'd like to make you aware of a new program that might just be perfect for you! Our Repeat Romancer™ program is specially designed for our clients who may need to kiss a lot of frogs in order to find their happily ever after! #puckerupprincess

For the small investment of only an additional $4.99/month, you can enroll in our Repeat Romancer™ program and be eligible to earn Exclamation Points™ for every arrow you place in someone's quiver and double points for every arrow you accept in your own. It's like being paid to date! #notadvocatingprostitution

Exclamation Points™ may be accumulated and redeemed toward your purchase of Click.com apps, e-books, style guides, dating retreats, and even the annual Click.com Cruise! Yes, you read that right—we have a cruise! #cruisinforlove #therealloveboat #thepatchisthenewblack

On behalf of everyone here at Click.com, I'd like to extend a very warm welcome back. Thank you for trusting me with your heart once again, Riley. I feel certain that between Click.com's proprietary matching software, my never-say-die attitude,

➤

and your willingness to "get back on the horse," as you say,
we will be able to set you on the path toward true love!
#welcomeback #ifatfirstyoudon'tsucceed #herewegoagain

Best,
Regina H.
Personal Romance Concierge, Click.com

Repeat Romancer™ and Exclamation Points™ are registered trademarks of
Click.com, a wholly owned subsidiary of the Click Thru Life, LLC, and may not
be used or replicated without the expressed permission of Click Thru Life, LLC.

Acknowledgments

Since this is the acknowledgment section, I would first like to acknowledge each and every person who read *The Good Byline*, because it was your support that made this second book possible. I have enjoyed hearing from so many of you, and am so grateful for your enthusiasm for Riley and her friends.

Thanks to my literary agents, Emma Sweeney and Margaret Sutherland Brown, for their tireless work behind the scenes. I feel so lucky to be a part of the stellar team at ESA. Special thanks to Margaret for letting me call her "M," because it makes me feel a little bit like James Bond.

A million thanks to my editor, Colleen Bates at Prospect Park Books, for her editorial direction, steadfast support, and patience with my emails that are always far too long. Every writer should be so lucky to work with a publisher as smart and talented as Colleen. Huge thanks go to Dorie Bailey for her insightful reading (and introducing me to a "dirty Shirley"), and publicist Caitlin Ek, aka the "real-life Riley," for working so diligently to spread the word. Thank you to designer Susan Olinsky and illustrator Nancy Nimoy for another fantastic cover. And much gratitude to Amy Inouye, Margery Schwartz, and Kirby Gann for their hard work and attention to detail.

As always, I cherish the support from my writing

beasties: Ann Breidenbach, Jennifer Gravley, Nina Muker-jee Furstenau, Laura McHugh, and Allison Smythe. Thank you for the support you have shown me a million different times in a million different ways.

To my girlfriends, who are by great good fortune too many to name, but who know who they are: thank you for all the times you bought a book, raised a glass, came to an event, posted a review, snapped a pic, told a friend, sent a text, gave a hug, consulted on an outfit, IKR'd, OMG'd, and LOL'd. I am profoundly grateful for your friendship.

I'd also like to thank the many mystery writers, book bloggers, reviewers, librarians, booksellers, and book clubs who have welcomed me to this industry so warmly. Your kindness inspires me to work harder.

And special thanks to my family for their unending reams of support: Neal Rosenfeld, F.E. and Jack Nortman, Cheryl and Scott Orr, Allison, Pete, Samantha, and Ava Fiutak, and Dawn, Eddie, Madelyn, and Jackson Orr. And of course again to Jimmy, Fletcher, and Ellie. I love you all so much!

Lastly, I'd like to point out that as I look back on this list of people who have helped me along my publishing journey, I see the names of so many strong, smart women. What a privilege it is to have you all in my life. So to end (and in the spirit of the pop-culture wisdom of Jenna B), I'll make a small modification to one of my favorite anony-mous quotes/Pinterest memes:

"Here's to strong women. May we know them. May we be them. May we raise them. And may we create them fictionally!"

ABOUT THE AUTHOR

Jill Orr is the author of *The Good Byline*, the first in the Riley Ellison mystery series. A board member of the Unbound Book Festival, she lives in Columbia, Missouri, with her husband and two children.